Book Four
Eclipse Pack

J.E Daelman

COPYRIGHT © 2025 J.E DAELMAN. ALL RIGHTS RESERVED.
COPYRIGHT PROTECTED WITH WWW.PROTECTMYWORK.COM,
REFERENCE NUMBER: 16538110225S033

This book is a work of fiction. Names, characters and events are the product of the author's imagination or have been used fictitiously. Do not construe them as real. Any resemblance to actual events or people, living or dead is purely coincidental.

This book or any portion thereof may not be reproduced or used in any manner whatsoever without the express written permission of the author. You cannot give for free on any kind of internet site.

This book is for readers over the age of 18 years. If bad language, violence, sexual encounters offend you, please do not read.

Business Manager: V. Saunders
Editor: R. Tonge
Alpha/Proofreader: G. Brockelsby
Proofreaders: L. Cameron Brashears & M. Vayer
Beta Readers: J. Spalding, S. Hazuda
Book Cover: Kevin Brand Graphics
Models: Shutterstock

Copyright Registered

IF YOU HAVE NOT PURCHASED THIS COPY YOU NEED TO DELETE THE FILE AS IT IS STOLEN. PLEASE RESPECT THE AUTHORS RIGHT TO EARN AN HONEST LIVING.

Signed paperback copies are only available from the author.

COPYRIGHT © 2025 J.E DAELMAN. ALL RIGHTS RESERVED.
COPYRIGHT PROTECTED WITH WWW.PROTECTMYWORK.COM,
REFERENCE NUMBER: 16538110225S033

Note

Please note, this author lives in the United Kingdom, and has Alpha and Beta readers who correct errors, but, as in other countries, it depends on which state you live as to how your slang or terms differ.

Therefore, although some words/terms you may think are incorrect are correct in one or more states.

No AI programme has been used in the writing of this book, the cover images or design.

Kingdom Of Wolves is best read in book order as book one is world building and helps the understanding in the books that follow.

COPYRIGHT © 2025 J.E DAELMAN. ALL RIGHTS RESERVED.
COPYRIGHT PROTECTED WITH WWW.PROTECTMYWORK.COM,
REFERENCE NUMBER: 16538110225S033

Table of Contents

Copyright Registered

Note

Table of Contents

Chapter 1

Chapter 2

Chapter 3

Chapter 4

Chapter 5

Chapter 6

Chapter 7

Chapter 8

Chapter 9

Chapter 10

Chapter 11

Chapter 12

Chapter 13

Chapter 14

Chapter 15

Chapter 16

Chapter 17

Chapter 18

Chapter 19

Chapter 20

Chapter 21

Chapter 22

Chapter 23

Chapter 24

Chapter 25

Chapter 26

Chapter 27

Chapter 28

Chapter 29

Chapter 30

Chapter 31

Chapter 32

Chapter 33

Chapter 34

Books by J.E. Daelman

Acknowledgments

You can find me here

Chapter 1

BRONZE

Standing in the office, I look around, taking notice of the bookshelves, filing cabinets and the two desks. I know I have a lot of work to do to learn all the aspects of what is essential to the upkeep of the pack. I learned much at Alpha training, but it's nothing like being in the pack and how my father, Alpha Chet, looks after everyone.

I don't want to be one of those Alpha heirs that come back from training and throws new ideas around undermining everything the last Alpha achieved. Each time a new Alpha is placed in a pack, things change. It's inevitable, but it's what, how, and even why.

My father is an excellent Alpha to the pack and I know he wants to retire and spend more time with my mother. They have always placed the pack's needs first, and now I am of age they are ready to do things they have wanted to do, and travel to other Kingdoms.

The office door opens and my father enters, giving me a solid look over from feet to face. "You have grown to be a good-looking male, son. I can see you've been training just by your size. Your mother and I are very proud of you and the reports we've been given throughout your Alpha training.

"I have plans to travel to the other packs, introduce you to the Alphas and that way you'll begin an alliance of your own, rather than using my reputation and old alliances. It's a good thing to create new bonds with other Alphas, and they are all younger, so will be more in-tune with you, rather than an old beat-up Alpha like myself." Not giving me the time or opportunity to say anything, he continues, "I want to speak with you about Taria. I understand why you are not wanting to bond right away, but it's going to get hard as time goes along. It's not natural to not claim your mate when you find them. But I agree that Taria has to learn to be a competent Luna. She is kind, caring, and works hard, so I'm sure she will be an enormous benefit to the pack. I have had a few reports that her fighting skills are coming along, but it is slower than we thought it would be."

"I want to claim her, but I need her to be fully understanding of her role. She is the most beautiful female I have set eyes on, and I know once we mate, we will be perfect for each other. My worry is that she has not had the responsibility she should have had at this point. Not her fault, I know, but it's something we can't overlook. If we don't teach Taria what's needed, she'll be overwhelmed, and I don't want that to happen." I lay it out the best I can for my father to understand why I've insisted on Taria having all the training I've stipulated.

"Don't leave it too long. Let's see if we can get Taria here with you so your mother can teach her all she needs to know about the pack. This will be her pack, not Blood Pearl, Blackshadow or any other, and I'm sure she'll be excellent in her role as Luna."

"Taria cannot visit Spirit Walker, as Lyle hasn't found his mate yet. He is happy for her to go along and see how he operates, though, but only for a day or two. But I'm not sure Titan will let that slide.

He's becoming edgy, wanting his mate, Maya. He knows why we haven't claimed our mate, and he truly understands, but at the end of the day he is an animal, he's a wolf and he wants what his instincts tell him." I look at my father and get an understanding nod.

"Today I want you to go through the filing cabinets, file-by-file, so you know everything there is to know about them. We can discuss anything you feel you need to know, and any more information to grasp a full understanding of any file. Once you have finished that, which could take you a week or more, I want to enlighten you on the library area of the office."

"Okay, let me get started, and we'll take it a day at a time." I walk over to the filing cabinets, and open the top drawer of the first one, and seeing it's bulging with files, I can't help but think I'm pleased there are only two cabinets.

The days pass agonizingly slowly. The desk I was given to work from is piled with folders, which are stacked as read and to read. I've read nearly every pack member's full history from birth to death in some cases. One thing is more than obvious is the fact the only ones that leave the pack are the females that have found their mate. It is rare for a male to leave to go to another pack, unless it is for a higher position in the pack his mate comes from.

The carpentry shop which the pack opened in Wolfsfoot Town is doing exceedingly well. The three pack members that work within that business are bringing a nice profit to the pack, and enough to top up their pack payment.

Our pack has used investments and bonds to create an income that can provide for pack members. Each member or family receive a stipulated amount and if they don't have a job of their own, they contribute to the pack by cleaning, cooking, gardening, warrior training, and even nursery nurse and doctor.

We now have the carpentry shop, and a clothing store which also does repair work. We give an allotted number of vegetables grown on the pack grounds to be sold at the grocery store, and have even started rearing chickens, pigs, and goats.

The door opens, and Savannah walks into the office. Now this female is doing her best to trap me in her bed. But she has no chance at all. My heart, mind and soul belong to Taria and I would never risk losing her.

"What do you need, Savannah?" I ask with a bored but firm voice.

"I thought we could get together; you know, spend some quality time together."

"You have been told no it's not happening more times than I can count. It's not happening, Savannah, now or in the future. I have found my mate, and she will be here soon to take her rightful place at my side. She will be your Luna once my parents step down, and do you really want her to have a grudge against you from the beginning?"

The stupid pouty look she has makes her look like she's eating something inedible, but she seems to think it makes her appealing. Stepping towards my desk, she hasn't noticed my father appear in the doorway behind her. As she reaches the desk and leans forward to place her hands on it, she jerks when my father, her alpha, snarls.

"Savannah, did you knock on the office door? Or did you just let yourself inside without being told you could enter?"

I lift an eyebrow as I'm waiting for her to lie so I can call her out for it, but it looks like she's swallowing the lie to avoid a punishment from her alpha.

"I entered, Alpha Chet. I'm sorry I just wanted to speak with Bronze as I've not had the opportunity since he came home from Alpha Training."

Oh my, she is simpering, and I'm interested to see what my father's response will be. I lean back in my seat and fold my arms over my chest, and wait.

"You walked into the Alpha Office, without knocking, because you wanted to speak to the Alpha Heir knowing he has a mate who is working hard to achieve what's needed to be the best Luna for the pack in the future... Is that right?"

While my father deeply cares for each member of our pack, he has no tolerance for foolish behavior. Savannah is on the verge of being punished by him, and I can sense that it's about to happen.

Savannah is looking at her feet, placing her weight back and forth, not knowing what to do or what to say as she has been caught out disobeying the command that her Alpha gave at the pack meeting when I arrived home.

"You will only receive half of your pack salary this month. You will work in the kitchen and if I hear one word of complaint that you are lazy, disrespectful, or anything else, you will be placed outside the pack boundary to survive alone for a specified time. You will only be allowed back into the pack if you survive, and if you show remorse for the bullshit you are pulling. Now GET OUT and report to the kitchen."

After Savannah ran out of the office, and my father's blank expression shows me he is relaying his orders. I smirk as I speak, "Well, that was interesting, but I have to admit, I'm grateful. I have had nothing to do with her apart from her being a pack member. She has chased me since," sighing, "since forever, but I've made it more than clear I am not interested. She knows I have found my mate but still came in here. It was harsh to tell her you'd put her outside the pack boundaries."

Taking a seat at his desk, my father chuckles, "Yeah, but what I didn't tell her was I'd put her out of our boundaries and right into Tati's. Can you imagine what she'd do with her knowing she's trying to split up mates."

Shaking my head in amusement because everyone knows that Tati is not a she-wolf to mess with. She is a magnificent Luna and a better friend you would never find. She is, however, a heck of a fighter, being taught by the best over several years now. I don't know her as well as I would like, and I will rectify that as I need to be on friendly terms with all the Alphas and Lunas, in our small part of the Kingdom.

Later that day, I thank everyone in the kitchen for the meal, and notice Savannah is elbow deep in a large sink. I can't help but smirk to myself as it seems she is going to have many of the hated jobs in the kitchen until she proves her worth.

Walking outside, I head for the training area, and stand watching the drill, noting who is doing well and who is struggling. Warrior Dixon, who is our Chief Warrior, is giving Ember tips on how to take down Eloise, but she's not cottoning on all that well, as she is for the second time while I've been watching, slammed onto her back and pinned down.

"Come on, Ember, jump up. Don't stay down. Keep springing back onto your feet and getting back into it."

Ember struggles onto her feet, giving Warrior Dixon a filthy look as she does so before screaming at the top of her lungs and lunging at Eloise who in turn spins, lifts her arm and elbows Ember in the face, knocking her out cold.

"I'm sorry, Warrior Dixon, I just reacted. It's been my homework all week, and it was just instinct to follow through," Eloise panics out, before bending and checking Ember.

"Don't worry about it, Eloise. Ember has to learn, and these are hard lessons, but I may give her a bat and let her hit any enemies with that instead of actual fighting." Warrior Dixon chuckles at his own comment, and Eloise giggles.

Stepping forward, I chuckle to myself. "You have your hands full with Ember, Warrior Dixon. Do you think she'll ever make the grade?"

"Unlikely, but she is fast on her feet so if we are attacked I've told her to make sure all nursing she-wolves, pups and elderly get to the packhouse. She can outrun most of the pack, so her ability would be best used that way."

Nodding in agreement, I look down as Ember starts to come around and Eloise helps her to her feet. "Come on, Ember, let's get you inside for a drink."

Warrior Dixon, and I watch the two she-wolves walk to the packhouse before turning to study the rest of the pack training. Discussing how the training is progressing, and the percent of casualties we could expect from the pack members I am watching, if we were to be attacked. All-in-all, we have work to do to get everyone at the ready, and I'm thinking it's a high possibility that the five packs in our part of the Kingdom will end up going to war with the no-man's-land rogues. If they have themselves a viable Alpha as leader then we cannot throw away any chance to be ready for war.

My mind wanders to Taria, and how I'm going to keep her safe. She's going to have to fight, and she's going to have to be good at it. She'll need to be as feisty as her mother has been, and I know she's got it in her, we just have to bring it out.

Chapter 2

TARIA

My first stay and learning experience was going to be with Luna Tati and Alpha Gabe of the Wolfsfoot Pack, but they have something pending and won't have the time right now. I'm at the Blackshadow Pack and following Luna Hope, who is showing, or rather teaching me, how she rules as Luna to the pack.

Walking into the dining room, I quickly take a bowl of oatmeal, drizzle it with honey, and sit at an empty table. I am trying not to take advantage of Luna Hope and Alpha Connell's kindness, allowing me to be here and learn all I can.

Gamzin, the Delta of the pack, takes a seat across from me, and I grin when I see his plate piled high with pancakes, breakfast muffins, scrambled eggs, bacon, and toast.

"I know what you're thinking, but I'm a growing wolf." Delta Gamzin chuckles, and I'm sure that's more for his amusement than mine.

"It's plenty to get you started for the day. Do you have a mid-morning snack, lunch, afternoon snack, and later, the main meal?" I ask, grinning because that would really be one heck of a lot of food for anyone to eat.

"How did you know that? Have you been speaking with Chief Warrior Oscar?"

"No, I have hardly spoken with anyone yet," I admit, but watch as he shovels food into his mouth as I responded.

He eats a lot of food. Maya, my wolf, speaks by mind linking.

'He does, and I think he's going to be amusing, too,' I reply to her. I can see she's sitting in the back of my mind, watching Delta Gamzin closely.

Looking up at me as I place the spoon in my bowl, Delta Gamzin grins. "You'll need more than that to eat once the training starts or you'll be passing out with hunger."

He's right, we need to eat more. We will use more energy, so burn more of what we eat. We can hunt and I'll eat more rabbits. Maya chuckles to herself as she lies down in the back of my mind, resting her head on her front paws. I quickly eat while thinking about what the day may be like.

"Morning, Taria."

Turning as I respond, "Good Morning," I give Luna Hope and Alpha Connell a small smile.

"We'll be walking around the pack this morning, so make sure you are ready in around twenty minutes."

"I'll be ready Luna Hope."

"None of that Luna Hope. You call us Hope and Connell. We are going to be allies, after all. Oh, and call that hungry monster Gamzin, not Delta Gamzin. We don't sit on ceremony here in the

Blackshadow Pack." Hope grabs Connell's hand and pulls him to the head table to have their breakfast.

Knowing I'm dismissed for the moment, I grab my bowl, give Gamzin a smile before taking my bowl to the kitchen, leaving it on a kitchen counter after thanking Nora one of the kitchen helpers.

Rushing to my room, I quickly freshen up before heading to Luna Hope's office. After knocking with no reply, I take a seat next to the office door. It's a bench and hard as all heck on your butt, but I sit quietly waiting for her to arrive. I'm happy that I receive smiles and *good morning* comments from pack members as they pass by.

Luna Hope arrives probably thirty minutes after I sat here, but I don't let her know I've been waiting that long. I don't want to look over eager and desperate.

"Come on into the office, Taria. We'll get down to it because I can imagine you have been waiting for me for a while. I'm not a very good timekeeper as I get easily distracted. Thankfully, the pack members now know me well enough that they don't stress when I'm late."

I don't hold back the grin on my face, mainly as she has a huge smile on her own after telling me this. Opening the office door, the first thing you notice is the smell of lavender. It's not strong, but is soothing as it seems to wrap around you.

"Okay, we are going to walk around the pack. I'll introduce you to people and point out places of interest. I won't try to fill you in on too much at once, as it's overwhelming. We, as Lunas have a lot to check, housekeeping, food supplies, nursing mothers, new pups, and the school. We also need to fight as we are protectors, the same as our mates, but we don't have the strength they have, but we can be cunning." Luna Hope checks over notes that have been left on her desk, but gives me a nod to follow her out of the office.

Walking beside Luna Hope, she turns and gives me a smile. "We are going to the kitchen. It appears some of the garden stock is not ready, so we have to do some menu changes."

Walking into the kitchen, it is bustling, and Luna Hope introduces me to Isla, Evangeline, Lorna, Nora, and Betina whilst we head to the office where all the kitchen assignments happen. "Knock, knock, are you free to look at the supplies now, Nessie?"

"Of course I am, Luna Hope. Come in, and bring the lovely Luna Heir Taria with you." Nessie holds her hand out to shake mine, and I give it easily, along with a broad smile.

I watch, listen and learn for over an hour as Luna Hope and Nessie discuss the garden, what is ready for harvesting and what is slightly delayed. They then run through the menu and what needs to be altered. I was amazed at the ease they worked together to achieve a new menu ready for the following week.

I don't know if the Eclipse Pack has a garden similar to Black Shadow Packs, but if not, I'm certainly going to discuss implementing one.

"I can see your mind working from here, Taria." Luna Hope smiles. "The Eclipse Pack has a garden that works for the pack and they have extra they sell in Wolfsfoot Town. But they could do with some diversity, and I'll show you what I mean when we go outside."

An hour later, we are walking through an orchard, with an area where mushrooms grow too. It really is an eye-opening experience and makes me realize how little I know and have been contributing to the Blood Pearl Pack over the last few years. I have to admit I'm rather ashamed of myself because I could have been helping my mother, taking some of the pressure off her shoulders.

After I've eaten lunch, I go to my room where I freshen up and make a call to my mother. It's too far to mind link her, but I want to discuss my feelings.

"Hi, Taria, are you okay, sweetheart?"

Hearing my mother's voice brings a huge smile to my face. "I'm good. I wanted to say I'm sorry, I should have been helping you. Watching Luna Hope has brought home to me how little I did to ease your burden, and I'm sorry."

"Listen, Taria, if I had wanted you to do more, I would have told you. It has been my wanting control over everything that has led to you not receiving the proper training you should have had. It really is my own fault that I did everything, but I'm also sorry that you now must go through all this training instead of being with Bronze, which is where you should be."

"Luna Aurora, we have a breach. Alpha Gerry wants us to go protect the pups." Hearing this in the background, I know something is happening again.

"I have to go, Taria, but I'll speak soon. Love you…"

Before I can respond the phone goes quiet and I know she has gone. I pray to the Goddess that everyone will remain alive and well. It brings home to me also that I need to learn to fight to protect the pack members. I have been training while here the last few days, but I need to step up my own commitment to becoming the best I can be.

Two hours later I am exhausted, but know I have given everything I have to the session. Chief Warrior Oscar gives me a grin as he walks beside me back to the packhouse. "You did very well today, Taria. You chipped four minutes off your run around the perimeter. That is superb and you need to recognize all the minor achievements as well as the large ones. Putting Weldon on his butt wasn't easy and I know he wasn't paying attention when you did it, but, let's be honest, that is the time that you get the upper hand in a fight. You did good, and I am looking forward to seeing you continue with the determination you showed today."

I shower, change and am brushing my hair when someone knocks lightly on the bedroom door. Walking over and opening the door, I give a smile to Luna Hope. "The Shifter Council will arrive tomorrow, Taria. I wanted to give you a pre-warning. They speak to all Lunas, so I'm not surprised they are going to come and visit you. Just be yourself and you'll be fine."

Now, that is something I wasn't aware happened, but I'm not particularly surprised either. The council seem to have a hand in all aspects of the packs, and more so since it came to light some of their members were not fully reliable or honest.

"Okay, thank you. I'll be ready for them."

"Come on, let's have our meal, then you can have the evening free to do as you like. Maybe Maya would like to go for a run. I'll make sure someone is available to run with you."

"I want to speak with Bronze later, but I would like to give Maya a run. She hasn't had one for three weeks and is well ready to stretch her legs and feel the wind in her coat."

Luna Hope tucks my arm with hers, and we head to the dining room, where Alpha Connell is waiting impatiently for his mate. I have heard the stories about his father and the way Tati was treated. But, while I have been here, I've seen nothing but good things regarding Alpha Connell, and I think he has redeemed himself in the eyes of the Goddess.

After I've eaten my meal, I excuse myself from Luna Hope and Alpha Connell and walk into the kitchen where everyone is bustling around cleaning as all the dirty dishes arrive from the dining room.

"Nessie, I'll help clear the dishes. I can rinse and place in the dishwasher as well as clear away the counters. If anyone needs an evening free from duties, I'm happy to give someone that opportunity."

"You don't have to do that Taria." Nessie is giving me a look full of shock.

"I know I don't, but I'd like to anyway, if that is alright with you, of course."

"Isla, get yourself off duty. You've gone the longest without a break, so take time out, but make sure you thank Taria for taking your duties over this evening." Nessie is giving Isla a look that says, *come on, make the most of it.*

"Thank you so much, Taria. This is a lovely surprise. I can spend some extra time with Baildon and my pup." Isla kisses my cheek before rushing out of the kitchen and leaving the kitchen ladies, all giggling.

"Okay, you need to roll up your sleeves and stand at that sink. Roll a cloth over the dishes in the suds, then dip in the second sink before placing in the dishwasher. Then repeat, you'll be at that for quite some time."

Nessie's not wrong either. I work for another two hours, filling and emptying the dishwashers, because it turns out they have three. Who would have guessed? Everyone is pleasant. They laugh as they work, helping each other when it's needed. I like this atmosphere and I'm going to make sure the Eclipse Pack has the same warmth.

We go run now?

'Yes, Maya, we can go for a run now.' I quickly head outside and shift, remembering at the last moment I was supposed to have someone run with me.

"You forget you were to be accompanied, Taria?" Chief Warrior Oscar asks, making Maya jump in the process. "I'll run with you, but follow along with me. No running off."

Maya gives Chief Warrior Oscar a nod by dipping her nose, letting him know she understands. We are not able to mind-link as I am not a pack member. But I'll make sure Maya follows his instructions.

I rest while Maya runs with Conan, Warrior Oscar's large gray and white wolf. My mind is running through all I've learned today, from the kitchen arranging meals right through to learning about the council coming to see me. Whatever happens, I will show myself in the best light I can. I don't want Bronze to be disappointed in me, and I don't want him to feel he has to reject me because I'm not good enough to do what is needed.

Chapter 3

BRONZE

Looking around the office, I have to admit to myself that two weeks in here has driven me a little stir crazy. Titan, my wolf, is whining and pacing for his mate, and I know he understands why Taria and her wolf, Maya, are not mated with us yet, but he could give it a rest. My head is constantly aching with the pity-party he has going on.

I want mate!

'I know you do, Titan, but we are doing what is right for us and the pack. I want my mate too, and we'll get Taria and Maya. We just have to be patient.'

In the back of my mind Titan huffs, circles a few times then lays down with his back to me. Sulking! Boy, I hope these next few weeks pass quickly.

Placing the last of the folders on my desk back into the filing cabinet, I let out a relieved breath. I hope I'm going to remember all the information, but I'm sure my father will remind me if I forget.

The door to the office opens and my mother walks inside. "Are you all finished, Bronze?"

"I am, and I'm hoping I remember everyone's information because there are a lot of members." I give her a kiss on her cheek when she lifts her face. I know what she expects and as her only pup, she was always very affectionate towards me.

"You will remember more when you get to know everyone in the pack personally. You have to make the effort to go to the garden, kitchen, training sessions, etc., etc. There is a lot to cover, but if your father and I can do it, so can you. You know the younger pack members, so that is not going to be an issue."

"I did as father asked and kept myself away from the she-wolves, and kept myself apart from the males. I only had a friendship with Xander and Wesley. They kept in touch with me while I was at Alpha camp, and I know they'll help me reach out to everyone." I know mother has more to say as she's settled herself into one of the easy chairs.

"I want to discuss Taria, and what I will need to teach her regarding our pack. She is learning from the other Lunas, as you well know, but all packs have their own way of doing things, and it's here that Taria will be the Luna. I want her to feel she can make any changes she sees fit, and doesn't feel she has to be answerable to me or your father. You, as her mate and the Alpha of the pack, will need to be aware that Taria doesn't become overwhelmed."

Taking a perch on the edge of the desk, I look at mother, and give her a slight smile. "I will be careful with Taria, but she is strong. She will be a great Luna. She has to learn to fight because of the war that is coming, and before you say more, mother, there will be a war because the rogue Alpha is not going to sit back for years to come. He has an agenda, and we know this from what developed with Luna Aurora, and the information she procured."

"I have been telling your father that we need to ensure more females in the pack can fight. Maybe not as warriors, but be able to do something, even if it's throwing pans and dishes accurately."

Now, I can't help the smirk that crosses my face thinking about the kitchen females throwing everything they can lay their hands on at a rogue enemy.

"Stop smirking, I know what you are imagining..." the giggle that my mother gives shows me she's imagining the same thing and also finding it highly amusing. Ash, our chief cook, is handy when she flicks her tea towel so I can just imagine how accurate she would be with a skillet.

"I'll speak to father about training, but as for Taria, let's see how she gets along at Blackshadow and Wolfsfoot Packs before we think of what she will need when she arrives here. I have no intention of not claiming her, mother. I just didn't want the bond to start before she was ready to show how capable she is. You and I both know the pack would jump on her if she wasn't confident and able. I have an appointment with the Elders, and I can tell you now that I will not take any idiocy from them."

Mother pats my shoulder while giving me a look that says she knows exactly what I mean. Then, after kissing my cheek, she walks out of the office, closing the door quietly behind her. I know she'll help Taria as much as she can, and if I'm totally honest, I can't wait to have my mate here alongside me.

Looking around the office, I know that I can do no more than I have at this time. Next on my list of things to look at and organize is the warrior training schedules. I'll need to watch a few sessions on the training field and speak with Chief Warrior Dixon. Now he has a massive wolf and his name 'Beast' portrays him perfectly. He is the best fighter and trainer I've encountered or even heard of, and I know that the Shifter Council have tried to lure him away with no luck.

Leaving the office, I think of mother's advice and head to the kitchen. Seeing Ash scolding someone at one of the sinks, I wait for her to finish and try not to smirk when I see it's Savannah that's getting the negative attention. Noticing me standing across the kitchen, Ash gives me an eye-roll and walks over to me.

"Why? Why do you do this to me all the time? What have I ever done to you as pack leaders that warrants punishing me with all the half-wits in the pack? I hope she finds her mate and he's from a pack far, far away." Taking a deep breath, she calms herself, and then her usual pretty smile resurfaces. "Now, to what do I owe the pleasure of your company?"

"I just came to see if there was anything my favorite cook needs or desires?" Smiling at Ash, I see the cogs turning before she replies.

"You could find another way of punishing people other than sending them to me. That would be an excellent start. The kitchen is running well otherwise. The teams are good and working well together. I don't need any more *helpers*, thank you very much. Maybe you could send them to warrior training or gardening for a change. Anywhere but here would be good." Ash laughs as she says this in an exasperated tone of voice.

"Cookies, Ash. That always works for me... Cookies," I suggest, grinning as I make my way to the garden.

Our garden has come on well recently. A pack member emerged as a keen gardener and to say he has green fingers is an understatement. He has taken the small kitchen garden we had and turned it into a business in its own right. I have to admit to being one of the doubters when he asked for the position of head gardener. His name, Herb, was just too funny at the time, but he has made all his doubters become the laughingstock. He has extended the garden into what you could only describe as a hobby farm.

He has left the kitchen garden by the back door of the kitchen for herbs and suchlike. He persuaded my father to give him some land by the edge of the forest and he cleared it and had vegetables in there within months. He now has three full-time helpers, and they've fenced it and erected two small greenhouses for potting and a large one for some more exotic, hotter climate fruits. I don't think there's going to be any limits to what Herb will achieve. He has plans for it to become both fully organic and self-sustaining. He even pays Ash for her waste vegetable peelings and as long as she separates the meat products, he takes her leftovers that she can't use.

I know his chicken coops paid dividends from day one and he has further plans for his goats, sheep and pigs. I haven't heard about any cows yet, but I won't be surprised to wake up one morning to the bawling of a few calves.

Hearing hammering and the sound of drills coming from the forest, I walk over and see Herb busily putting up a wooden building.

"Hi, Herb. Livestock pen?"

"Morning, Alpha Heir Bronze. No, not yet. Just a shed for all the tools we're accumulating. We've too many to keep leaving them out everywhere now, and I want to keep them clean and in good repair. If we do decide to go down the organic road, I want any councilmen to see that we take pride in everything."

"I think you should keep a log of all the improvements that you implement. A few photographs wouldn't hurt, either. You could use that when the time came to show them how much work you've put into it." I think that's a great idea and even if it never got used for that purpose, it would serve as an inspiration for any pack members in the future that took on a similar improvement project that these things take time.

Herb looks at me a bit shyly. "I have kept a photo history of everything from when I started as a personal record. I could do some copies and make up a project folder."

"You do that, and let me know if you need anything. I don't expect you to finance that as well. I know that you use some of your personal finances already, and I want that to stop." Wagging my finger at him has him blush and I know I've caught him out.

Leaving him to his construction, I finally make my way to the training area. As I approach, I hear Chief Warrior Dixon's voice boom out. "You're not in the schoolyard now! It's time you realized exactly what warrior training is all about and started taking it seriously. Form a circle as wolves, all of you."

In the training area, Dixon is now surrounded by his trainees, and he doesn't look happy at all. Before I can ask why, he shouts again. "Attack me!" The trainees tentatively move forward and he roars again, scaring half of them to within an inch of peeing their pants, I'm sure. "Attack me!" Seeing him shift into Beast has me worried for all of them.

This time they all rush at him, and I can only say it is a massacre. Within seconds, all the trainees are down and appear to be bleeding from some part of their anatomy. One springs back up, and despite blood dripping from her shoulder, faces Beast again. As

I see her muscles tense for her spring, Beast shifts to Dixon and he catches her by the throat in mid leap.

"Adaline! Stand down... You have been the star pupil in today's lesson. Please go and get your injury looked at. The rest of you need to take notice of Adaline's commitment. I will not tolerate this kind of lazy attitude towards your training. From now on, anyone that does not give me one hundred percent of their effort will receive extra duties within the pack. Dismissed."

"I'm sorry you had to witness that display, Alpha Heir Bronze. I assure you they will do better from now on." Chief Warrior Dixon shakes his head as he watches how slowly some of his class shift back to human form, and limp dejectedly away from the training area.

"I came to discuss the warrior training schedules with you. Do you need more time?" I raise an eyebrow because if this is where we are at in our training, we are in a far worse position than I thought.

"The schedules are drawn up and awaiting your approval. This was my newest class that have just reached the age to start their warrior awareness training. They treated the entire lesson as though it were playtime in one of their nursery classes. They needed the short sharp shock treatment, I'm afraid. I'm sure they will be more focused next time."

"I'm sure they will and if not, I trust that you will show them the error of their ways? Leave the prepared schedules in the Alpha office, and I'll look them over when I'm done meeting with the elders. I'm sure that you will have them as complete and satisfactory as always."

Receiving a head tilt from Chief Warrior Dixon, I head back to the packhouse and my meeting with the elders. The elders have had a place in the pack for as long as I can remember. History tells us that a pack Alpha was running the pack to further his personal wealth and not for any other reason. At that time, the elders came into being to prevent this ever happening again and to ensure that the pack was always the first concern of all those in positions of power.

My father considered disbanding this elder group several times, as he believes that they display the very traits that they were set up to prevent. When I heard this, I did some digging in our library archives and nothing states they are any form of legal body or that they are required at all. In one of the early Alpha diaries, I found the entry that describes their original purpose and it does not include anything that they have become over time. I had a certified copy of the entry made by the pack secretary, which I have in my pocket.

Entering the packhouse, I see my father waiting for me. "The elders are in the Alpha office. I'll escort you in and then I'll leave you to it. Don't forget that you are the Alpha Heir. They answer to you and the pack, not the other way around. They have only the power to report or suggest, not command or make demands."

Taking the certified copy from my pocket, I let him read it.

"Oh, brilliant, son. I wish I'd thought of that years ago. Damn, that's a subtle move. I almost wish I could stay in there now."

Pushing the office door open, my father ushers me in before him. I'm not fully in the office before one of the elders shouts at me.

"You need to knock before you enter an office, young man. Did your father teach you nothing?"

Sensing my father's fury, I merely step into the office before he knocks me to the ground in his haste to confront the speaker.

"I do not need anyone's permission to enter my own office and you, sir, need to remember that it is neither your office nor your place to speak to the Alpha Heir in such a manner. Address the pack's Alpha Heir, my son, in that way again and I will meet you in the training ring as is my right. Are we clear on that point?" It is obvious that my father is in Alpha Chet mode.

When there is no answer forthcoming, my father steps further into the room and addresses all the elders. "You will answer my question. Is that clear, or I will take it you as the elders, as a whole, wish to challenge my authority in the ring. What is it to be?"

Three of the members look at the fourth and he shifts uncomfortably in his seat. "We are clear, Alpha Chet."

"In formal proceedings such as these, you will address me as Alpha Blueblood."

"We are clear on both points, Alpha Blueblood. My apologies."

My father turns to me, gives me an outrageous wink that almost has me bursting out laughing, and then leaves the room whispering, "Give them hell, son."

Entering the room fully, I sit in my father's chair at his desk, and not in the seat at the table that has obviously been left in front of the four of them to be intimidating.

After formal introductions have been made, as if I didn't already know who they were, they begin making suggestions as to how I should proceed when my father steps down in a week's time. This surprises me, as there have been no discussions as to when I will formally take over the pack.

"Where did the timeframe come from, may I ask?"

"What timeframe?" Elder Francis asks.

"The one that you've just quoted. The one where my father steps down next week!" I try to sound confused, as if I'd missed something.

"We would expect you to take over as soon as possible. You want to get in the *big chair*, don't you?" Michael is the one that my father faced down. I've taken a very strong dislike to him and I foresee us having problems.

"Oh, I see. I'm expected to give him the date of his stepping down. Very well, continue."

Noting down their suggestions on my pad from my father's desk, I see a pattern emerging. Giving them a little more rope to hang themselves with, I sit quietly as though agreeing to all their ideas. When they suggest that I look for a mate from no-man's-land as a way to keep us out of the coming war, this is the last straw.

"Elder members of the pack..." I begin but am soon spoken over.

"We are the elder council, if you please." Michael again.

"Elder members of the pack, and if you interrupt me again, Michael, you will meet me in the ring, not my father. IS THAT CLEAR? You are only a council by your own choosing. There has never been an elder council and unless you cease this nonsense that you have made yourselves into, there won't even be any 'Elder members' meetings. That is what this is, after all, a meeting granted to you by the Alpha of the pack."

"There has been an elder council since time immemorial, Alpha Heir Bronze. There will always be an elder council and you will respect it." This elder has been quiet so far and appears to be the youngest of the elders.

"Jude, isn't it? History tells us that Saint Jude was the patron saint of lost causes, I believe, and you are certainly that gentlemen. I have heard enough of your self-righteous bullshit, and your demands that only benefit yourselves and your families since we sat down. I have scoured the archives and there is no elder council, nor has there ever been one. Elders' *meetings* were set up to stop a corrupt Alpha and prevent a recurrence. That was all there was, or ever has been. Over time, your predecessors have tried to become more powerful and wealthier by insinuating themselves into being more than they are." Taking the copy of the Alpha diary from my pocket, I pass it to Jude.

"Currently, none of you give to the pack. You have a wage, a substantial one at that, free food, free housing, free clothing. In fact, you pay for nothing. You gentlemen, are parasites, and are no longer to be tolerated as such. I will be drawing up an elder members' charter in the future that will determine what is required of you and what remuneration you will receive, if any. Living for free will cease on the day I take over the pack. That is a certainty."

Watching their faces go ashen as they realize that their days of lording it over the pack have ended with the paper they have been handed.

"You will not dictate to me who my mate will be. You are all well aware that my mate is currently preparing herself to become an outstanding Luna, and yet you have the audacity to suggest that I abandon her and my moral responsibilities to our allied packs by taking a mate from no-man's-land to save your wealth and future. That diary entry states that after five alphas have succeeded the corrupt one, the elders may be disbanded by any alpha that sees fit to do so.

"Gentlemen. If one word of this meeting leaves these four walls, you will find that I will be that alpha. Now get out of my office and prepare yourselves to once more be of some use to this pack."

Chapter 4

TARIA

As I am waiting to be summoned before the Shifter Council, I feel my nerves starting to get the better of me. I've seen the council at Blood Pearl Pack in the past, but they were always there to have dealings with my mother, never me.

You are strong. Don't let them take the lead.

'I hear you, Maya, but it's not that easy. I want to appear strong so they don't put obstacles in the way of me going to the Eclipse Pack and Bronze.'

Don't appear strong. Be strong.

Hearing my name spoken, I look up and see Councilman Flint standing by the Alpha's office door.

"Taria, please join us." Flint waits for me to proceed him into the office, and gestures to a chair at the table that Alpha Connell uses for his formal meetings.

The council members, Flint, Porter, Lykos, Roman, and Cinder, all introduce themselves formally, smiling and nodding. I must look a little puzzled, so Flint explains that not all council members are present. I certainly remember there being more when they came to the Blood Pearl Pack. There was one female member that my mother used to rant about whenever the council was mentioned. I wonder which she is?

"Taria, we visit all packs and especially when new leaders are emerging. As the Shifter Council, we try to encourage the best traits we can from each new Alpha, or Luna to benefit not only the individual packs but also the kingdom as a whole. The kingdom remains strong and safe for all when the packs are in harmony," Flint recites this as though it has been said a million times before, and it probably has.

"Ladies and gentlemen, let me assure you that not only do I have my mother's strength running in my veins, but also my father's compassion. That does not make me a tyrant nor a pushover. In the last few months, I have seen that I was unaware of responsibilities that I could, no... should have taken onboard to assist in the running of the pack." Taking the time to look each council member in the eye, I continue. "While being here, Luna Hope has opened my eyes further to simple acts that enhance the pack's morale, and their bond with each other. I have no doubt that with each Luna I visit, I will find things that will help me become the Luna that I'm expected to be, both for the Eclipse pack and my mate, Alpha Heir Bronze."

The next hour involves the council members asking me questions, giving me scenarios and them giving lots of umm's and ahh's. Councilman Flint is supportive of me throughout, and Councilman Lykos says very little but watches me like a hawk the whole time with an occasional grin.

I am surprised by the questions that are put forward, as they are far more insightful and not as personal as I was expecting. When they have exhausted their questions, I thank them for their time and ask several questions of my own. How did my answers compare to their expectations? Was there anything else they needed to clarify? Would I get feedback on this experience, and would each member care to give me their own thoughts of the meeting, rather than just a simple, 'It went well' or 'It could have gone better.'

Being escorted from the room by Councilman Flint, he asks if I would join him for lunch? He would be free in just a few moments and would be pleased if I would sit with him. Agreeing, I walk into the canteen area and find a quiet spot to wait for him.

Someone throwing themselves into the chair next to me has me letting out a little squeal and I turn to see Luna Hope. Eyes as wide as an owl's she starts to fire questions at me so fast that I can't possibly answer her. When she finally stops to draw breath, I can't help but burst out laughing.

"I have no clue what you've just asked me, Hope. The questions came so fast I don't know a single thing you said."

"Well, I want to know everything, of course." Luna Hope's excitement is interrupted as Councilman Flint asks if he can join us.

As he takes a seat, Hope jumps up to leave, but I grab her arm and pull her back into her seat. "I'm not worried that you hear anything that Councilman Flint has to say, Luna Hope. What I've learned since being here has only been positive, so any negativity won't reflect badly on you."

"First of all, Taria, let's dispense with the Councilman title when we're not being formal. The meeting went on longer than any of us expected, but in a purely positive way. Your answers were more in-depth than we expected, and this led to more questions being asked than normal. Lykos thinks that you and his daughter, Tati, will become great friends. He believes that you are so alike that you could be sisters."

"He didn't say much, but I was aware of how he observed me throughout, and he kept having a sly grin at some of the points I raised," looking from Flint to Hope to see what reaction they had to this.

"He said that some of your clarifications could have come straight from Tati's mouth, and he grinned when he recognized her frustration in you, too." Flint was also grinning as he passed this information on.

"Oh, I'm so relieved that it all went well. Not that I didn't expect it to, but when you're in front of the council, they can be so cold and impersonal sometimes." Realizing that she's saying this in front of one of them has Hope blushing furiously. "I have to get back to work," she squeaks, jumps up, and runs into the kitchen.

Flint laughs as he watches her back disappear and says, "She is such a good Luna you can't help but love her, even if she thinks I'm cold.

"You have impressed the council greatly, Taria. We have no doubt that unless something serious happens to throw you off track, you'll be a great addition to the Eclipse pack and an excellent mate to Bronze." Flint tilts his head to one side before uttering his next words. "Umm… Bronze asked me to ask you to contact him after the meeting, if you would be okay with it. He didn't know how to approach it directly without it appearing he was checking up on your progress, rather than it being a genuine case of concern on your behalf."

"I'll do it straight away and thank you, Flint. You have been very kind throughout this meeting and I hope that our friendship will flourish in the future. I'd be happy to count you as one of my circle of good friends."

"I have things to attend to, so perhaps we can have a rain check on lunch?"

"I can do that. Whenever you have some free time, let me know and I'll be happy to join you. I'll go put a call through to Bronze and let him know how the *'Cold and impersonal'* council treated me." Both laughing, we go our separate ways as we leave the canteen area.

Sitting in my room with my phone in my hand, I suddenly get butterflies and come over all girlie and giggly.

It's only a phone call. You're not going to mate with him.

'Trust you to jump straight to mating, Maya. You wolves have a one-track mind.'

Two, if you want to be precise. You forgot food. There's nothing like a warm rabbit in your teeth to make you feel good.

'I haven't fully got used to that yet. Not sure I ever will.'

When we're out in the forest and you're hungry, you'll appreciate it then. Now get this call made while I rest and don't have to listen to you gushing.

Maya turns around a few times and then throws herself to the floor of my mind with her back to me.

Placing the call to Bronze, it hardly rings when I hear his voice. "Taria, thank you for calling. Are you okay? Did it go well? How hard were you questioned? Flint passed my message okay, then?"

"Yes, yes. Not too hard and yes."

"I'm sorry. That was a bit of a mouthful, wasn't it? I was just concerned that they would find something to delay you coming here."

"Honestly?" I tease him, as I'm sure that he wants me there as much as I want to be there with him.

"Of course, honestly. I can't wait for you to join me here and start our lives together. I think you're going to be a top rate Luna for the pack, and you'll see where we can make improvements. I don't mean my parents weren't good for the pack, but there are always things that someone coming from the outside can see more clearly."

"I wonder what Luna Sage will think of me when we meet."

"Don't worry on that score. Mom is already excited about you coming here. She has been making lists of things she wants to show you, places to take you, recipes to teach you. She's confident that by the time you get here there'll be nothing left to teach you about being a Luna to the pack."

"You tell her together, we'll tick the boxes of everything on her lists. She sounds wonderful and I can't wait to join her." My laughter stops with his next words.

"I can't wait for you to join me, Taria. If there was a way to speed things up, I'd gladly do it. I wish we didn't have to go through this training period. And don't get me started on Titan. He's driving me insane with his constant whining for Maya. I wouldn't mind, but they have one-track minds!" He sounds exactly like I did when I spoke with Maya.

"If you say that to Titan, Bronze, see if he gives you the same answer that Maya gave me earlier when we had the very same conversation. She pointed out that she had a two-track mind, as I had forgotten about food."

"Give me a second to say that..." There's a brief silence and then Bronze is back. "He mentioned rabbits in his mouth and the salty taste of their blood."

"They'll get on well together. She said rabbits, too." I feel Maya stir in my mind.

Standing and stretching, she says, *I told you so. And we need pups, too. We should have heirs.*

"I'm not telling him we want heirs, Maya. That's a conversation for further down the line, not this soon."

Hearing Bronze laughing loudly brings me back to the phone call.

"What are you laughing at?"

"Oh, Taria. You said that out loud. I think that was a conversation that should have been in your mind and not to me. I must admit, though, I'm certainly with Maya on wanting a family. How do you feel about it?"

"Of course I want a family, but not within minutes of getting together. Jeez, you guys kill me."

Hearing someone in Bronze's background, he tells me he's sorry but has to go. Saying goodbye and hearing the silence has me feeling sad.

See! You, too, are ready for pups!

Walking from my room heading for the gardens, I see Alpha Connell by his office door. Waving for me to join him, I follow him into his office. Taking the seat that he indicates in front of his desk, I wonder what he wants me for.

"Hi, Taria. I've been talking to Flint and the other council members. It seems you have made quite an impression at your meeting. Porter made several complimentary statements about you, and for him to make a single compliment about someone is unusual. You should be very proud of yourself. Hope and I are proud of what you have achieved, and we think you have such a lot to give."

"I don't know what to say, Alpha Connell, except thank you for everything that you and Luna Hope are doing to help me develop myself." I feel a little embarrassed by the positive feedback I'm getting after the council meeting. I thought I'd held my own, but apparently, I excelled. Wow.

I told you, be strong and you were. Now you are reaping the benefits.

"I don't want to keep you, but I felt it wouldn't be fair if I didn't pass on the feelings of everyone that has been associated with your training. With everything that is being thrown at you, I think you are processing it all extremely well."

Standing up and offering my hand across the desk, Alpha Connell steps around and gives me a hug. "I think that deserves more than a handshake, Taria."

The door bursts open and the whirlwind that is Hope rushes in. "You spoke to her already? I wanted to do that, Connell. You stole my thunder."

Hope replaces Connell and gives me an enormous hug that almost takes my breath away.

"That's what you get for insulting a councilman to his face." Connell laughs at the shocked look on Hope's face.

"Oh, my God. He told you that? I was so mortified when I realized."

Slipping away as they discuss Hope's unintended insult, I finally make my way to the garden.

Chapter 5

BRONZE

Walking to the training area, I have arranged to meet Chief Warrior Dixon and see how the female training is coming along. I have an idea to try out, and I also have a surprise for one of the females that needs a bit of an edge, as her skills are not warrior based.

As I approach Dixon, he sees me and begins blowing on one hand, as if it was cold. "What are you doing?"

"I'm just warming my hand so I can do this…" He turns his hand palm up and then slaps himself on his forehead. "I believe I have the patience of a saint when it comes to training, but it must be on vacation every time it comes to the females. There is improvement, but by the Goddess, it's negligible. I don't know whether it's me or them, but something isn't clicking."

"Perhaps I can be of assistance," I say with a smug look on my face.

Dixon squints at me suspiciously. "Give it your best shot."

"Ember," I call out and one of the females jumps to attention as though she's been shot. "Come here, please, Ember."

Walking towards me, she looks terrified. Giving her my warmest smile, she stumbles as though I just snarled at her. Dixon bursts out laughing and tells me I look like I'm going to bite her head off and eat it.

"Ember, there's nothing to worry about, I have a gift to help with your warrior training." Still looking terrified, she flinches as I hold open a large carryall with my hands. Reaching in slowly, as though there's a bear trap or something inside, she finds the gift, slowly takes it out and then squeals with delight.

"For me? Truly, Alpha Heir Bronze?" She looks as excited as Titan with a rabbit.

"All yours. I hope it helps."

Looking at Dixon, she can't hold her excitement back. "Chief Warrior Dixon! Look what I've got! Isn't it fantastic? It even has my name on it! I love it. I am so gonna do better now!"

"May the Goddess help us all," Dixon looks at me and shakes his head as Ember rushes back to the training area.

"Okay ladies, who's first?" Standing there swirling her baseball bat like she's about to hit a home run, all the females look at the bat, then to me and back to Ember. "Well, come on. You were keen when I couldn't fight back. Let's see what you're made of now!"

Still shaking his head, Dixon punches my shoulder. "See what you've done now? You've created a monster. She'll have someone's head off by the end of training. You mark my words."

"I think you'll have to do one-on-one training with Ember. I think she'll surprise you with her confidence now, though."

Turning towards me, Ember shouts, "Thank you, Alpha Heir Bronze. I won't let you down if I have to use this in anger. It's awesome."

"Ember, your training is over for today. I'll arrange a training program just for you, and we'll work on your technique." Dixon watches her skip away and as she does so, swirling her bat, she sticks her tongue out at the rest of the class.

"I have another surprise for you," I tell Dixon and laugh as he groans out loud. "If you think that was good, wait till you see this one. I've excelled, even if I say so myself."

"Please, please, please, stop helping me. I don't think I can take much more of your *help*," Dixon watches me for any clues as to what I am about to inflict on him.

"Adaline! You're up!"

Watching Adaline retrieve another of my carryalls, Dixon is positively sweating gallons. I watch as his anxiety grows while Adaline walks up to the first female who takes something from the bag, and going around the class until they are all holding a small rucksack with a fluffy toy puppy sticking out of each one.

Adaline puts her rucksack on and instructs the class to do the same. Forming them into a circle, she explains the rules of the next exercise.

"You all have a pup. Your primary objective is to protect that pup at all costs. Your secondary objective is to get your opponent's pup away from them. Attached to each pup, there are two pieces of paper, one red and one green. The red one is a penalty for losing your pup, the green one is a reward for the one who steals it. To begin with, this will be a one-on-one exercise. Remember this. If it comes to war with the rogues, the toy pup you are carrying now could be a real pup in the future. Chief Warrior Dixon, would you call out two names, please?"

"Sofia and Eve, step forward. On my word you will commence... GO!"

Eve shoots forward and looks as though she has taken Sofia by surprise, but at the last moment, Sofia drops low and sweeps Eve's feet from beneath her. As Eve falls to the ground, Sofia plucks the pup from Eve's pack. Sofia stands there with a look of complete surprise on her face. Eve looks up from the ground and, seeing her pup in Sofia's hand, she rolls onto her back and slaps the ground in anger.

Holding her hand out to Eve, Sofia helps her up. Looking at the green paper, she carefully opens it and reads the reward out loud. "One day of my choice, free from any pack duties this week." Sofia squeals a yes, fists the air and the class cheer for her.

Eve reads hers to herself and then to the class. "Report to Lois, the housekeeper, for one day of toilet cleaning duties." The class give a chorus of 'Oh's', 'Ah's' and 'Yuk's'.

Dixon looks at me with a frown. "Where did you come up with that idea? I've never seen them so animated and engaged in the class before."

"I've just gone through all the personnel files and Adaline's school reports show she is extremely competitive and also states that she has high protective instincts. I called her to my office and explained that we needed to improve the female training, and within minutes she came up with this. The pups are something the females will identify with, and having both a reward and a consequence gives motivation. It took us less than an hour to get it together, and we had it perfected. It progresses into two-on-one, three-on-one, two-on-two scenarios, etc. Oh, and I created an assistant trainer's position too. Adaline's additional duties. You can thank me later."

Strolling away with the biggest sense of satisfaction I've felt in a long time, I decide it's time for lunch. Walking into the canteen area, I'm looking forward to a nice, quiet lunch. Loading a plate with a variety of meats, a touch of salad and some crusty bread and butter, I grab a couple of bottles of water and then find a table where I can watch the room. The pack interacts well, and it's good to sit on the sidelines sometimes and take it all in. Not quite a cafe on the roadside, but the next best thing.

There's a calm, relaxed feeling to the lunchtime crowd. Not the boisterous laughter that sometimes echoes around the packhouse at this time of day. It helps to see the different sides of the pack mentality, so I can get a feel of how things are in general. I have to visit Spirit Walker pack with my father this week, so knowing the pack has no issues will make the trip more enjoyable. No one wants to travel when there is trouble on the horizon.

Having enjoyed my meal, I remain a while longer and drink my bottled water. Just as I'm thinking of taking my plate away, I notice a chilly silence come over the room. Looking around, I see Savannah has entered and is walking to the serving area. Now, I say walking but I suppose sashay would describe it better, but it's not in a good way. It's so exaggerated that it doesn't look normal. I'm not the only one that thinks so either, as there are several comments directed at her relating to her *need for the toilet*, or that *it looks like she's too late, maybe should have worn a diaper*. The room is quickly filling with laughter and it's all at Savannah's expense.

Reaching the serving area, Savannah takes a handful of smashed potato and throws it at the nearest table. Before she sees where it lands, she grabs more and throws a second handful in the same direction.

"Ha! Not laughing so much now, are you?" She screeches at the room in general. The room is totally silent with all eyes on the person wearing the smashed potato. Cook Ash stands up and wipes the mash from her face, neck and hair. Looking from Savannah, then to me, she quietly speaks. "Alpha Heir Bronze. Her ass is mine and I'll still bake you the cookies." Launching herself at Savannah, she just misses as Savannah bolts for the kitchen, with Ash in hot pursuit. There's a scream and the sounds of pans crashing, so it sounds as though her escape was unsuccessful. Trusting that Ash won't actually kill her, I leave Savannah to her fate and head back to the Alpha office.

No sooner does my ass hit the chair than the phone rings. Answering, I'm surprised when I'm greeted by Shadow Warrior Xavier.

"Alpha Heir Bronze, just the person I was hoping to speak to. How are you?"

"I'm very well, thank you. And yourself?" I probably sound a little wary, as I'm not sure why a Shadow Warrior would want to speak to me about anything.

"I'm good. Thank you for asking. I was hoping we could discuss one of your pack members, if you have time?"

"I'm sure I can always make time for one of our most esteemed Shadow Warriors. Wouldn't you rather speak to my father, though?"

"Our discussion will, I feel, be relevant to some future event after your father has relinquished the reins to yourself, so I don't believe I'm being disrespectful by coming directly to the future alpha. This may also save some repeat conversations going forward." His voice appears calm, and I don't detect any kind of deceit.

"Very well. Though I should point out that I may still discuss this with my father at some point," I want it clearly understood that I will keep nothing from my father.

"I would expect nothing less. You've recently gained a new pack member, a young female by the name of Hannah, if I'm not mistaken."

"Yes, that's correct. She came from the Northern Parklands, as I recall. She was picked up by one of our warrior patrols at the border."

"It's come to our attention through our communication network that her brother has had a resurgence of interest in his sister's whereabouts. I thought I should pass this on to yourself should he decide to pay your pack lands a visit, and try to *persuade* her to return with him."

"Why would he want to do this?" I ask myself. "Have you any thoughts on this?" We're talking about a hell of a risk for someone to travel such distances, and cross borders to kidnap a sister that took such lengths to escape in the first place. She would not go back quietly, and for him to get caught would certainly bring death to his door.

Xavier surprises me when he says, "She ran because her brother was going to sell her into a mating, so he could gain power in the Northern Parklands. When she ran, she put him in a seriously bad position, he procured another bride and narrowly escaped an early grave. Instead of keeping his head down though, as any sane shifter would, he was caught bragging that his sister was far superior in every way to the new bride. This caused some consternation in the groom's quarter, and so he's been given an ultimatum. Supply the original superior bride or meet the Goddess with his head under his arm, and not on his shoulders. He may already be on his way to your lands."

I don't waste my time asking how accurate this information is, as I know that a Shadow Warrior wouldn't waste his time on uncorroborated intel. "I will speak to Dixon, my Chief Warrior, and have him make the border patrol warriors aware. I will also explain to Hannah that no matter what happens, the pack will not give her up."

"Those were the actions that I thought you would take. I respect your decisions, Alpha Heir Bronze. I will keep you aware of any further information, and be assured that should you require our assistance, the Shadow Warriors will be happy to oblige."

"Thank you for that, Xavier, and for the heads up on Hannah's brother. I seem to recall he's called Elijah, if my memory serves me." Something else recently gleaned from the files I so diligently read.

"Correct. You obviously pay attention to your pack members and any issues they may have. I'm impressed. You don't have a small pack, so to know such a level of detail is commendable." I almost blurt out how I know, but decide it won't hurt to be well thought of in such circles as the Shadow Warriors. "I'll leave you for now then, Alpha Heir Bronze. I'm sure you have a lot you wish to put in place before your visit to Alpha Lyle at Spirit Walker pack with your father."

Before I can ask how he knows about my impending visit, I hear a soft chuckle and the call ends. I shouldn't be surprised that he knows. There are probably Shadow Warriors in the pack that I am unaware of. I'll ask my father about that while we're traveling to Spirit Walker Pack.

CHET

Knowing that the pack will be in excellent hands with my Luna, Sage, and Beta, Xavi, I still couldn't help checking that Bronze had made sure everything was in place for our visit to Spirit Walker Pack. As we have six warriors accompanying us, he has audited the patrol rosters with Dixon to ensure there are no weak spots. *Check*. He has requested travel permission across Wolfsfoot lands, and arranged a stopover for us on the way to Alpha Lyle and on our return. *Check*. Alpha Lyle has agreed to the visit, its purpose and duration. *Check*. Communication protocols are in place in case of emergencies, either at the pack or on our journey. *Check*.

I haven't spent this much time with my son in years, if ever. The traveling alone, with breaks, will account for two whole days. I don't expect to see him much while he's with Alpha Lyle, but it will be good for him to see how a much younger Alpha does things. Pack life has a lot of custom and tradition within its culture. However, that doesn't stop change or evolution playing its part. It wouldn't do if we all still lived in caves or in the woods.

Alternating between human and wolf, we are making good time. Shaman and Titan are getting hungry and they both share their fondness for rabbit. It won't be long before we call a break and I know what that will entail for those two.

Titan has already discussed our food requirements, humans are not food focused enough. Shaman's statement echoes through my mind.

'Shaman, that does not surprise me. You should both be overweight with the amount of food you put away.'

We get to run more than most other pack leaders, so we burn off the calories. No chance we will get fat. Shaman snorts with some indignation.

'What do you say, Titan? Do you get to run more than most?' Waiting for his response, I'm taken aback when it arrives.

Running is all well and good, but need mate more than food. Wolf cannot live on rabbit alone.

Bronze bursts out laughing at the shocked look on my face. Through the mind-link, he states. *'You shouldn't be surprised, Father. We're a product of you and Mother, after all. And don't for one minute try to deny anything. I remember all the nights I heard you two at it, in both human and wolf form, some nights.'*

Blushing furiously, I try to deflect the conversation from my sex life. 'So... You guys like rabbits, huh?'

Finally reaching Wolfsfoot, after nine hours of running and breaks, I'm ready for a good rest and a hearty meal. Being greeted by Alpha Gabe and Luna Tati was very formal. I wasn't expecting it. They explained later that they haven't had many occasions to throw out the red carpet, and thought it would be good for the pack to be involved in some traditional practices. They certainly seemed to lap it up.

I would have been happy to spend more time at Wolfsfoot with Alpha Gabe and Luna Tati, but they have a busy schedule. I was informed by Alpha Lyle he also has a busy schedule and not having his Luna yet was adding to his duties. So, early the next morning, we were on our way again.

During our talks, it became apparent how hard it was for Bronze to have to wait for Taria. Titan might be desperate for Maya so they could start having pups, but Bronze was also desperate for his companion, and the bond that came with her. I'd forgotten what life was like without my Sage.

Sixteen hours after leaving Wolfsfoot and we arrive at the Spirit Walker pack house. We were met at the border by a group of warriors and escorted the last six hours. There was none of the fanfare that we'd had at Wolfsfoot, but as we journeyed those last hours we saw and felt the impact that the no-man's-land rogues were having. Everyone looked tired and run-down. Being on alert constantly was taking a terrible toll on the pack.

We were taken to the Alpha's office and Lyle was busy debriefing a patrol that had come back from their border. Although not attacked, they had been shadowed and taunted by rogues the whole time. Lyle thanked them, dismissed them, and told them to get food and plenty of rest.

"We can't keep this up. My warriors are doing an amazing job, but they can't keep this up. Being kept on high alert every minute of every patrol isn't sustainable, no matter how well trained or determined they are," Lyle slaps his desk in frustration. "The Council won't allow me to go on the offensive for fear of escalating the problem. If we allow this to carry on, the rogues will be able to walk through the border, and take the pack lands at any time they see fit. I may have to defy the Council, but if I do, they will certainly recall their warriors and that will leave us even more exposed."

"Surely, a couple of forays into no-man's-land and kill the rogues that are taunting will disrupt them enough to back off?" Bronze's suggestion makes perfect sense and I have to agree.

"I've told the Council this, but all they seem to want right now is a diplomatic solution." Lyle looks as though he's at his wit's end with the council.

"What exactly have they said to you? What are the specifics of their orders?" Bronze looks across at me and states, "Father, can you take our warriors and get them fed and rested, please? I have a feeling we are going to need them in the morning. I want to discuss something with Alpha Lyle. It may be best if you weren't present."

"Son, I think I already know where you're going with this. You're a product of me, don't forget." Laughing as I walk to the door, I give them both a head nod and search out our warriors.

The next morning we are gathered just out of sight of the Spirit Walker border patrol. Myself, Bronze and the six warriors watch as the patrol follow their usual routine. Seeing four rogues approach from the forest and begin dashing to the border, then stopping at the last second before crossing, we see how this causes the patrol warriors to tense. There is no wonder that they are all so run down.

Letting them get ahead, Bronze sends four of the warriors over the border to slip behind the rogues. As the rogues run towards the border a second time, the four Eclipse warriors make their own charge, forcing the rogues across the Spirit Walker border. Once they are across myself, Bronze and the two remaining Eclipse warriors fall on them and they are dead in moments. We spend the day following this simple yet effective plan, and four of Lyle's patrols have a far less stressful day.

Back at the packhouse, we brief Alpha Lyle on our day with his border patrols, and explain that we were attacked on four different occasions. Reporting to Councilman Flint, he asked us to be present so that we could best describe our day. Although the councilman was surprised that the rogues would change their tactics, I pointed out how the propaganda would look if the rogues had managed to take out an Alpha and his heir in one fell swoop.

I also suggested that perhaps Alpha Lyle needed to show a little more aggression going forward, to make the rogues think twice before trying something again. Following a short adjournment, Flint spoke to the rest of the council regarding these developments, and it was agreed that any rogue wishing to test the border patrols in the future would be fair game.

I didn't doubt for one minute that Flint believed any of my fabrication, but he was probably relieved that he could at least give Alpha Lyle some necessary leeway.

The next day, Bronze accompanied Alpha Lyle on his rounds and after a meal and brief rest, we headed back home. The stop off at Wolfsfoot was much more informal, and we gained a female for the return journey when one of my warriors discovered his fated mate. Luna Tati was ecstatic, Alpha Gabe a little more reserved and Poor Bronze, although happy for the couple, was even more determined to have his day with Taria.

Chapter 6

TARIA

Sitting at a table in the dining area, waiting for Councilman Flint, I realize that, without thinking, I have a full view of the room, exits and entryways with my back to a wall. This was discussed in one of my training classes with Chief Warrior Dixon, but I didn't know that I was doing it until just now.

Maya speaks out saying, *I have noticed. You do much more than you think.*

'Why haven't you told me this?'

You shouldn't need me to tell you. It is good that you do these things without conscious thought. You are being more wolf. It's a good thing.

'You're mocking me, Maya. You're trying to make me want pups!'

That would not be a bad thing, replies Maya, and continues, *but I am not mocking you. It is good that your mind is working that way. It shows that the lessons are worthwhile, and you have taken much onboard with little effort.*

'What else have you noticed that I haven't?' I ask Maya.

How many warriors are in the room?

'Seven.'

How many could you beat in a fair fight?

'Five.'

How many females in the room?

'Twelve.'

If you had to exit the room quickly, how would you do it and how long would it take you?

'Via the kitchen and less than twenty seconds to be on the lawn outside.' I reply without thinking.

Less than fourteen days ago, you would not have known this. Now you are aware of your surroundings, and the people around you. I am proud of my human to have come this far. Maybe I will ask the Goddess to leave me here after all.

'OH! Maya! That is an awful thing to joke about. The next time you are hunting, I'm going to trip you as you're about to catch a rabbit.'

And I will shift back with no clothes, Taria, my human.

Letting my laughter slip out as a horrified giggle, I see Councilman Flint approaching.

"It seems that you and your wolf are entertaining each other while I've kept you waiting. I'm sorry I'm a little late. I was on a call with Bronze, and he again asks if you could give him a call when you have time," Flint grins at me as I sigh, and join him as we go to the serving area and fill our plates with food.

"I need to have a talk with him about his communication style. It isn't necessary for him to keep passing messages through people.

He could just pick up the phone." Giving Flint a frustrated look, he grins again. We sit back at our table and begin to eat while continuing our conversation. I can't help but notice that Flint is eyeing the amount of food on my plate.

"He genuinely can't wait for you and him to become mates."

"Oh, really?" I bluster as I'm shocked that Flint would make that statement.

"No! Not like that. I meant as a couple, intellectually and emotionally. I wasn't referring to *sexually*." Flint blushes furiously as he whispers that last word, and I can't help but try to keep him on his toes.

"So, he doesn't think I'm attractive in that way? That's a shame because I know that our wolves are very drawn to each other, and have already agreed on pups."

"You are doing this deliberately now, I can tell. Changing the subject, how do you feel about everything that has been thrown at you so far? Are you coping with the barrage of information, advice, and training?" Flint raises his eyebrows, and I can see how much he wants to get away from being harassed.

"Funnily enough, that was what Maya and I were discussing just before you joined us." Throwing the same questions at Flint that Maya had asked me, he was only able to answer two correctly. The exit question and when he stated that he could beat all the warriors. I couldn't argue that point, but he was three off with his guess as to how many warriors there were.

Seeing him side eye my half empty plate, I grin. "All this extra training, fighting, running around."

"I understand that. I just don't know where it goes until it gets burned off," he says. "It's not as though you have anywhere that looks remotely like a *calorie storage area*."

"I take that as a compliment, I think."

While we eat, Maya and Bruno take the time to wolf chat and I'm sure there'll be some juicy bits for me to catch up on later.

Wolf chat is not for your ears, Maya states.

'Well, that told me, didn't it?' Maya shuts me out and obviously continues her chat with Bruno. Flint must know what just happened as he smirks at me.

"Wolves, eh? Can't live with 'em, can't live without 'em!"

Finishing our lunch, we take our dishes away and go our separate ways. I have some calls to make, so head to my room for some privacy, peace and quiet. My first call is to Blood Pearl, and Pops answers.

"Hi, Pops. How are you?"

"Hey, Sweetpea. I was just talking about you. Me and your Momma were wondering how you were getting on."

"I'm doing great, even if I say so myself. Maya has been telling me some of the stuff I'm doing subconsciously, and I can see it more and more as I think about it." Going over the lunchtime with Gerry, he sounds pleased with my cautionary table choice and my observations. Passing me over to Momma, I feel emotional when I hear her voice again. It seems like forever since I've seen her.

"Hi, Momma. Are you okay?" I feel near to tears and have to make an effort not to start sobbing.

"I'm good, but more important, how are you doing? It's very strange knowing you're so far away. I'm not used to this."

"I'm kept so busy I hardly have time to think. Last time we spoke you had to dash off. What happened? Is everyone there okay?" I don't remember how long ago it was when that happened.

"Oh, that. It was another skirmish with the rogues. We got information that they were going to try and snatch female warriors for that alpha of theirs. He's got himself a 'queen' but is looking to surround himself with a female royal guard, apparently. I think he's a sandwich short of a picnic myself. A right royal looney-tune. I don't know what his endgame is supposed to be, I'm sure. We only allow one female warrior per patrol now. The females aren't happy about it, but it's reduced the number of breaches we're having. Trying to form a royal guard by kidnapping a single female and losing three or four of their warriors has calmed the rogue attacks somewhat. Anyway, never mind him. What news have you got for me?"

Explaining my heightened awareness yet again and how well I'm doing with my fight training has her gushing with pride. I can't say that I don't brag a little either. It feels good to shout out my own praise, I have to say.

Finally running out of things to say, I tell Momma that I have to call Bronze. I swear she giggles. Pops has definitely had a positive effect on Momma, she's a lot happier in herself and so much more relaxed. It's a pleasure to hear her voice so chilled out, and not all tense and sharp.

Taking a swig from the bottle of water I keep on my nightstand, I settle my back against my headboard and try calling Bronze. I feel quite girly and giddy as I wait for him to pick up.

"Hello. Alpha Heir Bronze speaking."

"Hello. Possible Luna Heir Taria speaking."

"Taria, wow. I'm sorry, I didn't look at the caller ID, I just snatched it up. It's great to hear your voice. Are you okay?" He sounds genuinely pleased to hear from me, which is always a good thing.

"I'm good, but I have a bone to pick with you," trying to sound as stern and as serious as I can.

"Oh, okay. What is it?" It must have worked, because he sounds very worried.

"Stop asking people to ask me to contact you. Pick up the damned phone and just call me. You're going to have to have better communication skills than this if you have any hope of getting pups out of me." Bursting out laughing, I hear a sigh from his end and then he too, laughs.

"I'm sorry, I know why I started to do that, but I can just make the call in the future. How are things progressing? Very well, I'm sure."

Repeating myself for what feels like the tenth time today, I tell him about my day. During our conversation, we stray from one subject to another, and it all seems very easy and relaxed. When he mentions getting a second desk for the alpha office, I question why he needs another desk.

"Well, for you, of course. You'll want your own desk, surely?" He sounds surprised that I'd not thought of it myself.

"Of course I'd want my own desk, but I was rather hoping I'd have my own 'Luna' office to go with it. I don't mean that we stay apart all day, every day, but I am going to need a private place to meet with people, discuss Luna issues. I will want to meet all the pack members at some point early on so I get a feel for them, and vice versa. We're both going to be busy, active pack leaders, so there's bound to be times when we'll both need the office."

"You raise a good point there, Taria. I hadn't thought of that. I'll speak to my father and ask how they got round the problem. I'm not saying that you won't have an office, I think you're right, you will need one. I just never came across it before now."

"I'll leave you to puzzle over that one then while I go and carry on with my exploration of the gardens here. I'm looking forward to this. Right, I'm off and I'll wait for you to call me next time. Bye."

"Bye, Taria."

Popping into the bathroom, I get a quick freshen up, and then head out to find out all I can about the gardens here. I understand that they are well established and quite diverse. I guess if I head out through the kitchen, I'm bound to find a herb garden, and that will be as good a place as any to start looking for the gardener.

Seeing a female tending to the herb beds, I approach her to ask for the gardener. I heard somewhere that the gardener was called Silas, so I doubt it's going to be her.

"Hi. My name is Taria and I'm looking for Silas."

She jumps a mile and lets out a squeal when I speak to her.

"I was miles away then. You interrupted a wonderful daydream. I was on a beach with my soulmate and we were … Well, never mind what we were…I'm Dahlia. Pleased to meet you. You're the Eclipse Luna-to-be, aren't you?"

"Yes, I am. I'm sorry I interrupted you. Sounds like you were about to have some fun." I laugh at the dreamy look that comes over her face.

"Yes, I was. It's only a dream though, as my soulmate doesn't know he's the one. Yet."

"Oh, I see. Why don't you tell him then?" I find this a bit intriguing, to be honest.

"I wish it was that easy. I don't have a good enough standing in the pack to be able to do that. I was an ass for years and wasn't in a good place with myself. Unfortunately, I took it out on my staff and anyone that got within range, so to speak. I got demoted from my housekeeper position, rightly so, if I'm honest. I was a first-class bitch, but it was the best thing that ever happened to me."

"Oh dear. It sounds like you fell on your feet rather than being punished." I try to see her as a bitchy female, but it just doesn't come to mind.

"You won't see me like that. I look in the mirror every morning and I can't see the female I was back then. It's as though being in the gardens and the sunshine has transformed me from a weed to a flower. I don't mean I'm some fancy bloom like a rose, but I feel a bit daisy-ish. I've lost so much weight, too. I've had to buy a whole new wardrobe, and that in itself helped transformed me. I saw all these lovely colors that I'd never worn before. I always had dowdy gray stuff as my go-to color back then. I think that was the color that matched my awful mood." Blinking at me as though she's just seen me for the first time, she puts a hand over her mouth. "Oh, my goodness, I'm so sorry. Listen to me babbling on. I've never spoken to anyone about this before." She looks mortified that she has just revealed so much about herself to a total stranger.

"Dahlia, I think you live up to your name, and not daisy-ish. From just what you've told me, it appears that you've turned your life around. I don't know what you were like before, but I'd gladly call you my friend if you'll have me as such?" Holding my hand out, she stares at it for a few moments. Just as I think I should take it back, she grabs my hand and then pulls me into a hug.

Hearing her cry into my shoulder, I just stand there and hug her back. After a minute, she gets a hold of herself and looks me in the eye.

"I don't have a friend, so you don't know how much that means to me. I know you're not going to be here for very long and that you'll forget me when you become Luna, But I'll never forget you." Wiping tears from her cheeks, she smiles and it positively lights up her face.

"Right," she says brightly, "let's go find Silas." Walking through the herb beds, she takes my arm in hers as though we'd been besties for years, and it feels so natural I just go with the flow. She describes everything that they have done to improve the soil, plant yields and even composting leftover fruit and veg from their kitchen, and unsold old produce from the shop.

She talks knowledgably and with great enthusiasm. It's plain to see that whatever she was in the past, she's a vibrant but shy female now. I wonder how her wolf feels about all this? Stopping before we find Silas, I feel I have to ask the question.

"Dahlia, can I ask you something immensely personal? It's okay if you say no."

"I know what you're thinking, Taria. You want to know if I still have my wolf?" I immediately take both her hands in mine as that thought hadn't crossed my mind.

"I never for a moment thought you didn't have your wolf, Dahlia, not for a second. I was going to ask how your wolf felt now, with the new you."

"My wolf is called Maiden, and she never deserted me. She gave me a hard time and sometimes we didn't speak for weeks at a time. When I was demoted, she must have sensed the change in me before I felt it myself. She began to approach me more, and I found it very comforting that she had been there for me when I was so *evil*. I think that describes it best. Would you like to meet her? She's very social."

"I would love to meet her, if you're sure?"

Dahlia disappears behind a tree, and reappears as a stunning wolf. She is a mix of different blues and grays, but with a thick darker ring from her neck spreading across her shoulders. It's almost a lion's mane, yet not as long as that would be. The colors make it look longer than it really is. Her claws are like marble with their different colors and look incredibly sharp.

"Hello, Maiden, I'm pleased to make your acquaintance. You are a stunning looking wolf." Holding my hand out, she sniffs me first and then walks to me. I run my hands through her beautiful coat and it feels soft like.. I don't know how to describe it. It's not the sharp textured hair you would expect, it's strange, but it's almost like lamb's wool.

"Thank you for staying with my friend Dahlia. It must have been a difficult time for you. You have both come out of it in spectacular fashion."

Walking away, Maiden is replaced and Dahlia is back once again.

"Thank you for your kind words. Maiden was happy to meet you. She senses great power in your wolf aura, too."

"We'll have to get them to meet before I leave. Maya would like that. Just a quick question. How does Maiden feel about rabbits?"

"She loves nothing more than a freshly killed rabbit, unless it's the chase itself. She loves the chase."

"They'll get on famously." Laughing, we continue our search for Silas.

As we go through the gardens, there is still no sign of our illusive gardener, but Dahlia fills me in on each of the different areas and the produce they grow. The fact that they keep some ground fallow each year, and how they rotate the crops, keep fields productive almost all the time. Harvesting spring crops and then planting the fall or winter crop straight away. The use of differing crops to reintroduce nutrients like beans for nitrogen. Her knowledge is just amazing.

When we reach the orchard, we see someone harvesting windfall apples. I notice a change in Dahlia immediately. She straightens her stance, her breathing gets quicker, she twists her hands together in front of her as she walks. I believe this is who she sees as her soulmate.

Approaching him, he notices us and stops his collecting. Walking over to us, he greets me pleasantly and doesn't acknowledge Dahlia at all.

"So, Silas isn't it? You're the gardener I'm led to believe? What suggestions would you have if I was to start, say, an orchard from scratch?"

"Well, I would suggest you thought about what fruit trees you require first. Some varieties deliver a high-quality fruit with a higher-than-average yield…"

"Yes, I understand that. My friend here, Dahlia, explained all that as we walked through your orchard. I presume you know Dahlia, as you didn't greet her when we arrived?"

"Erm, yes, I know Dahlia. She works in the herb garden."

I'm sure Silas is a nice male, but I think he still sees Dahlia as she was, and not what she has become. I'm going to make it my mission to change that, but I don't have long left at Blackshadow to play matchmaker.

"Her knowledge far exceeds the herb garden. Have you used her skills and knowledge elsewhere?" I tilt my head to one side as I look at him and wait for his response.

"To my knowledge she only works the herb beds." He looks at Dahlia, obviously hoping for some confirmation that he's right.

"Dahlia, how do you know so much about the larger gardens, such as fallow fields or crop rotation, that you have explained to me?" Poor Dahlia looks as though she wants the earth to swallow her up.

"I work the gardens when I'm not on duty at the herb gardens. I listen to the other pack members when they talk, and I stay near the meetings they hold so I can learn from there, too."

"Has anyone taken you under their wing and mentored you?"

She looks at me in panic. "Oh, no, Taria. No one has left their duties or given me any help. I've learned everything myself. It helped pass the time when I was off duty rather than be alone in my room."

"Dahlia, would you go and finish collecting the windfalls please, while I speak to Silas?" Giving her an encouraging smile, she gives me a nervous one in return before almost giving me a curtsy and trotting off.

"You are wasting a valuable resource keeping Dahlia in the herb garden. Her knowledge is remarkable, as is her enthusiasm. Look at her and tell me what you see."

"What do you mean?" He frowns at me as though I'm speaking some alien language. I turn so that Dahlia is working behind me.

"Look over my shoulder and tell me what you see!"

"The orchard. Apple and pear trees. Grass. A female picking windfalls." He still looks confused, but I may be getting somewhere.

"Describe the female."

"It's Dahlia." He looks pleased with that answer.

"She's my friend, Silas. I know her name. Describe what you see."

"I don't understand. I said I see Dahlia."

"And I said describe what you see." I'm going to lose my patience if I'm not careful, so I'm trying my hardest to keep my voice light.

"I see Dahlia. She's wearing work boots., jeans, a pretty yellow tee shirt."

"Better. What about her size and shape, hair color, hairstyle? Give me more detail." Now I can see a light coming on. At last, someone is home, I think to myself.

"She's lost a lot of weight. She's quite shapely, in fact. She used to be fat and her hair was in a greasy bun all the time. Her hair is light brown and cut short on her shoulders." Watching him describe her, I turn to see what he's seeing. As I do, Dahlia looks at me and smiles. "She has a beautiful smile, she never used to smile, ever. She has caramel eyes that I could look at all day." Seeing him smile at Dahlia and her face light up even more, I could high-five myself.

"Dahlia, that will be enough, thank you. Bring the basket and we'll all head back to the kitchen." She scoops up the basket, and balancing it against her hip walks over to us. I could kiss her myself, and without knowing it, she looks amazing as her hips swing and it couldn't be choreographed any more perfectly. Joining us Silas immediately offers to carry the basket of apples for her.

"No, it's not heavy. I can manage." Giving her my best wide-eyed death stare, she looks at me and frowns, totally not understanding. Glaring at the basket and then nodding at Silas, the penny drops and she hands it to him.

"Well, as you're offering. Thank you." She gives him the basket and I grab her arm, so we are walking in front of Silas through the orchard. As we walk, I tell her she has grass and leaves on the ass of her jeans that she should wipe off.

Looking over her shoulder to try to see, she rubs her ass with her free hand. Taking a sly peek at Silas, I see his eyes glued to Dahlia. Ha! My work here is done. That was easier than I could have possibly imagined. All credit to Dahlia though, I think her total innocence was the clincher, and I don't think she knows even now the effect she is suddenly having on her *soulmate*.

Approaching the kitchen, I stop and take the basket from Silas. "Thank you, Silas. I wonder if there is something you could do for me, though. As the future Luna of the Eclipse pack, I would take it as a personal favor if you could mentor Dahlia yourself? I think you'll find her an exceptionally devoted student, extremely intelligent and full of ideas about how to improve your lives." Seeing the look of panic return to Dahlia's eyes, I pull her into the kitchen and watch as Silas walks away. I say walk, but I'm not convinced that his feet are touching the ground.

"Just be yourself. No airs or graces. No trying to impress. Just...be...yourself! You've got this."

"Taria. What just happened?" She looks so innocent standing there. Butter wouldn't melt.

"I simply got him to see the new Dahlia, that's all. He has never moved on like you have. His mind was in the past, but it sure isn't now. He's just seen you as a beautiful female, and the *bitch that was Dahlia* is no more. You owe me an invitation to the ceremony."

"How did you know? I never said who it was."

"Your whole being changed when we walked into that orchard. I don't know why the Goddess herself didn't see it, but anyone with a brain cell could see how you felt about that male. It's up to you now, but I don't think you'll have to do anything but be yourself."

Slipping her arm in mine again, I march her off to get some food.

"C'mon bestie. I need to eat. All this matchmaking has made me hungry. I could eat an orchard!"

Chapter 7

BRONZE

I'm sitting at my allocated desk in the Alpha's office considering pack issues. I can see why Taria, or any Luna for that matter, would need their own office. When she spoke to me about having her own office, I wasn't too sure, but considering the matter, I think she made a good point.

I raised it with my father, and he looked as shocked as I had been. When we spoke to mother, she had always wanted an office of her own but thought Lunas didn't have one, so had worked around it. Having looked at the space available in the packhouse, it won't be difficult to move things around and accommodate a Luna office.

Having just had a conversation with Hannah, I wonder if this is something that could have been handled better by a Luna. I received a call from the Shadow Warriors again this morning. Not Xander this time, a Shadow Warrior by the name of Travis. Hannah's brother, Elijah, has dropped off their radar, but they've received a report that he may have been seen in the south of the northern parklands. The Shadow Warriors believe he is coming for Hannah.

I called her into my office so I could explain what we know, and what we can do to prevent her from being taken away by her brother. Hannah ran away from him when he tried to marry her to gain a powerful position in the north. She was not prepared to be used that way, and it proved that she was worth more than he believed, when she reached our borders and we accepted her into the pack.

She has been a popular addition, and has become an accomplished member of the carpentry shop team with Cameron and Logan. She does all the detail work and carvings. Her skill is phenomenal for someone with no formal training. She made Ember's bat for me and put her name on it as an afterthought. She definitely went above and beyond with that.

I wanted to move her back to the packhouse for a time until we could deal with her brother's threat, but she would have none of it. She stated that he had forced her to change her life once already, and that she was not going to allow that again. She will carry on working at the carpenter's shop in the town, but will accept that she cannot travel back and forth alone.

I made her agree to change her routine, too. Occasionally she will stay over in Wolfsfoot rather than travel home. She and her travel companion will arrange different routes to travel home. She also has to work different hours so that as many patterns as possible are changed, to stop her brother from being able to plan her kidnap.

I think I was a bit forceful at times when trying to explain that it was for her own good, so that's why I think a Luna would have been able to handle it better.

You did good. She accepted your decisions as they were for her own well-being.

'I hope so, Titan. Although she hasn't found her mate here, she has proved popular and has many friends.'

Her wolf, Moon, is very reserved yet perceptive. She calmed her human many times during the conversation.

'We need to ensure her safety. I do not want to start my pack leadership with the loss of a pack member, that's for sure.'

A knock on the door interrupts my train of thought, and I'm surprised when the warrior on duty answers my call to enter.

"Your lunchtime meal has arrived, Alpha Heir Bronze," he says, looking at me as though I have two heads.

"I don't take my meals in here." I frown at the unexpected statement.

"I thought it strange, that's why I made her stay outside while I confirmed it. Shall I send her away?"

"She?" I think I know who this is going to be. "Would it be Savannah, by any chance?" The pained expression on his face tells me it is before he answers.

"Okay, let her in." I'll see how this plays out, I think to myself, but I won't be eating anything she brings in.

Seeing her walk in with a tray, I get my biggest surprise. She is dressed sensibly, in fact quite demurely. I'm shocked by the transformation, but only in a suspicious way, nothing else.

"I thought I'd bring you some lunch, Alpha Heir Bronze. You're always working so hard, and I don't know why, we hardly see you in the canteen anymore."

Whoa! There are so many red flags in that statement that alarm bells are almost deafening me. Savannah doesn't think! She wouldn't do something for someone else, even me. She never refers to me as Alpha Heir Bronze, despite being warned numerous times about calling me Bronze. She has no idea what I do, so doesn't have a clue how hard I work. *We* hardly see you in the canteen? *We*? She only has I or me in her vocabulary, so who is this we? She wouldn't see me in the canteen anymore as she was following my routine too well, so I changed it.

"I don't take meals in the office, Savannah, so please return it to the canteen, and I've already eaten, anyway." She obviously had high hopes for her plan to succeed as her face betrays her disappointment.

"Well, I'll wait and walk with you when you leave, then," she states brightly, or hopefully.

"No, you won't. I'll be here for some considerable time yet, and I have a meeting shortly." Mind linking to Xavi, the beta, I ask him to come to the office immediately.

Standing there with the food tray in her hands, I can see the cogs in her head turning furiously, to find a reason to stay in the office with me.

"You may leave now, Savannah. As you said, I'm working hard and have things that need my undivided attention." Walking past her to the door, I open it and gesture for her to leave. As she moves towards me I get the feeling this little play was not of her making. It's far too subtle compared to the normal brash attempts she makes, which gives me concerns as to where she is getting her ideas from now.

Xavi walks in, looking from Savannah, to the tray, to me and his brows furrow, as he seems as perplexed as I am. "Alpha Heir Bronze, you requested my presence?" He blurts out before Savannah is out of earshot, and I see her turn to look over her shoulder. Shutting the door quickly, I almost slam it in her face, which wouldn't have bothered me in the least, I must admit.

"Yes, I did." Walking back to my desk, I sit down and gesture for him to take the seat opposite. "You are aware of Savannah and her wish to become my mate and the Luna of the pack?"

"Isn't everyone aware of that? If not, it would be the worst kept secret in pack history since time immemorial." Grinning at his witty response, I stare back until he sees that I am not amused in the slightest. "Erm, yes, I am aware."

"She has changed her approach, and I want to know who is coaching her. There isn't a chance that she came up with such a drastic tactical alteration on her own. I can't believe she has the mental capacity for it. You have my permission, no my direct instruction, to use any, and every resource available within the pack to get me an answer. In fact, if we must, I'll call in the Shadow Warriors to get the job done." Taking a deep breath, I look him straight in the eye. "I'm done with this. I'm going to put an end to it if it kills me."

Explaining the latest encounter, I can see that he thinks the same way I do. "I'll get on it right away, Alpha Heir Bronze. This has the stench of a higher brain power than that of Savannah's, though I don't think we're talking *genius level* here."

Xavi leaves me alone once again, and I sit back and rub the back of my neck. I wish Taria was here. I could set her and Maya on Savannah.

That would not be a fair match. Would be worth seeing though.

'You think so, too, eh?'

Taking a moment to clear my head of any thoughts of Taria, I also clear my desk of all paperwork. Getting a pad and pen, I have to start thinking of who I want in my inner council, and what positions I need them in.

My beta will be Xavi, as I do not want to lose his experience or knowledge. I know he will continue to serve me and the pack with the devotion he has always shown. I'm surprised he has never found his mate, although he has never been one for going outside the pack lands for anything other than official business.

I would have liked Dixon to become my Delta and take over the Patrols, but he's such a good Chief Warrior that I'm torn between the two. It's certainly too much for one person to be both. I need to see how Adaline performs as his assistant, because she could very well be my solution. I don't recall any pack having a female Chief Warrior, but I'm only interested in the best person for the position. Gender doesn't come into the equation in this instance. I'll talk to Dixon and see how he feels how Adaline is progressing.

Next on my list of titles to appoint, so to speak, will be my Gamma. Someone to protect my Luna, should she ever need it. This is a tough choice as my Luna isn't known to anyone in the pack as yet, so has no bond for me to call on. Taria, I'm sure, will be a force to be reckoned with by the time she is by my side, and I don't know her well enough myself to make this choice an easy one.

I have one pack member as a definite for my inner council, though she has no idea that this is coming her way. I'm going to have Eve as my advisory member on the inner council. She is a powerful female that doesn't recognize her own strengths and abilities. I was watching the pups one day and her male pup, Coal, was getting into mischief. I say 'getting', his whole life is one mischievous adventure after another. The teacher was asking him about something and he had his hand over his forehead as he was answering, almost like a salute, but his palm was covering his forehead. I could see the teacher was trying desperately not to laugh, and he eventually admitted to whatever wrongdoing he'd been up to. When I spoke to the teacher, she informed me that Eve had told Coal, from him being able to speak, that when a pup lied, a star appeared on their forehead that only adults could see. Every time Coal tried to bend the truth, he slapped a hand across his forehead so no one would see the star.

That is just pure genius. I am so going to steal that when I have pups of my own. That is the sort of out-of-the-box thinking I want from my advisors. I can't wait to see what else she has come up with to keep that bundle of dynamite on the straight and narrow. Goddess help the pack when he gets his wolf, we'll all be in trouble from that day forward.

Xander and Wesley will have to have positions on my inner council. They are the two that I would put my life in their hands without hesitation, and I know they would die for me without a thought. Xander and his wolf, Scout, were always the ones that got us out of trouble when we were pups. They could come up with an escape route, or an excuse at the drop of a hat.

Wesley and his wolf, Duke, were always in trouble for fighting. The funny thing was, it was never either of them that would start it, but they would certainly finish it as the last ones standing. Duke is only a fraction smaller than my wolf, Titan, and I'm sure that it's only our Alpha bloodline that would give us the victory in an all-out fight.

Oh, what a dummy I can be. There's my Gamma staring me in the face. Wesley. He is perfect for protecting Taria. They will get along easily, everyone does with Wesley, and most of his fights have been with bullies or someone causing an injustice. That's such a weight off my shoulders right there.

So, Xander and Eve are two of my inner council, I need at least two more. Cameron and Logan spring to mind, but only because they work with Hannah, and we spoke of them this morning. Malakai? He's a tailor in the clothes shop alongside Reagan. Both are good pack members, but not as advisors.

Nathan, Jack and Ezra work in the garden with Herb. Good guys, but not for my council. Hannah would be a good choice, but she has too much going on to be able to take this on, and I wouldn't ask her to. This is far more difficult than I imagined. Serenity, Vivian, Daniel, Liam... I could throw names out all day without finding someone that I've interacted with enough to involve them in the pack's decision making.

'Titan, you need to think about this, and see if you can pinpoint a wolf capable of being on my council.'

Yawning, he stretches before sitting and giving me his attention.

I will give it some thought. It is not in my usual job description to choose council members, so it will cost you a run and a rabbit.

I can't help but chuckle to myself at Titan's sneaky way of getting an extra run and a rabbit.

Chapter 8

TARIA

Standing at the edge of the forest with Chief Warrior Oscar, I watch the dawn rise. It's such a beautiful time of the day, I never tire of seeing the sunrise. I see Dahlia heading our way, and I swear she's positively skipping. Since Silas recognized her for what she is and not what she was, she has just bloomed all the more.

"Morning Taria," she calls. "Morning Chief Warrior Oscar. Isn't it a beautiful day for a run?"

"Morning Dahlia," I suspect he's not a morning person, as he hasn't said a dozen words since we left the packhouse.

"Good morning Dahlia. What's put the spring in your step so early?" As if I didn't know already. They've been joined at the hip since Silas became her mentor, and not only during their work hours.

"Life is great and it's good to be alive. You coming here, Taria, has been the single best thing that has ever happened to me. I'd still be moping around alone in the herb garden if it wasn't for you. I owe you my new life." Watching her with all her newfound confidence and zest has me smiling, too.

"Shall we get on with our run then?" Oscar is not feeling it, obviously. "Do you want to shift here or deeper in the woods?"

"Let's go deeper into the woods first," I'm not shy to show Maya in the least, but as a future Luna, I think it is best to show Maya to the Eclipse pack before any other. Some here have seen Maya, but not all.

Linking arms with my bestie, we follow Oscar into the darker shadows of the forest. It won't be long before the sun invades the canopy, and the darkness is chased away. Once we're out of sight of the packhouse, Oscar stops and announces that we are good to shift.

Seeing him become Conan, a large gray and white wolf, I have to appreciate why he is Chief Warrior. Size and physical prowess alone would have him standing out in any pack.

Shifting to Maya, I look to Dahlia and see Maiden before me. Her coat is glossy to the point of shining with its own light, and the different hues of browns blend seamlessly. Her yellow eyes are so pale they don't look like normal yellow wolf eyes.

Following Conan's lead, we stretch our legs and begin our run through the forest. Nearing a creek, there is still a mist hovering over the ground, and it's like running through clouds in the canopy rather than trees at ground level. We run for thirty minutes before Conan slows and walks us for ten more.

Walking out into a meadow, we see deer feeding in the distance. Sensing or hearing us, they look our way and then dart into the forest and are gone in an instant. The sun lights up the tall grass as the wind blows gently through it.

Shifting again, we sit in silence, all three in our own little world, when Oscar breaks the moment.

"I come here to reflect on my life. It doesn't matter if it's a good time or bad, or just life in general. I sit here for an hour or so, watching all the different birds, animals and insects that call this home, how they interact with the meadow, and it never fails to inspire me to want to do more for myself and the pack, I can't explain how or why it motivates me, it just does."

"I can feel it, too. I've never been here before, but I feel its aura, its power. It's not a physical thing, but it's there, talking to me. Like you said, there's an interaction happening. I feel it. Thank you for bringing us here," Dahlia says all this without turning her head, she just stares out over the meadow.

"Ditto. Now, where can I find a rabbit for Maya? She's starving!" Laughing at the look of astonishment on both their faces, I burst out laughing. Receiving a punch on each shoulder from them, Dahlia laughs.

"How could you ruin such a beautiful moment? "

"A girl has to eat, you know. Now, show me the rabbits!" Shifting to Maya, I dash into the meadow and give her full rein to satisfy her hunger. Feeling Conan reach my side and Maiden just behind us, I let all Maya's instincts run free.

Bursting from the meadow grass into the forest, we surprise a colony of rabbits that have left it late to return to their warren. It isn't long before we're all sitting by the meadow's edge enjoying our warm breakfast.

Having eaten our fill, we settle into a steady lope back to the packhouse. No one says anything, but I think we all feel that we've just shared something special. Before reaching the forest's end, we shift back, and I can't help but give both Dahlia and Oscar a silent hug.

Walking into the canteen, Dahlia sees Silas and I just smile at her as she silently asks permission to abandon me. Smiling, I bid her farewell and grab myself a plate of breakfast. Toast, bacon, sausages, eggs, hash browns, and beans. A couple of bottles of water and my tray is full.

Looking for a table, with my newly acquired sixth sense, I see one by a wall with good views of the room. There's an elderly female sitting there alone. Even if it hadn't had the view of the room, I would have gone over to sit with her.

"Excuse me, but do you mind if I join you?" She looks up from her breakfast and smiles.

"Please, feel free. I'd enjoy the company. It's been a long time since any youngster wanted my company." She laughs, and it's a soothing kind of sound that makes you smile along with her.

"I find that hard to believe. I bet you could tell them some tales from your younger days." I must look horrified as I realize how I've just referred to her age. "I'm sorry, that didn't come out quite as good as it sounded in my head."

"Nothing to be sorry about. You're right. I've seen and done things that would make their hair stand on end. Pups these days hardly know they're born. Why, when I was your age, I was mated with pups and trained as a border warrior with skills they could only dream about. I was top female warrior for three years running. Would have been longer if my wolf hadn't been such a hussy and always trying for pups."

Her smile loses some of its sparkle when she talks of her pups, and I just know that it must be a delicate topic for her. I feel I need to change the subject.

"My name is Taria. I'm very pleased to meet you."

"Oh, I know who you are, young prospective Luna for the Eclipse pack. I know a lot about you and it's all been good so far." She gives me a sly look and has me on the back foot, so to speak.

"You know a lot about me? And who might you be, to know so much?" I can feel Maya paying attention now and I sense her unease.

"My name is Merry, and I'm a member of the Shifter Council."

Maya relaxes and, after pacing a couple of circles, she settles back down with her head on her paws.

"Well, I'm pleased to meet you, Merry. I wasn't aware that I was getting a visit from the Shifter Council?"

"I'm not here for you, per se, but thought as I was visiting my old pack, I'd take advantage of the opportunity to meet you. I wasn't available for the last Council meeting." She still looks like an old female but has a glint in her eye that I hadn't noticed before.

"If there is anything you need to know, or need clarifying, please don't hesitate to ask. I have no secrets to keep. Well, not yet anyway."

"After breakfast, if you've finished all that before they serve lunch," she says, pointedly looking at my loaded plate. "You can accompany me while I visit Alpha Connell. His mother and I were very good friends."

Clearing my plate in record time, I take the tray and dirty dishes away. Merry waits for me and then we head off to the Alpha's office together.

Watching the way Alpha Connell greets his visitor has me in awe. He is genuinely pleased to see Merry that it looks as though he'll hug her forever. Merry's eyes are watery at his heartfelt welcome, and I think I should leave them alone. Walking quietly to the door, I turn just as I am about to exit and catch Connell's eye. I see him mutter a thank you and then shut the door behind me.

Walking to my room to freshen up, my phone rings. Taking it from my back pocket, I see it's Bronze.

"Hi Bronze. Couldn't get a message to me, huh?" I laugh as this is the first time he has rung me directly.

"Hi Taria. Everyone was busy, so I thought I'd brave it and call you. How's things over there?"

"Everything is wonderful, thanks. Maya had a good run in the forest this morning with Conan and Maiden. Maya had her fresh breakfast, so she's in an excellent mood now."

"Conan is Chief Warrior Oscar's wolf if I remember correctly, but I'm not familiar with Maiden."

"Oh, she is Dahlia's wolf. I made a new friend and did a little touch of matchmaking. Maya and Maiden wanted to meet, so I cajoled Oscar into an early morning run with us. Oh Bronze, he took us to a private place he found, just a meadow, but so much more than that, too. We need a place to go, similar to that at Eclipse. It was fantastic."

Taking the next few minutes to explain my matchmaking, and then the beautiful meadow, Bronze listens and only when I've finished gushing does he say anything.

"I think that was a brilliant observation of yours with Dahlia and Silas. Well done for making him see the new Dahlia. As for the meadow, if we can't find one on the pack land then we should design and create our own. It sounds like a little piece of heaven."

"Oh, there's a member of the Shifter Council here, too. Her name is Merry, and she used to be part of Blackshadow pack. A friend of Connell's mother. She told me she has only heard good things about me, which makes me think I must be on the right track."

"I don't doubt that for a minute. I'm confident that you're going to be a great Luna and make me very happy as my mate."

"I truly hope so. I'm working hard to be the best at everything I need to be. My fitness and fighting skills are far beyond the level I expected them to be now. I don't think you'll be disappointed." I can't help but speak with a measure of pride in my voice.

"It won't be too long now, and I'm so proud of you and cannot wait for you to get here," Bronze states with a rumble in his voice, showing me his wolf Titan is to the surface.

Ending the call, I sit on my bed and reflect on how far I have come to date.

You are head and shoulders above where you were, there is no doubt. You are naturally more confident and you give off an aura of self-assurance.

'That's quite a change you're describing there, but I don't feel it in myself.'

Perhaps not, but just your actions with Dahlia and Silas show how your awareness of the world around you has evolved.

Diving into the shower and freshening up, I dry myself off, put on clean clothes and listen to my stomach complaining. Seeing it's lunchtime already, I head back to the canteen and wonder what's on the menu this time. I hope there's a good dessert selection as I am feeling my sweet tooth at the moment.

Chapter 9

BRONZE

Walking with Dixon to the training area, I'm going to see how the females are progressing. Hopefully, they will have shown considerable improvement since my first visit, when Dixon took the floor and challenged them all.

He has been very vocal about his assistant Adaline, and the way she has motivated the females. Dixon introduced her to the males at their last session. When there were several smirks and comments, she immediately stepped forward and asked for a wolf volunteer to meet her in the ring. Wylder stepped forward and when Dixon noticed he groaned, then he looked at Adaline to see if he should stop the challenge, but she slyly shook her head.

Wylder's wolf is called Goliath, and Dixon knew that he was going to dwarf his opponent. Wylder and Goliath were accomplished warriors and had been at the top of their game since qualifying.

Watching Star, Adaline's much smaller wolf, circle the ring, no doubt assessing her opponent, Dixon said he was genuinely concerned for his trainer. Before he could call a halt though, Goliath lunged at Star. There was a sudden flurry of bodies and then Goliath was standing there, apparently alone.

Everyone was stunned when Star was gone. It wasn't until they looked closer at Goliath that they saw that Star had her legs firmly clamped around his body as she hung below him, and her jaws locked on his throat. If she shook her head, his throat would be ripped open. Goliath lowered his head, and Star released him and dropped to the floor.

Once shifted to their human form, Wylder looked at Adaline, stepped forward, took her hand in his and raised it high in the air. When he released her hand, he bowed then scooped her up in a bear hug, laughing. The entire session erupted in cheers. There were no more smirks, and when someone made a comment, Wylder immediately challenged them, to which they quickly withdrew their remark, and offered an apology to Adaline.

Arriving at the training area, I'm pleasantly surprised to see everyone waiting quietly for Dixon, a full three minutes early. In front of each female at her feet is a backpack containing the toy pup. I look quizzically at Dixon and he laughs.

"They bring the toy pups to every session without fail. Adaline asked for them back at the end of that first training session, and they simply refused to part with them. They bring them every time and occasionally we run that scenario after training has finished. The contests are nothing short of brutal, short of an actual death. I think we've had every injury from any medical journal. They fight with a ferocity you won't believe, and yet as soon as the contest is won, or lost, they help each other in true warrior fashion. I wouldn't hesitate to put any one of them forward for warrior training if we needed them," Dixon shakes his head, but I can see the pride he has for them, and for his new assistant.

Watching them walk away, I see a lone female waiting at the far side of the area. When she sees me looking her way, she waves excitedly with her bat.

"How is Ember coming along?" I ask.

Dixon gives me a grimace. "You created the greatest monster of them all when you gave her that damn bat. I get bruises on muscles I never knew I had after training with her."

Seeing the way she strolls across the training area shows a confidence that she never had before. The bat is swinging in her hand as though it was part of her, an extension of her right arm. As she reaches the halfway point across the area, someone streaks across from the shadow of some trees, and launches themselves at Ember. In a move so nonchalant that neither myself nor Dixon can believe it, Ember takes the head of the bat in her left hand, pushes with her right. The thick head lands in the stomach of her attacker, who drops and writhes on the floor in agony. Without batting an eyelid, or even looking to see who her attacker is, Ember mutters quietly, "Better luck next time, bitch."

As Ember approaches, I see another shadow by the trees, but it seems to be making a fast exit.

"What was that all about?" I ask when she stands in front of us.

"Since you gave me the bat, and I've been having my one-to-one training with Chief Warrior Dixon, there appears to be a certain amount of jealousy. Several times now, some female has tried to take my bat either by force or deception. As you can clearly see, I will not be giving up my bat anytime soon to anyone, unless it's over my dead body," she says all this in a sing-song voice that has me believing every word.

Looking at her attacker, I recognize her immediately as she limps away. I need to speak to Xavi again.

Ember asks, "What do you need me to learn today, Chief Warrior Dixon? Maybe we could demonstrate what I've learned already for the Alpha Heir to see that his gift has been more than appreciated." Her enthusiasm doesn't seem to infect Dixon as he groans and agrees to the demonstration.

Stepping forward, Dixon enters the training circle and Ember skips to join him. Skips! She would have to be dragged kicking and screaming not so long ago. Dixon does a fantastic job of dodging most of Ember's attacks, however, he has to block several hits, and the odd attack does get through his defenses. Watching the new Ember is exhilarating. I never in my wildest dreams expected her to become so violent and bloodthirsty. I see what Dixon meant when he said I'd created a monster.

Calling an end to the demonstration, before Dixon gets seriously hurt, I watch as Ember walks towards me, examining her bat. She herself has some cuts and scratches, but she ignores her own injuries while she makes sure her bat isn't damaged. Oh...My...Goddess.

"What did you think, Alpha Heir Bronze? Am I worthy of carrying your bat? I practice every day, and I study weapons and tactics in the library during the week. Some sword tactics can be transferred to my bat, and throughout history, many other weapons can be assimilated into my bat training." Her eyes are wide with excitement and enthusiasm. "I'm looking into getting new bats made, too, in different materials. I have one in a lighter wood, but it doesn't stand up too well when I get excited."

"Neither do I, Ember," Dixon pipes in and laughs. "Your skill with that is something I would never have believed possible. I'm one hundred percent sure that there isn't anyone in the pack that could stand in the training ring with you and come out unscathed. I think there are those that could beat you, but they would certainly have scars, bruises or broken bones as souvenirs."

I watch as she swells with pride at Dixon's words. "I am pleased that my gift has had such a positive impact on you, Ember. You looked frighteningly competent out there, and I wouldn't want to upset you to the point that I had to stand against you. I may even have a bat made for my Luna." Seeing her laugh has me remembering her only a few months ago. Terrified of her training, being ridiculed by some, and almost afraid of her own shadow. I know that she was being bullied by a couple of the females. I bet they don't dare bully her now.

Heading back to the packhouse, I mind link with Xavi to meet me in the alpha's office. I also ask my father to join us. Dixon, I notice, has slipped off to visit Doctor Gideon, though I suspect he thinks Nurse Elana would be a better healer for him. I'm sure he has a soft spot for her, but they haven't become fated mates which, when you see them together, you'd think they would have been a natural choice by the Goddess.

As I approach the warrior at the alpha office door, I receive a slight nod which tells me my father is there ahead of me, so I knock before entering. Xavi and my father are laughing at something, and both look up as I enter.

"Well, my son. What do you want us for? I was just going to get my lunch, so I hope it's nothing that will spoil my appetite," Alpha Chet says with an eyebrow lift.

"In all the years I've known you, I've never known anything that could do such a heinous thing," Xavi says this almost under his breath and we all laugh.

"Depending on what Xavi has to tell me, I think it might even enhance it, if that's possible." Taking a seat by Xavi at the front of my father's desk, I turn and ask him, "Did you find anyone that was in league with Savannah?" I think I know the answer already from the incident earlier.

"You have that look that says you already know something and just want confirmation. Has something else happened that I'm not yet aware of?" Xavi squints at me suspiciously.

My father sits there quietly but intrigued.

"Savannah tried to pull another stunt today and when it failed, spectacularly I might add, I saw a figure sneaking away in the background," I quickly glance at both my father and Xavi, "Before you ask, Savannah tried to take the bat I gave to Ember away from her. Ember literally stopped Savannah dead in her tracks with no effort whatsoever. She didn't even break her stride, as she did it. It was a thing of beauty to behold."

"Everyone in the pack is talking about Ember and her bat. She is never seen without it and brags that she sleeps with it in her bed. Goddess help the male that becomes her mate because that bat is going to be stiff competition. Who did you think it was sneaking away?" Xavi asks me.

"I think that she is in league with..." I pause for effect... "Elder Michael."

"My sources have reported that they have been seen together quite often of late, so I would have to concur with your suspicions there," Xavi agrees.

My father explodes from his seat and I wait for the anger to burst forth. Instead, he has a huge grin on his face and says quietly, "Got the weasel at last. Now I can do something that will give me great satisfaction and save you a job in the future, son. Xavi, round up the four council members and bring them here immediately for an emergency meeting. No excuses. They come now, in fact, wait. I'll call them here as an Alpha order. Even better..." He sits and grins. It is only a matter of minutes before the council arrives, and they look puzzled, and more than a little apprehensive. Elder Michael, however, looks at me and grins.

Francis, Jude and Isiah, the latter who is certainly the quietest member, take a seat at the table. Michael looks as though he has prepared a speech, and as he opens his mouth my father says quietly, "You have nothing to say at this point, Elder Michael, that anyone wishes to hear. You will take your seat just as the other more respectful members have done, and you will remain silent until such a time as I wish to hear from you. You will know when that time comes, I assure you.

"You have been summoned before me because a very serious matter has been brought to my attention. A pack member is scheming against the pack leadership, and although I have no documentary evidence, I do have witnesses to this scheming. As Elders, I want to know your opinion as to what punishment would best serve the purpose of the pack? Any form of such action would reasonably be deemed traitorous, surely. Would you agree?"

There are three yesses and one attempted speech by Michael. Alpha Chet continues, and I quietly enjoy the squirming I notice. "Elder Michael. Every question that I am going to put to the council, and I use that term purely as a courtesy, as we all know that there is no such thing as an Elder Council, will be a yes or no answer. This is not a debate, argument or even a conversation. I will ask a question, you will answer yes or no, is that clear?"

Four yesses echo in the room, although one is a little later and not as clear. "I am informed that a pack member has begun to recruit others to their treason, and is directed at a singular member of our leadership. Would it be correct to say that anyone joining such a scheme willingly would also be regarded as a traitor?"

Yes, yes, and yes come from the Elders. Michael remains silent. I believe a light is coming on in his, 'I'm so high and mighty' brain. Watching the beads of sweat form on his brow, my father smiles, and it is one of the most frightening things I have ever seen. The hunter has his prey, and they both know how it is going to end. Sensing the tension in the air, the other three Elders all turn and look at Michael. Shaking his head, Isiah says to Michael, "What have you done this time?"

"For once in your life, Michael, you have no words?" My father gives him a moment to answer but he sits there quietly. "You don't wish to tell the others that you have been conspiring with a young female? A young, misguided slip of a female, that you could have helped see the error of her ways? No, not you, Elder Michael, all you saw was a weapon. An opportunity to try to either embarrass or mislead my son into some kind of indiscretion, that would give you some sort of perverted satisfaction. Perhaps you sought to gain some further measure of power for yourself? For the council as a whole, maybe? No, you are not that noble that anything you do is for anyone else."

Jude speaks up. "Is this true, Michael? Have you done what the Alpha accuses you of?"

Michael begins to speak. "I…"

Jude stops him. "It is not open for discussion, it is a simple yes or no answer."

Michael looks around the room, obviously hoping for some form of escape, but there is nowhere for him to go. "Yes, it is true. She came to me…"

"Liar!" Xavi spits the word with more venom that I have ever heard in his voice before. "Savannah did not approach you. She wouldn't dream of approaching you for such help. You, an Elder of the pack? No, Michael, even now you cannot be truthful. If I had my way, I would put you before the pack and let them decide your fate. You yourself have made the Elders unapproachable to the pack. Not one of them would think to ask for your help, any of you, even if you were their last hope of life itself."

Xavi's hands have become claws and I see his wolf fighting to get out. If he does, Michael will die where he sits. Placing my hand gently on Xavi's shoulder, his head snaps to me and I see his wolf's eyes blazing back at me.

Titan comes forth, and speaks to Cerberus, Xavi's wolf. *Let the Alpha handle this. Do not lower yourself to that human's level. We are above his dishonor.*

Cerberus replies to Titan, *I hear you, Titan, but it is difficult to understand why his wolf has not stopped this behavior. I have tried to reach his wolf but cannot get a response, though I sense he's there.*

"Wolfsbane. That's why your wolf couldn't stop you. You've been using wolfsbane against your own wolf..." The words are torn from me and even as I speak them, I know their truth.

I see my father's eyes blaze, and within seconds, the office door slams open. Four warriors rush into the room, and my father points at Michael. "Take him from my sight immediately, before I administer my own justice."

Taking the Elder by his arms, they have to almost carry him from the room, he is so docile. The three remaining Elders watch and shake their heads as he is removed.

Francis turns to my father. "Alpha Chet, we had no idea any of this was going on. I assure you that none of us were involved."

"And there, Elder members, is the problem. You have no idea what is going on within your own council, never mind the pack itself. How could you not see what he was doing? Drugging his own wolf and not one of you could see that?" My father shakes his head and takes his seat at his desk. "I was going to remove Michael as an Elder member today, for his actions against my son, but in light of what I have seen today, I am going to go one step further."

The Elders look at each other and Isiah speaks for them. "Please don't put Michael in front of the pack. They will kill him, we are all certain of that."

"Your concerns are noted but that was not my intention." My father stands and looks each elder in the eye. "As of this moment, there will be no more Elder Council, Elder meetings or indeed Elder members. I am disbanding the Elders as of this instant. I cannot and will not, in all good conscience, stand by and waste pack funds, or resources for something that will turn against the pack, or the pack leadership, my family. It ends here. From the end of the month, you will receive none of the remunerations or gifts that you have been getting. I suggest that you look at what talents you have that will benefit the pack going forward. You are dismissed."

Fortunately, none of the Elders argue with my father. We can all see and understand his decision, and his reasoning is solid. How could they not know that one of their own was subduing his wolf? I watch as the Elders leave the office, and have to wonder what they will tell their followers. Some have developed what could almost be described as congregations. They will not be able to hide Michael's actions.

We all sit silently as we digest the recent events. None of us had foreseen such a dramatic conclusion to the Michael and Savannah issue. "Savannah?"

My father looks at me. "Already taken care of. I'm having her transported to Wolfsfoot to spend time with Luna Tati. I mind linked your mother and she has made Luna Tati aware of what has been going on. Luna Tati is looking forward to pointing out the error of her ways to Savannah."

Knocking at the door has us all looking that way, and I'm sure we're all wondering what now?

The door bangs open and Cook Ash comes bowling in like a whirlwind carrying a large plastic tub. Beaming at me in particular, she stops dead, holds out the tub and literally shouts...

"COOKIES!"

Chapter 10

TARIA

Sitting alone in the canteen, having finished a huge breakfast, I think about how I can make small but visible changes when I join Bronze at Eclipse.

I like the way you are thinking. Maya's voice interrupts my thoughts.

'Oh yes? In what way?' I'm intrigued.

You obviously realize that if you go in there guns blazing, the pack will immediately think you know better than them. The pack has customs, traditions, and ways of doing things that may be centuries old. Charging in and changing things will not be received well.

'That's what I thought, but if I go in and make no changes, they will think I can't stand on my own two feet. It won't be easy, but I'm going to take some time-out for myself today, and make a list of my ideas in my notepad. Once that is done, I can prioritize what I think will be the way forward.'

You won't need me for that, so I'll just have a nice, long nap. Our run with Conan and Maiden this morning was enjoyable, and I got to chase rabbits. The amount you are eating these days, I don't need to catch them every time!

Thinking back to our run this morning, there is no wonder I'm eating like a horse. With my morning run becoming a regular thing, and getting longer, I might add, the training sessions are becoming far more warrior based, rather than defensive. I must be burning calories at a hell of a rate.

I know I feel better for it, and my body is definitely liking all the exercise. I noticed when I got out of the shower a couple of days ago, although I still have all my feminine curves, they have firmed up and look toned. I made myself blush when I thought of Bronze finally getting his hands on me.

Clearing my table, I head outside to go through the herb garden. Seeing how it is laid out, I make a quick sketch in my pad. Noting what herbs are in close proximity and which are planted separately. I notice that the various mints are in their own bed yet still in pots. I remember Dahlia saying how they take over if left 'loose' in the soil.

One bed has lavender and rosemary in it. I bet that smells divine when it's flowering and ready to harvest. I notice it has a bed of stones so the soil drains well, and it's also well away from the building where it will get the most sun throughout the day.

Cilantro and dill dominate another area and I remember another of Dahlia's lessons about how these attract predatory insects that eat aphids, and they also attract pollinators like bees and butterflies. She is an encyclopedia for beginners like me.

Walking further, I pass through the vegetable garden and see the raised beds full of carrots, there's another of Dahlia's pearls of wisdom. Carrot-fly can only fly around sixty centimeters high, so raised beds above this height prevent them from reaching the plant. Also, tagetes give off a scent that repels them.

Making notes, I'm filling my pad quickly and wondering how much the Eclipse head gardener already knows. Even if he knows every bit of information I gather, it will, at least, show them I have an interest in what they do.

Realizing the time, I rush back to the packhouse to change into my training clothes. Arriving at the training area, I see Chief Warrior Oscar finishing a training session with a female warrior.

"Ah, Taria. Come and meet Iona. I don't think you've been introduced as yet. Iona, this is Taria, soon to be Luna of the Eclipse pack."

"Pleased to meet you, Taria. I have heard good things about you. I particularly liked your matchmaking with Dahlia and Silas. None of us saw that coming, and we should have. Unfortunately, like Silas, we did not see past our blinkered vision of the old Dahlia. Well done, you."

"Thank you, Iona. It was just a fresh pair of eyes, that's all. Dahlia has certainly come out of her shell though, I must admit." Looking closer at Iona, a thought strikes me. "Aren't you on the warrior council that Gabe set up before he became Alpha at Wolfsfoot?"

"I have that distinction, yes." Iona bows slightly and we all laugh.

"Could I steal you away at some point so you can explain what that's all about? I'd be very interested in your thoughts and perspective." The warrior council at Blackshadow is something that I have not seen or heard of in any other pack, so it could be something, or nothing.

"Well, I'm going to eat lunch now, but I can be back here for when you've finished your training period, if that suits?"

"Oh yes. That would be excellent. Thank you so much. I'll see you then. Oh, and enjoy your lunch. I'd join you if I didn't have this session?" I look at Oscar and give him my pleading puppy-eyed look.

"Not a chance. I went by the canteen earlier and saw what you ate for breakfast. You don't need lunch," Oscar grins at me. They both laugh, and I see that my appetite is becoming common knowledge amongst the pack.

During the training session, I seem to be picking myself up off the ground more times than I care to remember. I'm not normally getting my ass handed to me so many times in a session. I am determined not to lose every attack and give it my all. All to no avail, however.

When Oscar has had enough of watching me struggle to my feet, he stands there looking down at me for the last time.

"I don't know what's got into you, Taria, but you are trying too hard to win every fight. You are not normally this focused on trying to win, and it's making you careless. If any of today's fights had been the real thing, you'd be dead. No two ways about it and no way to sugarcoat it. You wouldn't stand a chance if an assassin came for you right now."

"I could tell that I wasn't doing well but thought that you had introduced something new that I wasn't seeing." I roll my neck to try to free up some of the knots I can feel. Sweat is running down my chest and back in rivers.

"Nothing new here. In fact, I didn't even have to try. You left yourself wide open to my moves. Stop trying so hard. You'll find your moves will come more fluidly, if they are more instinct than thought. Does that make sense?" Oscar smiles at me and then I see his eyes flick behind me.

"I understand, but I'm not sure what's made me this way just now. I'll think it over before our next session." Turning, I see Iona waiting. "I hope you didn't see too much of that," I smile, and she nods her head.

"Enough to know that it wasn't pretty, and you were not at your best. I've seen you fight better in other sessions, I must admit." Giving me a sniff, she says, "Would you like a shower before we have our question and answer session? Please...because you stink."

"I guess I need one, huh?" Heading briskly back to the packhouse, I agree to meet her in the canteen in a few minutes after I shower and change.

Walking back into the canteen, I spy Iona sitting at a corner table, in pretty much the same sort of position that I would choose now. She is not alone, there is a male with her. As I approach, the male stands and introduces himself as Hallec, Iona's mate and fellow warrior council member.

"Pleased to meet you, Taria, however, I must leave you two to your lunch. I want to surprise the border patrol with an inspection. Enjoy your food, I'll see you later, Iona." Seeing the look in her eyes as he walks away, I have no doubt that they are a fated pair, and I feel a pang of jealousy.

"I am not a weak female, Taria, by any means, I can hold my own against anyone, but there goes my rock," she whispers.

"I imagine he feels the same way about you, Iona. He should have kissed you before he left. He wanted to." Taking a seat beside her, I wait for her to come back to earth.

"So, the warrior council. Let me tell you what I know and then we can go from there. Beta Gabriel, as he was then, wasn't happy with the way the pack had been run by the then Alpha Torrence, and none of us were sure how Alpha Connell would shape up. None of us doubted that he wanted the pack to thrive and become a great pack once again. We were just not sure that he would be up to it. His friends were not friends, but users. They abused his friendship and bullied the pack. Beta Gabriel wanted a way to stop them, and the easiest way was to somehow curb their power over others. As most were warriors, taking away that status would rob them of their power.

"By forming the warrior council, he could give the pack a way of deciding who should warrant that power. Warrior training has improved. The standard has been raised and we once again hold each other in high esteem. We know our borders are protected and that our pups can once again sleep safely."

"I don't believe the Eclipse pack has those issues, but I like the warrior council format. I think all packs could benefit from having a standard that is upheld by a group rather than a single Chief Warrior. Not that I'm casting aspersions on any Chief Warrior..." I can certainly see how Gabriel came to his decision and can only marvel at how he managed to implement it.

"Remember, Taria, that the Delta is also heavily involved with the warriors. They regulate the patrol schedules, take all reports from them, investigate discrepancies and any border infringements. It is not always necessary to have more than those two officers involved. It can quite easily have an adverse effect if you have people on the council with too strong of an opinion or ego."

"Oh, my goodness. This is like my fighting training," I say, laughing. "I think I'm trying too hard and overthinking everything."

Iona grins, "Go chill out, you'll think about what you've heard and mull it over I'm sure. You have plenty of time before you leave for the next pack you are visiting, and then you will have even more information to think about."

I can't help but look at Iona in horror, and as she throws her head back laughing I watch her leave, laughing all the way.

Chapter 11

BRONZE

Sitting at the alpha's desk, munching cookies down as though it's my last meal. I'm thinking of punishments that don't involve Cook Ash or her kitchen. So far, it looks like Herb the gardener is going to be taking the hit with anyone that gets disciplined. Although, unlike Cook Ash, I don't think Herb will ever run out of tasks that need extra muscle. If anything, I believe he'd lap up any extra pairs of hands he could get. He's doing a fantastic job with the gardens and his future plans are all ahead of schedule, his enthusiasm is an absolute joy to see.

Wolfing down the last peanut butter cookie, I look at the white chocolate cookies and sigh. I can't face another cookie, I think to myself, as my hand reaches out and takes one. They are so tasty that I can't help myself.

The office door opens and my father, Alpha Chet walks in. I jump out of his chair and take one in front of his desk.

I notice him smirking at my move, before he speaks. "It won't be long before you don't have to do that, you know? You don't have to do it now unless there's someone else around. I appreciate the courtesy though, son."

"Sitting in the Alpha's chair on a permanent basis will take some getting used to. I still see it as your chair, your desk, and your office. Even though I'm in it such a lot these days, it's not mine yet," I grin at my father and see the humor in his eyes. "I'm going to miss the pair of you when you join the council, you know that don't you?"

"It's going to be strange for us too, son. Not having to be up at the crack of dawn every day. Being waited on hand and foot. Undisturbed meals cooked by a chef. Free time to do as we like and not wonder who is going to disturb us. I just don't know how I'll cope in such a stress-free environment, I really don't," Putting the back of his hand against his forehead for dramatic effect has me laughing.

"Being with Mother twenty-four seven. Never being alone. Hearing her voice in your ear all day, every day. Eating all your meals together. Not forgetting her boundless energy, of course, that will have her volunteering the both of you for any and all committees, fundraisers, and events. I just don't know how you'll fit in *any* free time, I really don't." Slapping my hand to my forehead, I see the reality of my words hitting home as my father's face drops.

"Aw, shut up! My dreams of a tranquil life have just been shattered. Torn asunder by my evil-minded son. If you're not careful, words like that may cause me to rethink my retirement, and then where would you be? Huh?"

"Oh, Father, please have a rethink. I could take Taria as my mate immediately, and we could do diplomatic visits to the other packs, maybe even to the Northern and Southern sectors. We could be gone for months at a time, enjoying ourselves while you watch over the dreary day-to-day pack tasks. That sounds appealing," I grin at him and seeing his eyes flare, I know that Shaman is enjoying my teasing.

"Typical only child. Got an answer for everything. It's at times like this I wish we'd had a dozen pups!"

"It's a bit late for that now," We both jump as we hadn't heard Mother enter the office. "You wouldn't have coped with a dozen pups, you old fraud. You struggled to help with the one we had when it came to diapers. You gagged and faux vomited so much every time you had to change him. It was amusing that we kill to eat when in wolf form, that you made such a fuss over a dirty diaper."

"You pair have always ganged up on me. I wish I'd at least had a daughter as well. She would have stuck up for her dear old dad."

"Oh yes, I can just see it now." Raising her finger, she pretends to wrap something around it and smirks at him. "That's where she would have had you. After all, it's where I've had you for the last twenty-five years." Bursting out laughing at my father's horrified face, my mother winks at me. Taking a cookie from the plate on the table, she takes a nibble from it and then pops the rest into her husband's still open mouth.

"Oh, and while I remember. Xavi asked me to tell you that Michael the awful elder member that you had locked in his dwelling, is dead. They found him as I was coming to get you for lunch. I said I'd tell you rather than him mind-linking such a thing to you." Seeing mother taking another cookie, I look at my father and he spits his cookie all over the desk.

"Dead? He's dead?"

"Xavi said there was a note. Apparently, as soon as his wolf became free of the wolfsbane, he told Michael what he thought of him and his actions, and begged the Goddess to remove him from such a dishonorable host. Hearing it from his wolf struck home more than anything you or the other elders had said to him, and he took his own life. Losing his wolf may be why none of us felt him leave the pack? Losing his wolf probably did us all a favor. I'll visit his family when I leave here, see if they need anything."

"Mother! I've never heard you sound so callous about anyone in my whole life." I'm at a loss for words. She has always been positive about everyone and genuinely upset whenever someone passed on.

"Oh, come on, Bronze, he was a nightmare, he didn't have a redeeming bone in his body. His family will be better off without him." Finishing her cookie, she takes another and heads out of the office.

I sit there staring at my father, who hasn't said a word as yet. He just stares back at me, trance like. It only takes a few seconds for him to shake his head, and he's back in the real world.

"Well, I never saw that coming. I've asked Xavi to give me his report as soon as he can, but I'm sure your mother will be correct in her summary." Looking at me for a comment, I don't have anything to say, so I just shrug.

I'm surprised no one knew he was using wolfsbane. His family, or closest friends, must have noticed his wolf was quiet or absent, Titan speaks to Shaman.

Shaman responds, *I also think that this should be so. We will see what Cerberus can uncover while his human investigates.*

Taking a cookie from the few remaining on the plate, my father stands and starts to walk to the door. "Lunchtime, these cookies are making me hungry. Coming?"

"No, thanks. I've had so many cookies I don't think there's even room for a glass of water in my stomach," I rub my stomach to show it's slightly bloated.

Once my father has left, I sit back at the alpha desk and try to decide what I need to do next. I'm still two members short for my inner council, and I want to have them all attend a meeting before we go live, as it were. They at least need to be introduced to each other formally, and as to what their duties will be.

You asked me to suggest someone for your inner council. I have someone but you may not be happy about it. Titan sounds hesitant, and that is not a trait I have ever seen in him.

'Why would I not be happy about one of my pack? They are from the Eclipse pack, aren't they?'

Yes, and no. They are Eclipse pack, but also a Shadow Warrior.

'There's a Shadow Warrior in the pack? Does my father know this?'

Oh, Bronze. Come on. There are several Shadow Warriors in the pack. There are several in every pack by necessity. How could they be effective if they were not readily available?

'So who do you suggest then?'

Valor. His human is Ethan. They are highly respected among the Shadow Warriors. They are honorable and have had difficulty not going to your father and telling him what they are.

'You know them well?'

Well enough to suggest that they could be of great use to you as advisors.

'Okay. I will speak with Ethan and then make my decision. That still leaves me with one more seat to fill.'

I would have suggested Ember, but I think her bat would sway the other members' decision-making processes.

'You're joking, right? Ember on my inner council?'

Yes, I'm joking. If you were to have Drake from Wolfsfoot perform an assessment on Adaline to be your next Chief Warrior, and she passed his assessment. She would be good on your council. She is like Eve in that she can be creative and think outside the box.

'You are being very helpful with your suggestions, Titan. Am I missing something?'

You promised me a run chasing rabbits if I suggested a member. I have now suggested two and both for good reason.

'Ah, yes, I did.' I can almost see him smiling as I recall the conversation. 'I suppose I owe you two runs, then. Is that how you see it?'

It would seem fair to say that, yes.

Seeing him lay down, I accept defeat, pick up the phone and place a call to Wolfsfoot. Tati picks up, and as soon as I speak, she launches into me. Comments like, I thought better of you, what were you thinking? Taria will be furious.

When I can finally get a word in, I manage to stop her and ask what she is talking about.

"Leading a female on, thinking that she is going to be your Luna and then dumping her for another. I never saw that in you, Bronze."

"Oh, now I understand. Savannah! Tati, I am not like that, and she was never going to be anything. Far from leading her on, I have spent years fending her off. You should speak to Luna Sage about Savannah."

"Well, she certainly has a lot of detail with her story," Tati sounds a little less certain now.

"Tati. I have never had any interest in Savannah. It's all in her head. The next time you speak to her, you'll be able to recognize when she's telling lies."

"Oh? How so?"

"Her lips move! She can't tell the truth if her life depends on it. If she tells you it's raining, look outside. She's that bad," Laughing, I'm amazed that she got one over on Tati.

"Her life will be a misery from this moment on. I don't appreciate being made a fool of. I'm sorry, Bronze, she was so believable," Tati sounds both upset and angry at the same time.

"Don't worry, Tati. I forgive you. I didn't call about her though, I'm asking for a favor."

"Well, I can't very well refuse now, can I? Having doubted your gentlemanly conduct, I'll have to do something to make it up to you," Tati made it sound worse than it was.

"I want to promote someone to my Chief Warrior position, but they haven't been a warrior, as such. They are an excellent trainer, and I don't doubt that if she was sent to a border skirmish, she would acquit herself favorably."

"You want to send me another female problem? Is that it?" I hear Tati sigh, which makes me smirk before I respond.

"No, not at all. I was going to ask if I could borrow Drake so he could come here and assess her skills for me. Now that you mention it, though. Sending her to you might be a better way to accomplish it. No one would know about the *trial by combat*, and if Drake doesn't think she's ready, the pack won't need to know about it. He can also suggest where she would need to improve. That would be a great way to get her promoted. What do you say, Tati? Is it a goer?" I'm very excited about this now and think I'm definitely onto something.

"A *goer*? Where did you get that from? You've been spending too much time with the pups, I'm sure. You realize that Drake is a hard taskmaster? I know from personal, firsthand experience, he'll want her for more than just an assessment. To give her the best chance, which I think that's what you want, you'd best send her here for a week. I'll discuss it with him and put a plan in place. Send her in two weeks and we'll smooth any rough edges and make sure she does you proud." Tati has certainly picked up on my wanting Adaline to succeed.

"Thank you, Tati. You're an angel. I remember you saying how hard Drake worked you to make you the best he could."

"One last thing before I hang up…"

"Okay, what's that?" I ask, intrigued by her tone of voice.

"Make sure she can climb trees…and damn fast!"

The phone clicks and I'm left thinking…climb trees? Then I laugh as I remember.

Chapter 12

TARIA

Waiting for Alpha Connell to arrive at his office, I sit quietly and reflect on my time here. I've learned so much that I couldn't begin to list it all. Once I'm at the Eclipse pack, I'm hoping that most things will come naturally without having a blank moment at a time when I'm needed to stand up and be counted.

My fighting and fitness training has improved so much that I don't recognize myself in the training ring anymore. I do so much by reflex now that I would be happy to be helping on border patrol. I asked Chief Warrior Oscar if I could go on a patrol and he outright refused and told me not to ask again.

Luna Hope has been a marvel. She flows through the pack like a tornado wherever she goes, but instead of leaving a wake of destruction, she leaves organization, peace and tranquility. You'd never know it without experiencing it. Her admin skills are out of this world. If there's paperwork involved, it's done to the highest standard, schedules are met, journals are kept.

I've been to every department and spent time there, occasionally left in charge while someone had a day resting, or they were concentrating on a project they hadn't had time for. I've learned about things I'd never thought about before, and I wonder how

Momma ever coped with it all by herself. I should have been there for her.

Alpha Connell's voice brings me back from my thoughts as he invites me inside. Following him into his office, he motions to a chair in front of his desk. Taking his seat, he smiles at me.

"So, Taria. What can I do for you today?"

"I was wondering if you could spare someone to go with me to Spirit Walker pack? I know how busy Alpha Lyle must be and was wondering, with everything I've learned so far, maybe I could be of help to him for a couple of days?" I thought about this last night after supper and decided to see if it would be viable. "What do you think? I haven't spoken to him, obviously. I wanted to speak to you first."

Looking at me with an intense stare, I feel uncomfortable and perhaps I've overstepped a boundary or something. "I think the idea is extremely noble and if it was me, I'd accept your offer. I will need to speak to Alpha Lyle and see what he thinks. It may be too dangerous for you to be there right now with all the rogue issues he's currently battling with. Let's give him a call and see if he's free."

Picking up his phone, he presses a single digit, which tells me he has the Alpha's on speed dial. Something else I can use when I get into my own Luna office, I think to myself.

I listen to half a conversation as Alpha Connell talks with Alpha Lyle. It appears to be a positive reaction to my idea and I'm keen to hear how it plays out. The call ends and Alpha Connell looks at me with an expression I can't read.

"Lyle could use some help from someone with your newly acquired experience and is grateful for the offer. His concern is the rogue infractions across his borders are more frequent, and driving further into Spirit Walker pack lands at the moment. He wants you to speak with Bronze first, and if Bronze is good with it, you can go for two days. In two days, you should be able to ease his workload significantly with regard to admin tasks, and a few other issues that his Luna would normally take care of, if he had one."

"Why do I need to speak to Bronze about where I go and who I help? We are fated mates, but I'm not a member of the Eclipse pack, yet! He does not control my actions, or where I go. I am doing everything I can to be a good Luna, but I'm not at his beck and call, or under any obligations to him, as yet. If I needed to speak to anyone it would be Luna Aurora, my mother." I'm feeling more than a little feisty being told that I have to ask permission to help someone or go somewhere, and it manifests in my tone of voice. I think I'm doing enough on the Luna learning front, without having to ask to be allowed to go somewhere.

Alpha Connell seems a little surprised by my response, especially my petulant tone, and he sits back in his chair and watches me closely.

"I don't think you've thought it through, before you gave that display of the old Taria." Leaning forward, he rests his elbows on the desk and links his fingers. For some reason, just this posture makes me nervous. "It isn't so much asking permission, as it is doing the right thing, morally and politically. How would you like it if your betrothed, and let's face it, that's what you are as fated mates, suddenly went off and stayed at a female's pack, without your knowledge, or having the courtesy to explain this action? Lyle is a single alpha male, don't forget, and don't try telling me you wouldn't mind." His voice has risen only slightly, but with a dramatic effect. "You wouldn't be worth a damn as a mate if you didn't care.

You're asking to go into what is basically a war zone between the rogues and the rest of us. Spirit Walker are currently under the rogues' microscope, and you are aware that there are skirmishes on a regular basis. I've just told you that they have become more frequent, and are penetrating deeper. You are the fated mate of not just a pack member, but an Alpha Heir. If you were to be injured or killed while staying at another pack, without that mate knowing you were even there, you could potentially start a war between those packs. Lyle will be held responsible for your safety while you're at his pack, whether you like it or not. As none of this seems to sit well with you, Taria, I deny you permission to leave Blackshadow pack lands. You are currently under my protection and as such will remain here until I have spoken to Alpha Gerry as your pack alpha."

I am completely taken aback by this turn of events. My outburst seems to have touched a raw nerve, and I don't know what to say or do to make things right. "I apologize, Alpha Connell, if I spoke hastily and without thinking. I have been trying extremely hard to prepare myself for my role as Luna, so I didn't think of my own importance as a shifter. I was only thinking of others and how I can be productive for them. My importance as a mate or as a Luna was not in my thoughts."

A sudden weariness comes over me and I feel myself begin to sag under its weight. No. I'm not giving in to it. Taking a deep breath, I pull my shoulders back and look him in the eye.

"It happens to all good leaders at some point. Go get some food and then get some rest. You have indeed been putting a lot of effort into everything since you arrived, and you're looking tired. You'll take tomorrow off from all training, learning or Luna related activities. I order you to have some 'Taria time'. Do something for yourself, as long as it does not involve work. Now, go."

Entering the canteen, I realize it is only lunchtime. While grabbing a small selection of meats, I spy the desserts. That's what I need. Sugar, cream, sweet stuff. Loading every inch of available tray space with desserts, I spy a corner table and prepare to gorge myself silly. I don't care if I spend the rest of the afternoon being ill. I'm going to demolish it all.

Laying on my bed in my room, I'm seriously regretting my sugar rush. I cleared my tray and was silly enough to go back for more. Having seen some of the other pack members watching me, I couldn't bring myself to waste any of my second helpings. I feel so sick right now. Oh. My. Goddess!

Hearing my phone ring on my bedside table, I debate whether to ignore it or not. It keeps ringing so my decision is made for me. Reaching over, I see it is my Pops. Grabbing my phone, I quickly sit up and take the call.

"Hi Pops. Is everything ok?"

"Hello Sweetpea. Everything's good here. Me and your momma are doing fine, Raina says hi, too." I'm not sure, but I think I detected a slight emphasis on the word, 'here'.

"I take it this isn't just a social call, Pops. I think you've had a call from Alpha Connell." I wait for confirmation and to see what he has to say.

"I called Connell to see how things were going before I rang you. It was an interesting conversation, and he was very complimentary about you and your progress. I'm very proud of how hard you've worked and so is your momma. I hear you've been playing cupid too." He gives a small laugh at that, and I wonder just how much everyone discusses me.

"It didn't take much, believe me. It was more of a gentle nudge than a match make. One party just needed to see the wood for the trees, that was all. They certainly suit each other and are a wonderful pair together." I smile as I recall how Dahlia and Silas are now joined at the hip, and you rarely see one without the other.

"Has something happened that you think Connell needed to call us about?" I'm not sure if this is a test or not, but I don't see Pops as that type, so I explain the recent conversation, including my attitude.

"Well, Sweetpea, I can see where you would jump to that conclusion, and I don't think that's a bad thing. You're becoming a strong, independent, and confident female. Making decisions for and about yourself is part of your learning curve on this journey. You've just learned that you don't always take everything into account at a moment's notice. Welcome to the world of leadership. You're not being trained to be infallible. None of us are."

"Thanks, Pops. I've been giving myself a hard time about my reaction and lack of thought. I feel better having talked to you. I do miss you and momma, though I don't have a lot of spare time to think of anything but Luna stuff." I smile as I hear him laugh.

"As I said, welcome to the world of leadership. You do, however, need to make time for yourself, occasionally. I'm sure Bronze will encourage you to take time out when you can, and do something just for yourself." Listening to his voice, I get a lump in my throat as I realize just how much I miss him. We haven't been Pops and Sweetpea that long, yet he seems to have been in my life as long as I can remember. How someone can become so important in such a short time is just amazing to me.

"Unfortunately, I have to go do some leadership stuff, but I'll call again when I can. Don't forget we're behind you one hundred and ten percent in everything you do, Sweetpea. You're making us all very proud. Bye for now."

"Okay Pops. Now you need to go before you make me cry! Love to you and Momma. To Raina too. Bye."

The call ends and I feel a tear run down my cheek. Now I have spare time for myself, what the hell am I going to do with it?

We need to run and chase rabbits!

'Oh, my Goddess, Maya. You and rabbits. I couldn't eat another thing after all that sweet stuff, and I doubt you could either.'

Nobody mentioned catching them, but we need to run off some of that sugar.

'Ugh. Just the thought of running right now makes my tummy roll over. You can be so mean at times.'

I know. It's a gift.

Chapter 13

BRONZE

Standing in front of Lincoln and Madison, our two schoolteachers that look after the pup's educational needs, and Eve, I'm desperately trying to remain straight faced. The schoolteachers asked for my presence to discuss a serious disciplinary matter, and when I got here, they were struggling to remove what appeared to be paper towels from their hands. Eve stands there, wringing her hands in despair.

"Alpha Heir Bronze. Honestly...this can't be allowed to continue. We insist that you take action immediately. He's a monster! The spawn of everything evil!" They both look at me with such conviction that I know they believe what they are saying.

Eve can't contain herself. "He is no such thing. He's... high spirited and has an active imagination."

Turning to look at the object of their outburst, it looks like butter wouldn't melt in his mouth. The huge, wide, innocent eyes look back at me and I'm almost taken in.

"Coal, did you replace the soap in the dispensers with glue?"

Slapping his hand to his forehead so fast that it's a wonder he doesn't knock himself out, "No, sir. Wasn't me, sir."

I have to place my hand over my mouth and look as though I'm thinking hard as I force back the laughter that is trying to burst forth.

"Let's try this again, Coal, without covering your forehead. Did you swap the soap for glue?" I look at him as he desperately wants to raise his hand to his head.

"Yes, sir. I done it. But it was just a joke. I didn't mean for no one to get hurt or anything." His enormous, now guilty eyes seem to get even bigger as he admits to his prank.

"Okay. That's better. No one got hurt, but you mustn't play pranks on the teachers. They are here to help you learn, and you need to respect that. And you should never lie. You know that you will get harsher punishment if you're caught telling lies."

"I do respect them, sir, but school is so boring. Maybe if it was more interesting to learn stuff, I wouldn't want to get into so much trouble."

He sounds so genuine and honest that I can't help but turn to both schoolteachers. "And there from the mouths of babes, as they say. Perhaps the pup has a point that we all need to take on board. Learning should be fun. Look at the lessons and see what you need to bring some fun into their learning. I'll authorize whatever we need to get them motivated to learn." Turning to Eve, "Take Coal home for the rest of the day and see if you can think of anything that will help Lincoln and Madison with the pups' learning."

"Not calling them names might be a step in the right direction," she mutters as she reaches out for Coal's hand and gives both teachers her best stink-eyed sideways glance. You can see Coal doesn't want to hold his momma's hand, but when she turns to look down at him, he grabs it quick and gives her a nervous smile.

As Eve walks away with Coal, I turn to Lincoln and Madison. "I'm available at any hour, any day or any night, for the benefit of the pack. However, I don't expect to be called to deal with something so trivial ever again, or that you insist on me taking action. If you cannot handle one strong-willed pup with an overactive and healthy mind, I'll find someone who can, and you pair will be training fodder for the warriors. Am I perfectly clear?"

They look at me in horror. "Yes sir," they both echo, imitating Coal's reactions to my questions.

As I walk away, I just want to laugh loud and long. That pup gets into so much mischief you could write a book on it. He must drive Eve to distraction, but you can't deny the love she has for him. I would not want to be the one that hurts him or tried to keep her from him.

Heading back to the office, I detour to the training area as I remember I need to arrange a meeting with Adaline. Arriving at the end of a female training session, I grin as I watch all the females picking up their backpacks and toy pups before heading off.

Adaline smiles as she sees me grinning. "You may well grin, but it worked better than either of us would ever have imagined. You know they've all given the toy pups names now, too? One of them happened to mention Pedro, and when they realized that she had named her toy, they all went mad at the idea. We had to hold a contest between two females because they wanted the same name and neither would yield. We had to do a 'winner takes the name' fight to settle it."

"I was going to arrange a meeting with you in my office, as there are a couple of things I need to discuss. Nothing you need to be concerned about, but they are important. When are you free?"

"I can make myself available to suit you, Alpha Heir. I'm free for the rest of the day now." Adaline looks at me and I think now's as good a time as any.

"Okay. Let's do it now then."

Walking to the office, Adaline points to a few of the changes in the grounds that Herb has been making. Although I've noticed some, I've not noticed all of them. I'm impressed that Adaline has though, and her enthusiasm for them has me surprised too. She describes how the new flower beds and borders that have appeared have made an astonishing visual impact as you approach the packhouse. She's quite right too. The whole place has taken on a colorful and vibrant feel. I need to speak to Herb and give him some praise for the work he's doing.

Once we're in the office, we take a seat, and I dive right in. "Adaline, I want you to be part of my inner circle. One of my trusted advisors, a counselor. Someone to bounce ideas off and someone that will tell me how it is. I don't want people that will tell me what they think I want to hear. I need people that will be truthful and straight. Are you in?" Looking at the shocked look on her face, I might have dived in at the deep end, I think to myself.

"Wow. I wasn't expecting that. I don't know what to say, Alpha Heir Bronze. It's not long ago that I was just a female warrior trainee. Now I'm Warrior Trainer, and you're proposing to make me Chief Warrior if I stack up. To be asked to be on your inner council is such an honor that I don't know if I can live up to it." She looks at me with huge owl eyes, and I wouldn't be surprised if her head did a three-hundred-and-sixty-degree rotation.

"Being on my inner council has no bearing on anything else you've mentioned. The warrior achievement is completely separate. That is something you have earned with hard work and dedication. My request that you join my council is based on my own observations of your character and inner strengths." Did I just say those words? I sound like my father.

"I would deem it my honor to be a member of your council, Alpha Heir Bronze. I hope I can live up to your expectations." Adaline is beaming with pride.

"Talking of your Chief Warrior status. I have arranged for you to go to Wolfsfoot and spend a week with their trainer. He is an exceptional warrior and you will learn a lot from him. He is a hard taskmaster, but he will evaluate your capabilities and then report back to me. He will work with you for a week and be sure he will also work you hard. I have no doubt that you will return fully prepared for the role of Chief Warrior." Even as I say it, I know Adaline will give it her all and will pass Drake's assessment.

"When will this be? Do I have time to prepare?"

"Oh yes. You have two weeks to prepare mentally and physically, for probably the toughest assignment I'll ever give you." I have to laugh at the pained expression on her face.

"Two weeks? Seriously? Wow, that's not long. I guess my meditation starts after I leave here then." Adaline laughs too, then I thank her again for joining my council and she heads for the door. Just as she goes through the door, I call to her.

"Adaline?"

"Yes, Alpha Heir?"

"Just one last thing. Can you climb trees?" I smile at her shocked expression at my random question.

"I haven't climbed a tree since I was a pup. Is that some kind of requirement?"

"Oh yes. You definitely need to do that for the next two weeks. Climb as many trees as you can and as fast as you can. Have a good day, Adaline."

Frowning so hard that her eyes are almost closed, she states, "You too," and closes the door behind her.

Taking a few moments to gather my thoughts, I then mind link with Ethan and ask him to join me. My dilemma here is do I tell him I know he is a Shadow Warrior, which I feel would betray Titan, or do I wait and see if he tells me?

I would not feel betrayed. I knew the consequences of my revelation and am happy to face Valor.

A knock at the door comes sooner than I expected and when Ethan enters, I stand and greet him. Deciding not to have the desk as a barrier between us, I gesture to the armchairs near the fireplace. I've never had any dealings with Ethan and even during warrior training, we never came against each other in the ring. Nothing unusual about that though. There are many males in the pack that I have not trained with or against.

Ethan sits quietly, waiting to see why I asked for him. He exudes a calm confidence that, if I had not known he was Shadow, I could easily have mistaken for arrogance.

"I would like you to join my inner council of advisors. How would you feel about that?" He doesn't show any signs of surprise at my request.

"Yes, I can do that. I would like to be more involved with the well-being of the pack. When will you hold the first meeting?"

"Now that I have all the members that I feel I need, I will look at scheduling a meeting for next week. I will do formal introductions at that time so you all know each other." That went easier than I anticipated.

"Alpha Heir Bronze. You are aware that I am a Shadow Warrior. Certain responsibilities come with that title. You should know also, that I will never do anything that would hurt or endanger the Eclipse pack. If I have knowledge that will affect the pack, I will share it with you, though it may at times appear that this information has come to you anonymously." Ethan stands, tilts his head to the side and offers his hand. I take his hand and we both give a firm shake.

As he leaves the office, my desk phone rings so I return to the alpha's chair and take the call. "Alpha Heir Bronze speaking. How may I help?"

"Bronze, it's Lyle here. How are you?" His voice sounds strained and I detect a level of weariness there too.

"I'm good, thank you. More importantly, how are you? You sound tired."

"Definitely tired but good otherwise. Have you spoken to Taria recently?" Now that's a question I wasn't expecting.

"No. Why? Should I have? Or should I be worried about something?"

"No, not at all. She kindly offered to come here and help me out, which I said I had quite a backlog of things she could do for me, if she spoke with you first. It would only be for a couple of days and she would be at the packhouse the whole time, so safe. I've tried to call her but she hasn't picked up." Lyle is speaking fast but I don't think it's nervousness.

"It's the first I've heard of it, but if she can help and be safe, why not?" I'm a little surprised that she has made that offer, but I'm also proud of her.

"Well, that's just the thing. We caught a rogue spy trying to make his way across our border, and when we interrogated him, he was supposed to be observing our packhouse defenses. As I said, we got him at the border, so no worries there, but he may not be the only one. If you speak to Taria, can you explain and thank her again for the offer, but I can't risk her being here at the moment."

"I'll contact her immediately and thank you for your concern. What if I were to send you our Beta for a few days? Would that help you?" I'm thinking of ways to support Lyle in any way I can.

"Thank you, but there's nothing that can't wait. It's mainly admin stuff. I can get one of my inner council to step up if it gets too much. Please express my thanks to Taria though for the offer." Lyle sounds like he needs to get off the phone, so I quickly say bye and cut him loose, as it were.

Sitting back in the chair, I steeple my fingers and think about my future Luna. That was a good offer to help another pack leader, and that's the sort of thing that would sit well with the Eclipse pack. I think I'm going to leak that bit of information out while I'm at lunch.

Rising from the chair, the phone rings again. Picking it up and answering as always, I hear Alpha Gerry on the line. "Hello Bronze, how are you? Is this a good time for you to chat?"

"To chat? Gerry, I don't remember the last time I had a chat! What would you like to chat about?" I genuinely don't remember having a chat, let alone with an alpha. I'm not sure I'd call the times I've spoken to Taria chatting.

"How about Taria and when we can call it a day on her training period? That sounds like a fit topic." Gerry sounds very upbeat and in a positive mood, so I wonder where this has come from. And I mean the topic, not the good mood.

"Fine by me. I was just talking to Lyle and Taria was the topic of that conversation, so I can roll with this."

"Why were you discussing Taria with Lyle?" Ouch. That soon cooled his mood to frosty.

"Lyle was explaining that Taria had offered to go to Spirit Walker Pack and give him some help. He's tried to ring her but she didn't pick up, so he called me and asked me to pass a message on."

"Yes, I was aware that she had."

"It seems then, Gerry, I was not on the memo, because I knew nothing of it." I'm getting a little touchy with this now, and I feel it could be a tinge of jealousy. I'm not liking being the last to know, so to speak.

"Bronze, can I be frank with you?" Gerry has that tone of voice that my father uses when he wants to give me advice, without it sounding like advice.

"I'd prefer that to beating around the bush, any day, Gerry. What's on your mind?" Well, here goes. I asked for it.

"How much do you know about Taria's journey so far?" That took me by surprise, I wasn't expecting that.

"I have checked on her progress on a regular basis." That sounds all wrong. "No. Wait. I haven't checked. I have followed her progress, to be more accurate. There have only been good things said about her, and it seems to me that rather than learning new skills, she has awakened skills she hasn't used before. Does that make sense?" As I try to explain, that feeling of pride comes over me again.

"I understand exactly what you're saying, and I feel the same way. I've only been her Pops for a short time, but I've seen the change come over her. Her level of maturity is far beyond where she was when I became Alpha of Blood Pearl, yet she still retains all the things that make her who she is," He takes a deep breath at this point. "So, don't you think she could awaken these things as your Luna, now, rather than in a few months' time? I haven't spoken of this with Taria or anyone else. Not even her momma. I do believe, wholeheartedly, that this is a journey that you should now be making together."

Oh, wow. Gerry's last statement hits me like a sledgehammer. I think he's right. No. I don't think, I know what he's saying is right.

"Gerry, I need to speak to my parents. Thank you for the call and, more importantly, thank you for being frank." Closing the call with the usual byes, I go in search of my parents.

Chapter 14

BRONZE

Sitting in the alpha's office with my parents, I don't know how to begin this conversation, so I'm going to dive right in. They have always been supportive, so unless I've missed something important, I don't see them having any issues with what I want to discuss with them.

"I want Taria to join me as soon as possible." There, it's out. "I know we said six months, but I think she's already shown that she is capable of taking on the Luna position. Everyone that speaks of her has nothing but praise and positive things to say. What do you think?"

Watching as they look at each other, then look at me and back at each other, I feel sure I've missed something important. But what? Suddenly they both grin and high five each other like a couple of teenage pups.

"Fantastic idea," my father states.

"When do you want her here?" Asks my mother.

"Seriously? That's it? No discussion, arguments, just 'when'?"

"Arguments? Oh no. We've been hanging around waiting for you to come to your senses for the last few weeks. You have been working hard while running things, and we've allowed you more control over the pack. The sooner Taria gets here, the sooner you can officially take over the pack, and the sooner we can be out of here and start our retirement." My mother sounds ecstatic at the prospect.

"I hadn't thought of that," taking over the pack... I hope I have not just told my parents I want them gone!

"I'll call Flint and let him know. He can get accommodation arranged for us with the Shifter Council. Let us know when Taria will arrive. We'll hang around and get to know her for a week or so, and then we'll be out of your hair. You can always call us if you need anything but I'm sure you'll both be fine." My father stands to leave and offers his hand to my mother. "Come on, *ex Luna* Sage. Let's go make those future plans we've always talked about."

"Whoa... Hold on... Just a minute," I stare at them both as if they have gone mad. "This isn't how I was expecting this to go."

"Welcome to the world of leadership. Expect the unexpected. You don't want us hanging around when you take over, Bronze. That will affect the transition from one alpha to the next. It needs to be a clean break and we're only staying to get to know Taria. If she was already your marked and mated, we'd be gone in an instant." Mother smiles at me and, taking my father's hand, they walk towards the door.

Well! I'm so taken aback, I just slump back in my chair and sit there, gulping air like a fish out of water.

I've summoned Beast and Star to attend your office immediately. We need time to digest what you've just instigated and as you still owe me two runs, we'll have one now. It will be good for you to take a back seat for an hour or so and let me have the reins.

'Yes. Okay. Let's do that. I've been preparing for this moment all my life and now that it's here, it's happened so suddenly.'

A knock on the door, and before I get chance to say enter, Dixon and Adaline burst in.

They both scan the room and when they see I'm alone, they speak in tandem. "What's happened? Are you okay?"

Standing in front of my desk, they both look anxious.

"Yes, I'm fine. Why wouldn't I be?" Why would they think I'm anything but fine?

Dixon flops into a chair, and Adaline drops into the other.

"We both thought there was something seriously wrong. We've never been summoned by wolf to wolf in that manner before. We thought that Bronze was incapacitated and that's why Titan was reaching out. Don't do that! My heart can't take the strain," Dixon does look a bit pale.

Adaline shakes her head at me. "Men! Always so dramatic, but I have to agree with Dixon. It was so out of the normal for you that you had me worried. What was so urgent, anyway?"

"I need to go for a run in the forest and, obviously, you need to accompany me. I can't run alone."

Dixon looks aghast. "You scared me out of ten years of my life because you want some exercise?" Adaline and Dixon stare at each other, then me, and it's just as I stared at my parents when I thought they'd gone mad.

"Let's go for a run, and I can explain while we're in the forest. I need to get away from everything for a while." Standing, I lead the way out of the office, away from the packhouse and into the woods. Shifting, Titan takes over and we run. I relax back into my mind and let him run while I link with Adaline and Dixon to explain where my head is at. Giving them their due, neither interrupt and only when I'm done do they say anything.

Adaline is excited and her focus is on Taria and the relationship side of things, though she does make it clear that she is aware of the bigger picture of when I take over the pack.

Dixon, on the other hand, immediately goes into the logistics of the pack handover and what do I want to do as the new alpha. Traditionally, a new alpha will announce some form of change, if only to show the pack he is the new force to be reckoned with. I think my announcement of change will be the members of my inner council, so that the pack is aware of who else they can turn to for help if needed. I'm well aware that no matter how good an alpha you may be, there is always someone too shy or nervous to approach you directly.

Giving Titan free rein certainly helps me relax and get things squared away in my head. Perhaps it's just the freedom of the forest, though.

Hey. Don't try and steal away my contribution.

'Ha. Snooping on my thoughts, eh? I wouldn't dream of deflecting the credit that's due to you. It was a great idea to get away for a while. And don't think for one minute that I missed those rabbits that you chased down.'

That's my reward. You can't deny a wolf his rabbit once in a while.

'I suppose that won't suffice once Maya is here! You'll want more than a rabbit then, you sly wolf.'

There may be talk of pups, yes.

'Talk? You'll do more than talk.'

Realizing we are approaching the edge of the woods where we started, we shift back and I return to the packhouse and the alpha's office.

Alone again and clearer in my thoughts, I decide to call a meeting of my inner council. Time to get them introduced formally, and then let them know that their services may be called on sooner than originally planned. Mind linking with them all, I give them an hour to clear their schedules and be in my office.

I'm not surprised when the first to arrive is Eve, ten minutes early. She sits outside the office quietly, but the warrior at the door lets me know she is there.

Opening the door, I look at her, raise my eyebrows and tell her to come in. She is such a lovely, warm female and the way she manages with Coal, her pup, makes me wonder why she isn't gray beyond her years. He runs her ragged. I never see her mate having any dealings with him, though. That might be something I'll look into at a later date.

"Take a seat, Eve. How are you? And how's that little terror of yours doing?" I see the defensive look flash in her eyes.

"I'm fine thank you, Alpha Heir Bronze. Coal is...well, Coal. A handful at times, but most of the time, at home anyway, he's an adorable pup. He wouldn't thank me for calling him that, though."

"There was no harm done the other day, and it wasn't as big a problem as it was made out to be. I'm sure other pups have done as much, if not worse." I give her my warmest smile and I see her shoulders relax slightly. "I don't recall seeing his father lately." There. I've put my foot in it now, I think to myself.

"No, you're not likely to, either. He stays at the border when he's not on duty as a border warrior," she spits it out and I see the regret as soon as she's said it. "I'm sorry Alpha Heir. My issues with my mate are not your concern."

"Eve, I think you'll find that everyone's issues are my concern. Especially my Inner Council members. If I expect the best from you, I need to know that you are at your best, mentally and physically." Linking to the warrior outside, I inform him to hold the rest of the council until I'm ready. "Why would your mate stay at the border and not come home?"

"Honestly, it's not a problem. I cope well enough on my own. Thank you for asking, though." Eve is looking more than a little embarrassed, but I have a lot of respect for her and I'm not letting this drop.

"What's going on, Eve. Tell me," I throw a little of my alpha aura at her, and I see her begin to respond automatically.

"He never wanted pups." It's out before she can stop it. "He never wanted pups and never told me that fact until I was already in pup with Coal. His wolf, Lobo, let it slip one day, and when I confronted Miles, he told me it was true. When I told him I was in pup, instead of it being a happy day, it turned into the beginning of the end for us. We're together in name only."

"I'm sorry to hear that, Eve, I truly am. No matter what his feelings are, though, he is a father and should live up to his responsibilities. He needs to be teaching his son how to be a good pack member, and father for the future of the pack and his family name. Abandoning his mate and son is not the way forward. I need to reflect on this and see if there are others in your position." I will look into others, but first and foremost I will be looking into Eve's situation.

"Please, Alpha Heir, I am coping very well without him. I don't want him back in our lives." She almost pleads with me and although I sympathize with her, I still don't see that this is the best thing for her son.

"We'll talk about this again, but for now, let's see about getting the council meeting underway."

Once everyone is seated around the conference table, I apologize for keeping them waiting and begin with the introductions. I sense some surprise from Xander as I introduce Eve and Adaline as council members, and I hope I haven't misjudged him. I see Ethan has noticed something there, too. Taria will be my final council member when she joins the pack.

Explaining to them all that their role as my inner council will be advisors, eyes and ears, ideas, and if and when necessary, to keep me grounded. Oh, and anything else that I may think of in the future, has them smiling.

I'm pleasantly surprised by the enthusiasm when I tell them I am going to speak to Taria about joining Eclipse sooner, rather than later. There are congratulations all round when I notice both Adaline and Dixon behaving as though this is the first time they've heard the news. Brownie points for those two, I think to myself.

The only thing left to do now is speak with Taria, probably the only one that doesn't know yet, and see if she's okay with all this, too.

Chapter 15

TARIA

You need to eat more or let me run, one or the other. All this fitness training and improving your fighting skills is using a lot of energy and burning calories. At this rate, you'll look like a broomstick when you get to Eclipse.

'Well, thank you for that. I'm sure your compliments are well meant, even if they are a bit off target.'

I'm hungry and so are you. Let's go eat. Please.

'Very well. You're right though. I am hungry now you mention it.'

Walking into the canteen area, the smell of food has my stomach rumbling immediately, and it is loud. The pack members sitting at the table I'm walking past laugh loudly as they hear my stomach shouting for food.

"Did you miss breakfast, Taria?" One of the female warriors I recognize as Swan asks.

"Famished, Swan, and you are partly to blame. Both you and Nightshade have put me through my paces this morning."

Swan gives me a huge grin, and taking my wrist to stop me, says, "You did very well this morning. You anticipated most of our moves and defended extremely well. Your attacks weren't far off the mark, either. I would be happy to stand with you in a battle, and Nightshade would stand with Maya, too." The rest of the table give a little tilt to their heads at this statement from her, and I give them all a head tilt in return.

Her statement takes me by surprise as she has said nothing like this before. Swan is an exceptional warrior and is at the top of the warrior list. Gaining praise from her is not something to be taken lightly, and I place my hand over hers as she squeezes my wrist.

Grabbing a tray, I walk along the serving counter and load up my plate with various meats and a tiny portion of salad. I feel Maya's approval at my tray and add a couple of bottles of water before looking for a table. Seeing Gamzin wave me over, I head that way to join him. There is another male at the table, he looks stern and hard faced, and I'm not sure who he is. I've seen him around and he follows Luna Hope around like a puppy dog. Gamzin slides a chair out for me next to him and I slide in easily with a thank you.

"This is Baildon, Taria. Don't think you've been formally introduced yet. Baildon, this is Taria, who is the soon to be Luna of the Eclipse pack."

I stick my hand out and get a good, firm shake in return. "Hello, Bailman. Pleased to meet you."

"It's Baildon. Pleased to meet you, too." He gives me a frown as I've mispronounced his name.

"Oh, I'm sorry. What do you do around the pack then, Bay Leaf, other than follow Luna Hope around?" I give him my cheekiest smile and wait to see how he takes my sense of humor. Gamzin, I notice, is having difficulty not spraying his lunch all over the table.

"Well, Taria, it's my job to follow the Luna around. It's what I do, and I'm damned good at it, too." He gives me a sarcastic look back and I'm not sure my humor is his kind of thing, assuming he has a sense of humor, that is.

"Oh, really? And where is the Luna right now then?"

"She is with Alpha Connell in his office. While she is in his company, and thus protected, I'm allowed some me, BAILDON, time." Carrying on with his food, I get the impression that the conversation is over.

"So, Gamzin, your friend here, Baillif, is Luna Hope's first and last line of defense, eh? Is he good at his job?" I see Baildon stiffen as I mispronounce his name yet again, but he carries on eating.

"Taria, Bailjumper is very good at his job. I would trust him with my family, if I had one, and would be confident that they would come to no harm. What he lacks in a sense of humor, he makes up for in raw courage." Gamzin smirks at Baildon and I see a crack appear in the veneer that is his face.

"Don't you start, Gamzin. Little miss soon-to-be-Luna here is doing alright on her own. She doesn't need any help needling me." Seeing him finally smile, I smile back and give him a cheeky wink.

"You looked like you needed cheering up." I begin attacking my food, my hunger getting the better of my sense of humor.

"That's a new approach on me, but it worked, I'll give you that. I'm out of my mood now. Thank you."

Avoiding the obvious question of what put him in the mood in the first place, we enjoy lunch and when Luna Hope comes looking for Baildon, she sees me at the table and joins us.

"Hi Taria. A rose between two thorns here, I see. Don't let them get you down. They're a right miserable pair, I'll tell you." She gives one of her beaming smiles and I notice how Baildon looks at her. He adores his Luna, that's clear. Not in a love type adore, but an adore the ground she walks on, type of adore. I can see that she would be safe with him around. When he's not watching her, he's scanning the surroundings. I wonder if my Gamma will be that dedicated? If he's not, he's not going to be my Gamma for long. Baildon has certainly set the bar high.

"Taria, I have some news for you. Walk with me and I'll tell you," Hope says as she jumps up.

Taking my tray away, we walk out of the packhouse and into the walled garden. It is beautiful in here, and I'm going to speak to Bronze about having one at Eclipse, if they haven't already.

"You will never guess who has been to see me today?"

"I have no idea. Who?" Why I would know who would go and see Luna Hope I don't know.

"Dahlia and Silas, of course. They asked if there was any reason that they couldn't take each other as chosen mates. How wonderful is that? It's all your doing, too." Luna Hope is so excited. "You're better than holding a mating ball, Taria!"

"Are there any reasons?" I feel queasy waiting for Hope to answer.

"None. They have both had fated mates. Dahlia's rejected her after a year, probably why she became so horrible and Silas's rejected him immediately because she was already sleeping with someone she thought was higher in the pack. Now they've found each other, or more accurately, Dahlia found Silas and you nudged him, they can make each other happy. I love happy endings." Hope is positively giddy with excitement. "I'm going to speak to Connell and he's going to give them a place to live near the forest."

"That's so good of him."

"Oh, he doesn't know it yet, but he will when I've spoken to him."

I burst out laughing at her enthusiasm and know that Connell won't stand a chance. Not for one minute though, do I believe he would seriously deny Hope anything she asked.

Hope excuses herself and after looking around to make sure her gamma, Baildon, is in attendance, she dashes off to whatever it is she has planned next.

Heading off to my room for a shower and a change of clothes, I wonder what this afternoon will bring. I had my day off yesterday as ordered by Alpha Connell and although I rested up, it was such a long boring day. I just didn't know what to do with myself. Apart from eating three square meals and trying to read a pretty average novel, the day dragged by. I can't think how poor my daily life was at Blood Pearl. No wonder everyone had such a low opinion of me.

Laying out my change of clothes, I strip off for my shower and catch sight of myself in the full-length mirror.

'A broomstick, huh? No broom I ever handled looked that good. You need to be careful or I may have a nice rug for my fireplace!'

No matter how much training you do, you'd never be able to make a rug out of me. I can hear Maya giving her wolven chuckle, which always amuses me.

Stepping into the shower, I laugh as Maya preens and then lays down with her head on her paws. Realizing what she looks like, she pops into a sitting position and looks away. I take my time with the shower and enjoy feeling the hot water soak into my aching muscles. Getting my scrunchy all soaped up, I start to wash myself. All too soon, I start to wonder what it would be like to have Bronze soaping me and…

Pups. We'd soon be having pups.

Washing quickly, I hop out and grab a towel, rubbing myself dry in double quick time, hearing Maya laughing the whole while. Dressed, I lay on the bed, debating whether to call Momma when the phone rings. Seeing its Bronze I lay back and take the call.

"Hello Bronze. To what do I owe this honor? I've just been thinking about you," I say playfully.

"Hi Taria. How are you? I was just thinking about you too and I've got something I want to run by you, so I thought I'd see if I could catch you at a good time." I wonder what he wants to run by me?

"Well, you've caught me at a good time, I've just got out of the shower and I'm feeling all warm and fuzzy. What would you like to ask me?"

"You were thinking about me in the shower? Hmm. That sounds like something I could delve into at another time." Damn, he picked up on that fast, I think to myself. "Yes. I've been thinking about us and how much progress you've made in such a short time. I was wondering if the timescale we set wasn't perhaps a bit too long."

"Well, *we* didn't set a timescale, *you* did, and I always thought it was too long, but it wasn't my call. Why has this come up now?" I sit up with my back against the headboard, as I'm not sure where this is leading. "What were you thinking about us?"

"I was thinking that perhaps this was something we should be doing together now. You've made such a good impression on everyone that you've come into contact with, and I am so proud of you I thought we should stand together at this stage. What do you think?"

"Are you asking me to join you at Eclipse now?" I'm stunned and not sure if I'm understanding him correctly.

"Yes, that's precisely what I'm asking."

"Just give me a minute." Putting my phone on the bedside table, I bounce up and down on the bed like a child on a trampoline. Getting too close to the edge in my excitement, I slip off the edge and land on the floor with a tremendous crash, knocking my phone off the table.

"Taria! Taria, are you okay?" Hearing Bronze shouting, I snatch my phone and I answer breathlessly.

"Yes, I'm fine. Why would you think I'm not?"

"You fell off the bed, didn't you?" How could he know that?

"Of course I didn't. Why would you even think such a thing?" I brazenly deny his suggestion.

"You so fell off the bed. I used to spend hours bouncing on my bed as a kid. I'd recognize that sound anywhere, and I fell off more times than I can count." Hearing him laugh, I know I'm busted.

"Are you saying that I'm a kid? That's a quick swap from 'come and be my Luna' to 'you're bouncing on a bed like a kid', isn't it?" I can't put a harsh tone in my voice because I'm so damn happy.

"Guilty on all charges. So, when I can expect you to arrive?" He sounds as excited as I feel.

"Do you need to run this by anyone else before we get carried away?" How will his parents react? Or the Eclipse pack? Or my parents?

"Everyone will be fine with it. Don't worry about them."

"You've already spoken to your parents! I know you have," I accuse him.

"I've already spoken to your Pops, too. It was him that made me see how much time we were wasting that we could be spending together. He called me, and Taria, he was so right. We should be making this journey together, not so far apart. Don't be angry with him."

"Angry with him? I could kiss him. I'll speak to Alpha Connell immediately and I'll let you know when I'll be arriving, but it won't be too long."

"Yes, and I'll go tell my parents it's on the cards for the next couple of days or so. Bye, Taria. Talk soon."

Staring at the dead phone, he didn't even give me a chance to say bye. He must be excited. Sitting on the edge of the bed, I stare at my reflection. I'm going to the Eclipse pack!

Chapter 16

BRONZE

Waiting for Flint to pick up his call is killing me. This is the third time I've rung and he hasn't picked up. It's not like him not to answer a phone call. If he doesn't pick up this time, I'll have to try to speak to another council member, and I don't want to do that if I can help it.

"Hello, Flint speaking."

"Is everything okay there?" I don't bother with a greeting.

"Oh, yes. I went for a ride on my motorbike and forgot to put my phone in my pocket. Sorry about that."

"I didn't know you still had that old thing." I remember him riding it when he visited the pack when I was a pup.

"I'll never part with it. I love my bike. I haven't had her out for a long time though and as I had a very rare free day, I thought I'd let her stretch her legs a bit. What can I do for you, anyway. You only get in touch when you want something." I hear him laughing down the phone and think, yes, he's probably right.

"I need you to clear your schedule for two or three days if you can, and come visit the Eclipse pack."

"Two or three days from when and what for?" He asks suspiciously.

"Two or three days from tomorrow. My Luna is joining me any day now and my father will be handing over the reins."

"That's fantastic news, Bronze. Congratulations. Does Taria know?" Again, in his suspicious tone.

"Of course she knows. How would she not know?"

"I didn't know if you'd just decided yourself and were going to Blackshadow Pack, throw her over your shoulder and drag her back, kicking and screaming. I wouldn't have put it past you."

"If she'd refused, that may have been an option to consider, but fortunately she is as keen as I am to be mates, and get on with our life together." I don't see myself doing that to my female somehow.

"I can certainly clear my schedule for something as momentous as that. Do the rest of the council know?"

Oh, my Goddess. What is with his suspicious nature today? "You're always the first port of call when it comes to such ceremonies, you know that, Flint. I don't think there's a pack leader or heir that wouldn't reach out to you before any other council member." I'm happy that he can attend, although I doubt wild horses would've kept him away from a ceremony.

"Well, I'd better go and get packed if I'm going to be spending a few days with you. I'll see you soon and thank you, Bronze."

"See you soon, Flint." Ending the call, I wonder where to turn next.

I should let the pack know there's going to be a change, or should I leave that to my father? Yes, I think he should do that. I'll mind link him and let him know it comes under his realm of responsibilities. First of all, I think I'll grab some lunch.

Stepping into the canteen area, there's a sudden silence and then a raucous cheer. I guess my father is a step ahead of me on the announcement front.

Taking a tray, I looked at the assortment of food available on the serving area and made my choice. Adding a bottle of water and a glass of fruit juice, I see Wesley gesturing for me to join him. Taking a seat, I don't get a chance to say anything before I'm verbally accosted. He's talking so fast I can't follow what he's trying to say.

"Hang on there, Wesley. Take a breath and start again, slowly this time, eh?" I don't know what has got him so excited because he's usually a laid back, placid and calm sort.

"Sorry, Alpha Heir Bronze. I was just saying that if Luna Taria is joining us earlier than expected, and coming straight from Blackshadow Pack, where she is currently, then perhaps it would be best if I head over there and begin my duties immediately. A lot could happen between now and her reaching Eclipse lands. I could take a couple of warriors and provide a safe escort for her. Giselle and Wylder are not on border patrol for the next 5 days, and if it's okay with you, I'd like to take Ember, too."

"Hold on a minute. Why do you think Taria needs to be escorted from the Blackshadow Pack? They will provide adequate protection to our border and then we'll take over from there, surely?" This statement makes him look at me in horror, as I was hoping it would.

"No, no, no. That's not good enough. This is our new Luna, your mate. We cannot trust her protection to others, Alpha Heir. What are you thinking? If necessary, I will go alone. I have no duties to perform until Luna Taria arrives, so I am surplus to pack requirements. Our new Luna needs to know that we, the Eclipse Pack, are there for her from the beginning, not just when she turns up at our border. No, no, no."

"Also, I'm intrigued by your choice of escorts. Giselle and Wylder I understand, but Ember? She has not yet qualified as a warrior. Why take her?" I am genuinely curious as to that choice.

"Have you seen her wield that bat you gave her recently? She is the Devil incarnate with that thing, I swear. And she has more of them, too. She has been talking with Hannah from the carpenter's shop and between them, they have designed other bats that are suited for various purposes. She has a small one, like a cudgel, that she says is for personal defense. There is a longer one for taking into battle or on border patrols where trouble is to be expected. She has hard wood bats, aluminum bats. She even told me she was saving for a carbon fiber bat." If I didn't know better, I'd say he was in awe of Ember and her bat.

"Very well," I say, and he looks at me, perplexed.

"Very well? What do you mean, very well?"

"Do it. Go meet our future Luna and accompany her safely back to the Eclipse Pack. I think it is admirable that you have already taken on the role of Gamma and thought through your first assignment so thoroughly."

Jumping to his feet, he lets out an ear-piercing whistle and then heads for the door. Looking around, I see three pack members rushing to follow him through the door. No surprise for which three they are. The third one looks me straight in the eye and has an enormous smile on her face. I certainly created a monster with that bat, I think to myself.

After finishing my lunch, I take my tray and Wesley's to the kitchen, then head back to the office. Checking in with my father, I'm correct in assuming that he has informed the pack of the impending change in Alpha. He has also taken the liberty of announcing the earlier arrival of their new Luna. Well, one task less for me.

Informing Alpha Connell of the warriors heading his way to escort Taria here, I find that she has requested to go to the Wolfsfoot Pack before coming here. I'm surprised again that I'm not aware of her movements and decide I need to broach this subject with her. Mind linking with Wesley, I let him know that he will need to meet up with her at Wolfsfoot and escort her from there.

Next, I call Alpha Gabriel, who is aware that Taria is going to visit with Tati for an overnight stay on her way here. Letting him know that Wesley and three others will arrive as her escort, he states that he also has a designated escort for her, so she will have at least eight warriors in her protection detail.

I think my next call is going to have to be with Taria. She needs to tell me where she is going to be at any given time. If there is ever an emergency, I need to know where to get hold of her, or where to send help. I can feel my stress levels rising as I think of her needing my help and not being able to give it. As I reach for the phone, yet again, it rings before I pick it up.

"Alpha Heir Bronze speaking."

"Hello, soon-to-be-alpha. Soon-to-be-your-luna here." Taria's voice floating down the phone has me smiling and some of my stress floats away with it. Some but not all.

"Taria, I was just going to call you. I hear that you are going to the Wolfsfoot Pack before coming here," my tone is a little sharper than I intended, but I put that down to my concerns.

"How on earth have you found that out so fast? I was just calling to discuss it with you. I've only just got off the phone from Luna Tati and left Alpha Connell's office. I wanted to know your thoughts before I fully committed to the journey." Taria sounds quite put out that I know before she has had a chance to tell me herself.

"I've just spoken to Alpha Connell and Alpha Gabriel to let them know that there is an escort of four Eclipse Pack warriors heading their way. I didn't want any incidents when our warriors turn up at their borders. That's how I found out."

"Oh, well, in that case. I thought for a moment there, you had spies watching me, or shadow warriors or something. I was about to throw my toys out of the stroller."

"Toys out of the stroller? I've not heard that before. That sounds like something Eve, one of my inner council, would say." I can't help but let out a small laugh as I imagine her saying that after Coal had done something.

"Obviously I don't know this Eve, but she sounds like someone I could get on with."

"You'll like her. And her pup, Coal. He's so full of mischief, I don't know how she hasn't gone gray yet." Thinking back to the soap dispenser episode, I tell Taria all about it and she is in fits of laughter.

"He actually did that? That is so cool that he thought of it by himself. And he actually hides his forehead so no one sees this star? Oh, my Goddess, that is genius on Eve's part. I can't wait to meet them."

Hearing her laugh is like music to my ears, and I have the biggest grin as I listen to her.

"So why the visit to the Wolfsfoot Pack? Any special reason I should be aware or worried about?" Nothing springs to mind, but I don't want to be blindsided by anything.

"I wanted to meet Tati and then, apart from your mother, Luna Sage, I will have met all the lunas in the surrounding packs. Is there something you're not telling me I should be aware of?" I think the suspicion in her voice is playful rather than serious, but it does jog my memory. Savannah!

"There is something you should know before arriving at the Wolfsfoot Pack. My father sent a female there as punishment, because he knew that Luna Tati would be able to punish her for her actions here at the Eclipse Pack, better than he could." Explaining the Savannah saga to her, she listens silently to the incidents that Savannah has caused over time. When I tell her about Ember and her bat, she bursts out laughing again.

"Oh, I so want to meet Ember and her bat. That was priceless. To be knocked flat by her nemesis and with a bat given to her by the object of her desires! What a double shock that must have been for her."

"Oh, you don't have to worry about meeting Ember. She is part of your escort. You'll meet her soon enough. You just don't want to meet her bat." Listening to her, wanting to meet the characters of the Eclipse Pack, I can't help but believe Taria is going to be good for the pack, as well as good for me.

Chapter 17

TARIA

Having spoken to Bronze about my visit to Wolfsfoot, I was annoyed that he knew before I had a chance to speak with him. As much as I hate to feel that I'm asking permission, I'm going to have to discuss any of my plans with him before I talk to anyone else. He must get fed up with hearing things from other people. I know I would.

Before setting off for Wolfsfoot this morning, I had a chat with Alpha Connell and Luna Hope and they were both very positive about my stay there. Alpha Connell told me that when I first arrived I had an abrasive manner, but during my stay it has improved, and was replaced by a much more approachable one. That was a surprise until I thought back to how my behavior has changed for the better, too. Luna Hope was just gushing with the positives and must have mentioned Dahlia at least a dozen times. That had Alpha Connell rolling his eyes after the third one.

I was sad to be leaving Blackshadow Pack, not in a 'I wanted to stay forever' kind of way, but I'd made some good friends there, I thought, and I know how little the packs get to mingle with each other. It wouldn't be difficult to lose touch. Maybe that could be something else to be put under the Luna umbrella of responsibilities?

I was surprised that I had a six-warrior escort to Wolfsfoot's border, as it is only a couple of hours' journey, especially when I saw who they were. It's more like an honor guard than an escort. Chief Warrior Oscar, Iona from the warrior council, Swan and her brother, Ryan, both at the top of their warrior game, and then Brian and Theo. Theo I like, Brian, I am not so sure of. I know he came from the rogues and that he was originally associated with a Blackshadow Pack traitor, but I don't think it's that which has me on edge around him. It's hard to put my finger on it, and I honestly just believe it's a personality clash. Swan, I have a high regard for and I think she's where she is because of her competitive nature with her brother. There is definitely an air of *anything you can do, I can do better* between them.

As we travel through the forest towards the border, I notice Brian stays close on my left flank. Swan stays close on my right, and Chief Warrior Oscar stays in front of me. Iona, Theo and Ryan are further forward, with one of them always scouting ahead. As we run, I marvel at how my stamina has improved in such a short length of time. Running as Taria, I feel much more confident in my abilities. Running as Maya makes me realize, even more so, what an impressive wolf I have.

About time I got some appreciation in this relationship.

'What? You have never been under-appreciated. How can you say such a thing!' I'm appalled at Maya's statement.

When you were a selfish pup, you appreciated nothing, especially not me. We went for weeks without speaking and without me running. You are much better to be around now that you have been awakened to your true potential. I am so stunned by this that I don't have anything to come back with. If we'd been running as Taria at this point, I think I would have stumbled and fallen flat on my face.

Brian's wolf, Deefer, suddenly sprints forward to Chief Warrior Oscar's, Conan. We are all signaled to stop and we shift to our human form. Brian motions to the trees and we all scramble upwards into the dense foliage. Taking something from his pack, he spreads it across the ground and then climbs into a tree.

As we all watch from on high, we hear movement coming towards us. Four males appear and one is definitely excited about something.

"I can smell them, I tell you. They are nearby." He is speaking in the loudest whisper you can imagine.

"I don't smell anything. I think you're imagining things again. You've been overdoing the wolfsbane again," one of the others comment, and they all laugh at him.

"That's not funny. My wolf would have left me by now if I didn't sedate him. Failing my shadow warrior training, all but had him leave then. When I became rogue, he swore he would leave, so I started taking wolfsbane to keep him."

"That was over a year ago. It's a miracle you haven't killed him, never mind him leaving you." Listening to the disgust in their tone should have told the failed shadow warrior how they truly felt about him.

"That's none of your concern, anyway. I tell you I can smell those you seek. They are near."

One of his companions sneers, "You can smell old guts from an old kill. Look around you. Something had a killing spree and there is evidence everywhere. We're wasting our time. Our information was wrong, or we arrived too late. We missed the Luna this time. We need to report back to Alpha Arric and be sure that when we do, we tell him we arrived in plenty of time, but the information we were sold was wrong. I'm not having my head on a block because we were too slow."

Watching as they disappear back into the forest, we wait until Brian drops from his tree and confirms that they have left the area. Oscar joins him on the forest floor and then signals it is safe to join them.

My first question is, how did Brian know they were close by? No one else suspected a thing, or was aware of their presence. Seeing me looking at him, he speaks before I put my question into words.

"Luna Taria, if you suspect me of anything, please say so. Before you do, think of this. If I was a part of some plan to kidnap or kill you, why would I have warned you? That would defeat the purpose of being their informant. I knew they were there because the forest was too quiet. There were none of the sounds of animals or birds scurrying away from us. They were already silent and in hiding. I lived in the forest when I was with the rogues and it is my first home. Also, one of them was shadow trained, if only in part. That would explain how your escort didn't sense them." Brian looks at me, and I sense the hurt as well as see it in his eyes that I should feel this way toward him.

"Luna Taria, I don't have any doubts that Brian is anything but loyal. When we reach the border we will not return immediately to the Blackshadow Pack. I will speak with Alpha Connell and we will continue your escort until you are safely at the Wolfsfoot packhouse and your own Eclipse Pack warriors are present. Only then will we return home. I will also inform Alpha Connell that either Blackshadow Pack or Wolfsfoot Pack have an informant in the pack. Someone knew of your travel schedule and where you would be at a given moment in time. Failing this time does not mean they won't try again." Oscar looks at all of us individually until he is sure we are all aware of the danger.

"Chief Warrior Oscar's word is good enough for me. Brian, my apologies for having any doubts." Seeing him tilt his head slightly, I understand that he accepts my apology. "So, what do we do now? Continue our route or divert to a new path?"

"Diverting to an alternative path would mean that the packs would not know where we were, also it would mean a longer journey and more exposure to a second attempt. I suggest we carry on as planned and stop for irregular breaks." Oscar makes perfect sense and we all agree.

Taking a break now, as we're already stopped, Oscar contacts Alpha Connell through the pack mind link, and advises him of the incident. When he has finished his mind link, he tells us how it went.

"Not surprisingly, Alpha Connell is furious. The fact that rogues have penetrated the border is one thing, but to attempt to kidnap or kill someone under his protection has him raging. He wanted to send more warriors to escort Luna Taria, but I have told him that by the time they reached us we would already be at the border with the Wolfsfoot Pack escort. He is going to notify Alpha Gabriel immediately, so don't be surprised if we arrive at the border with half of the Wolfsfoot Pack in attendance."

"Why would the rogues be interested in me? I am not yet a Luna and the Eclipse Pack is the furthest from their lands. It makes no sense." I am confused as to any benefit that I would present to them.

"You are already the Eclipse Luna, in everything but the ceremony. You are the Alpha Heir's mate, everyone is aware of that," Swan explains to me. "Alpha Arric has already tried to get a Luna of the correct bloodline. He wants to be seen as a legitimate alpha, or as he puts it, King of the pack lands when he succeeds in his war. He is the only one that believes he can win. All he will do is get a lot of innocent shifters killed in his greed for power." Swan watches for my reaction to her statement.

"I'd die fighting. They would not take me to their rogue king. I give you all this Luna order. If I am unable to defend myself and they are going to take me, you are to kill me. You are not to allow me to be taken." I watch the look of both horror and respect cross their faces. "Now, can we move along?"

We reach the border with the Wolfsfoot Pack without further incident and although we don't meet the entire pack, we do have an escort of eight warriors, including their legendary fight instructor, Drake, their warrior trainer, Thomas and Flint's Shadow Warrior friend, Xavier.

The Blackshadow Pack escort stays with me, as promised, until we reach the packhouse. As soon as I have been introduced to Alpha Gabriel and Luna Tati, we head to their dining room for some much-needed food. Everyone seems very friendly, and the pack has a relaxed feeling about it.

Once our meal is done, we take our trays and join the queue to clear up after ourselves, before rejoining the Alpha and Luna. As I'm standing there, I notice a female watching me, and so does Swan, who's at my side.

"I think that is a female from the Eclipse Pack that was causing Bronze some minor irritation," I whisper to her. "Alpha Chet sent her to Luna Tati to learn some manners."

"I see that has failed miserably," responds Swan, grinning. "Oh. She's heading over here. Shall I stop her?"

"Let's see what she wants. I'm sure I can handle this." Watching her walk towards me, I smile at her with my best down-my-nose look.

"You must be the Savannah I've heard about," I say as she stops in front of me.

"It's good to know that Alpha Heir Bronze speaks highly of me," she preens.

"Oh, no. You misunderstand. None of it was good, and it wasn't from Bronze." I shouldn't taunt her, but I can't help myself after the things she's done. Seeing her stiffen, I prepare for the fight that I'm sure she is going to start, however she surprises me when she leans forward and whispers, "I don't know how the rogues missed you, but I'll be sure they don't next time."

Seeing Swan tense by me, I know she heard Savannah. "There won't be a next time." Grabbing her head, I twist it viciously and she drops at my feet, dead.

The dining room is deathly silent as I step over her, leave my tray on the counter, grab her by the hair, and drag her lifeless body out of the room. The guard by the alpha office door sees me and immediately slams open the office door, shouting for Alpha Gabriel.

Alpha Gabriel rushes out of the office with Luna Tati on his heels and sees me dragging the body to the main doors.

"You no longer have to worry about the informant. It's been dealt with," I can't help but snarl.

Alpha Gabriel signals to two pack members and they take the body from me. I smile at them both, as though this were an everyday occurrence, yet inside, I'm trembling with the knowledge that I just killed someone without a moment's hesitation. Swan must see this and gently takes my arm as she guides me to the alpha's office and onto a couch.

Swan asks for a glass of water, which she immediately hands to me. Luna Tati sits by me and asks if I'm okay and what happened. I look to Swan and she recites the incident and the brief conversation. With a tremendous show of pride, she tells them how I calmly dispatched Savannah by breaking her neck with the smoothest move that Swan has ever seen.

I can see the shock and horror on Alpha Gabriel and Luna Tati's faces at this incident so soon after my arrival, and whilst under their protection. I assure them they could not have known that this would happen, or that Savannah would be so twisted. If there was any blame, it would lie with the Eclipse Pack for not recognizing how dangerously unstable she had become.

I have just begun to calm down when we all hear a scuffle at the door. Alpha Gabriel's eyes show that he is linking with his warrior guard and then smiles an unhappy smile.

"Taria, it appears your Gamma has arrived and is not happy that you have killed someone to protect yourself. My warriors have them subdued in the hallway for the moment. All except one female that is standing alone and has injured two of my warriors with a stick that she refuses to relinquish. Could we take a moment to calm the situation, please?"

Jumping from the couch, I rush to the door and dash into the melee that is Ember. "STOP! That's enough. I am safe and was never in any danger while I have been here. Ember! Stand down at once. The rest of you behave in a manner befitting your position." Ember turns to me, stands with her feet apart, rests the head of the bat on the floor while leaning on the handle. She gives me a beautiful smile that looks so innocent, you wouldn't think that only moments before she had been trying to decapitate half the Wolfsfoot Pack.

Looking at the Wolfsfoot warriors, I see four of them restraining one of my Eclipse Pack escorts, two more of my escort restrained by two Wolfsfoot Pack warriors each, and the two on the floor injured. Ember is surrounded by what looks like a dozen others, but I don't take the time to count them.

"Release them, please. There will be no repeat of this incident. What are you thinking of, coming here and behaving like rogues? You bring shame on the Eclipse Pack with your actions. Go seat yourselves in the dining room, and wait until I call for you." Pointing at the escort that had been restrained by the four warriors, as he tries to speak, "Not a word until I call for you, do you understand?"

Nodding, he turns and walks into the dining room, where he gestures the others to a table that gives them a clear view of the alpha's office door.

Back inside the office and I can't help but smile when I see Luna Tati laughing with tears on her cheeks. Alpha Gabriel is smiling, but definitely not laughing.

"Well, Taria. It's never going to be boring having you visit us. I'll give you that. One death and one riot in less than two hours of your arrival in the packhouse. I'm confident that is going to stand as a record for some time." Luna Tati wipes at the tears as she speaks.

Alpha Gabriel then joins in. "Apparently, my pack members were a little too enthusiastic when explaining the incident in the forest, and what happened with Savannah. Your Gamma was concerned that you were in very real danger and my warriors wouldn't allow him to speak with you, because you were with their Alpha. I think we can say that both parties were responsible for the riot. I must say that I'm impressed that it took four of my warriors to subdue your Gamma. Impressed with your Gamma, that is, not my warriors. I think I'll be speaking to our trainer, Thomas, about that."

"Speaking of which, do you have somewhere private where I can speak to my escorts? I haven't met my Gamma yet, so this should be interesting, to say the least. Before that, I'd like to contact Bronze and let him know what happened to Savannah."

"Use my Luna office for both. I'll be busy for a while now, so it will only stand empty." Luna Tati smiles again and I just thank her. I don't know what I'm going to say to the escort team other than well done. Seeing Ember, the only one still standing in that hallway, will be an image burned into my mind for a long time to come.

Seeing a bench outside the Luna's office, I fetch my four escorts and have them sit on it, like naughty pups awaiting my displeasure. Sitting behind Luna Tati's desk, I pick up the phone and call Bronze. He answers almost immediately.

"Alpha Heir Bronze speaking."

"Hi, Bronze. How's things there?"

"Taria! How wonderful. I wasn't expecting to speak to you until tonight. I thought you'd be far too busy with just arriving at the Wolfsfoot Pack to take time out for a chat with me." He sounds excited to hear from me but I think that will die off shortly.

"Just arrived and very busy, you are correct in that. Time for a chat, no. This isn't a chat, more of an incidents report." That certainly curbs his enthusiasm.

"What incident? Are you okay?" Now he sounds worried.

"Incidents, plural, and yes, I'm good," Taking my time so I sound calm and okay, I explain the incident in the forest. Fending off his questions about the possible informant and their location, I give him the lowdown on Savannah.

"Your stalker Savannah, remember her?"

"Oh no. What has she done this time? I thought Luna Tati would have her reined in by now," He sounds exasperated at the mere thought of her.

"You won't have to worry about her as an issue anymore. I've dealt with it," I think a little bit of pride may have slipped into my voice, that I didn't mean to.

"You've solved it? Oh, well done you. How?"

Taking a deep breath, "I broke her neck. She's dead."

"No. Seriously. If you've solved it, how did you solve it?" I knew he wasn't going to believe this.

"Yes. Seriously. I broke her neck in the middle of the Wolfsfoot dining area, in front of everyone having their lunch." I then explain what happened and that Swan, from my Blackshadow Pack escort, heard and saw everything. There's a stunned silence and then an enormous sigh.

"Wow. So, she was certainly unhinged. I'm glad that you dealt with it as you did. That prevents any further future issues with her. Are you okay in yourself with taking her life?"

"Strangely, yes. Ultimately, it was going to come down to her or me. In fact, it was already at that point after the rogue attempt, so I feel completely justified in my actions."

"Well, I didn't see that coming, but I'm glad that you're safer now, with her out of the picture."

"I have something else you didn't see coming," then proceed with the story of the near riot in the packhouse, and of how Ember was the last man standing!

Once the call is ended, I take on the next task of speaking with the escort. I need to speak with my Gamma, alone first, and will then deal with the rest in one fell swoop.

Opening the office door, I give all four my sternest look, which I feel backfires when Ember beams at me. What on earth am I going to do with her never ending optimism and boundless enthusiasm?

"Gamma, come in." Sitting behind the desk, I watch him march in, close the door and stand in front of the desk. Sitting there, staring at him in silence, I realize I don't even know his name.

"Name?"

"Wesley, Luna."

"Wolf's name?" I snap.

"Duke, Luna."

"Show me Duke. I'd like to meet him. See if he's as dim as you are."

"He is certainly not dim, Luna."

"Neither is Alpha Bronze, but he made you Gamma!" I see him flinch at that comment and take note.

Watching closely, it is certainly a fast shift, and Duke stands before me. I have to force the stern look to stay on my face as I want to smile at the size and color of him. He's a magnificent wolf.

"Alright, Wesley, come forth." I watch as he shifts back and their transition again is both slick and smooth.

"I don't expect a repeat performance of today's debacle. Do I make myself clear? You will perform your duties, not only to the best of your abilities, but you will make all other gammas pale in comparison. This is not for my personal gratification, it is for the honor of the Eclipse Pack. Wherever I go, I want all other Lunas swooning in envy at the way you take care of my protection. I don't want a butler, but I do want the best from you at all times, day or night. Are we perfectly clear on that, Gamma Wesley?"

"Yes, Luna. My life is yours to command."

"I don't want your life, but I do want your mind, your body and your wolf at my disposal, twenty-four-seven. Now. When you fetch the rest of my escort in, you will seat them and then stand at my right shoulder, slightly behind me. I intend to show everyone that we are on the same page and are united in our roles. Bring them in."

Wesley steps to the door and invites the other three in. Sitting them in front of the desk, I ask him to introduce them and their specific talents.

He introduces the female that is unknown to me first, as Giselle, and she is a high-ranking warrior. Her wolf is called Fox. Next is

Wylder. Another high-ranking warrior whose wolf is called Goliath. Presumably then, another large wolf. Finally, he introduces me to Ember. Ember is a pack member who hasn't qualified in her warrior training as yet.

"How on this green earth has Ember NOT qualified in warrior training? You were all subdued, and yet she had disabled two warriors and was the last man standing. Ember, I will be taking you under my wing as my personal project when I get to the Eclipse Pack."

"Thank you, Luna Taria. Chief Warrior Dixon has been giving me one-to-one tutoring with my bat, as the normal warrior training doesn't cover it. There isn't a qualification for bats, either, so that's why I haven't qualified." There's that smile again.

"Just because there isn't a bat test doesn't mean you are not a warrior. I want you on my protective detail from now on. Gamma Wesley, make sure that Bat Warrior Ember is now on my detail."

"OH! Bat Warrior Ember! I love it. I'm exclusive. I'm the only Bat Warrior in the Eclipse Pack. That is awesome!" Her excitement is catching as I see Wylder and Giselle grinning from ear to ear. "Oh, I'm sorry, Luna Taria. I get carried away at times."

"So, I see. Right, down to business."

I spend the next half hour explaining to them what my expectations are going forward when they are chosen for my protection detail. I let Wylder and Giselle know that they will take turns with the other warriors fulfilling this task. I can't help but see the pride bursting from Ember that she is on full time Luna protection.

Chapter 18

BRONZE

Talking with my parents in the office, I can't believe my mother is laughing and my father is high-fiving me when I tell them about Taria killing Savannah, in a dining room full of pack members trying to have their lunch. I'm not convinced that I know my parents as well as I thought I did. They were aware that something had happened when the pack link broke for Savannah but thought that they'd been lucky and she had left the pack for pastures new, thus resolving the problem for me. They are positively glowing that Taria was so decisive about her actions and can't wait to tell her how proud they are.

The border warriors have announced that Shifter Council member Flint is on his way, and I know I'll have to explain this all again shortly. I wonder what his reaction will be? Not a high-five, I'm sure. Although looking at my parents and their obvious delight, I'm not sure of anything anymore.

Leaving my parents in the office, I take a walk through the gardens and get some fresh air. Taking some time to myself will help me get a clear head before I have to speak with Flint.

I spoke to Alpha Gabriel about the incident and he was apologetic that Savannah had managed to contact the rogues and pass on

Taria's travel arrangements. We'll probably never know how she managed it, and I assured him it was not a reflection on him or his pack. If we'd known that she was that mentally unstable, we would have dealt with her ourselves. He did tell me a bit of the riot scenario and that he was impressed with our gamma. Four warriors to subdue him would not surprise me knowing Wesley as I do. I had to smile at his description of the female maniac with the stick. That sounds like the sort of thing that Ember would do. Being the only one still standing surprised me, even when Taria told me, but that stick, as he put it, of hers is very unnerving in her hands.

Taking a walk through the gardens, I see how much more Herb has done since I last saw him. If I'm not careful, he'll turn the whole pack land into a farm and garden. I should catch up with him and his project folder, see how everything is going. I don't want to put a dampener on his enthusiasm by not showing an interest.

One thing I do notice as I enjoy my walk is the lack of flowers. Everywhere is clean and tidy but there is a lack of color around the packhouse and grounds in general. It could be that there is nothing in bloom yet rather than nothing planted, so that's another thing to discuss with Herb.

Walking by the children's nursery as I return to the packhouse, I hear raised adult voices and children's giggles. Immediately my thoughts turn to Coal and I wonder if he's behind another prank. Entering the building I see an enormous pair of eyes stuck to the doors of the building. I have to smile as they appear to watch me as I walk in.

Inside the hallway, I see what appears to be a black hole in one of the baseboards. Examining it more closely, I see a pair of eyes looking back at me. What? Surely we don't have mice or rats in the nursery? Getting down on my knees, I see that the hole is just black paint or marker and the eyes are the googly sort from a craft set. It was done very well because it had me fooled for a moment.

I see a pattern emerging here, and I start to smirk as I sense Coal's hand in this. Moving to the classroom door, I peek through the window to see what the raised voices are. Seeing Coal standing at his desk with his teacher, Lincoln, leaning over him, I realize my suspicions are correct. As I open the door, Lincoln raises his hand to Coal, and I see Coal flinch.

Before I can stop him, Titan bursts forth, has Lincoln on his back with his paws firmly on his chest, holding him down, snarling. The children are all staring wide eyed, and Coal has flopped back in his chair, mouth hanging open.

Shifting back, I order Lincoln to report to my office immediately and wait for me there. As soon as he has scurried from the room, I turn to the class of pups and apologize for Lincoln's behavior. Speaking to the pups, I find that this is not an isolated incident and that their teacher has disciplined more than Coal recently. I have to calm Titan before he bursts forth again and goes to discipline Lincoln himself.

Mind linking with Madison, I give her an alpha order to report to the nursery classroom immediately. Talking with the pups, I find that they are all bored with their classes with Lincoln, but they all get more enthusiastic when Madison's lessons are mentioned. It appears that since my last conversation, she has introduced many new teaching methods, even taking them outside the classroom on field trips to the orchard where Herb had given them seeds to grow, such as sunflowers and beans.

Madison rushes into the classroom and slides to a halt when she sees me standing there, addressing the pups. Instructing the pups to sit quietly while I speak with Madison in the hallway, I turn and walk out. When Madison has joined me and the classroom door is closed, I do nothing short of interrogate her.

After only five minutes of this, I am satisfied that she knew nothing of Lincoln's behavior towards the class and explain what I witnessed. Seeing the horror on her face, her first concern was for Coal and the rest of the pups. This puts my mind at ease and I ask her to consider who would be a suitable replacement for Lincoln as I have no intention of allowing him anywhere near the nursery ever again.

"I think you should approach Coal's momma, Eve. She would be good with the pups and also curb some of Coal's mischief." Madison has a thoughtful look on her face as she continues, "She has accompanied us on field trips, as Lincoln was always too busy to help, and I believe she enjoyed it as much as the pups."

"I'll speak with her and see what I can arrange. I'm not sure what other commitments she may have." I think that sounds like a great idea, and why am I not surprised that Lincoln was too busy?

Madison almost raises her hand as she states, "I don't think she has much in the way of other commitments, and seriously believe that she and Coal could use some extra funds. I've noticed that Coal doesn't attend birthday parties for the other pups and without speaking out of turn, I think it's because Eve can't send him with a gift."

This reminds me of the absence of his father in his life. Mind linking with Miles, I tell him to report immediately to my office and wait for me there. Fortunately, he's not on border patrol and is paying one of his rare visits to the packhouse, so I won't have to wait long.

"Madison, can you continue here until I can get a replacement, please? I'll see that you are rewarded for your dedication."

"Alpha Heir Bronze, I don't teach for financial reward. My reward is seeing the pups become valuable members of the pack," she splutters this out in indignation and it makes me smile.

"I never mentioned financial reward, Madison. There are better ways to reward someone than with money. I applaud your attitude, though."

Walking back into the classroom, I am about to address the pups once more when I hear a giggle behind me. Looking over my shoulder, I see Madison covering her mouth, trying not to laugh. Following her gaze, I see two more large googly eyes on the slowly spinning ceiling fan. There are two more on the top corner of the blackboard and now that I'm looking for them, I see them everywhere. Coal watches me and I give him a pretend fierce scowl before I can't hold back any longer and burst out laughing. The entire class is soon laughing as one.

Walking back to the alpha office, I feel Titan starting to tense up and tell him he's had his turn with Lincoln, now it's mine. Arriving at the front of the packhouse, I hear the roar of an engine and turn to see Councilman Flint arriving on that beast of a motorcycle of his. He gives me an enormous grin, which soon fades when he sees my scowl.

Pulling up beside me, he hops off his machine and asks, "What has happened? That face doesn't match the voice that invited me here."

"Come inside and you can witness me discipline one of my pup's schoolteachers. You can get the gist of it as we go. It's not something you need to be involved in as a council member, but your feedback later as an observer would be appreciated."

"Lead the way. You have my full attention." Flint follows me to the office where a sweating Lincoln is waiting outside.

Ignoring Lincoln completely, we go into the office, where I give Flint a brief explanation of what has gone on. Knowing that seeing me with Flint will have raised Lincoln's concern to a whole new level, I leave him a few more minutes.

Finally calling Lincoln into the office, I ask the warrior to remain and have him stand behind him. Making sure that I look as though I am struggling to contain both my temper and my wolf, I wait another minute before speaking.

"I have no words to describe the utter contempt and disgust I feel for anyone that would strike a pup. You are fortunate that Titan was able to control himself or right now, we wouldn't be having this conversation, we would be burning your remains." Pausing a moment and taking a couple of very audible deep breaths, I continue. "Do you have anything at all to say about your behavior before I decide what should be done with you?"

"Alpha Heir Bronze, I wasn't going to strike him, it was just a warning…"

"Don't you dare lie to try to protect yourself! The entire class of pups has stated that it wasn't the first time, and that Coal wasn't the only one to be subjected to your temper." Every fiber of my being wants to rip this idiot to pieces and I can feel Titan encouraging me to do it.

"There is no place for a shifter like you in the Eclipse Pack, therefore you will be…"

"Alpha Heir Bronze, if I may interrupt you for a moment. I may have a solution for this poor excuse of a specimen."

"What might that be, Shifter Councilman Flint?" Using his formal title may just have Lincoln losing the last bit of control he has left.

"Send him to the shifter council. We are always grateful for candidates for the council warrior training school. If he proves inept at the task, it will probably kill him, anyway."

"An excellent idea, Councilman. As he seems to enjoy the disciplinary life, it should suit him to a tee." Watching the color drain from Lincoln's face, it comes as no surprise when his eyes roll back into his head and he slumps to the floor.

Looking at the warrior, who is grinning like a fool at Lincoln's prostate form, I say, "Get that trash out of here and arrange for it to be transported to the council lands immediately. He goes with the clothes on his back and nothing else."

"At once Alpha Heir Bronze, and with pleasure. With your permission, may I divulge why he is going there?"

Flint speaks before I get a chance. "Consider that a direct order from the council, and warrior? Let's not be too gentle with any handling involved, eh?"

My warrior steps on Lincoln's hand as he grabs him by the collar and begins to drag him out. There are a series of 'Oops' comments as Lincoln bumps into furniture on his way out.

"Send Miles in, on your way out, please." I look at Flint and wiggle my eyebrows at him, making him smile in anticipation of another encounter.

Miles enters, and I direct him to stand before the desk. I feel contempt for this so-called warrior that won't step up and help raise his pup.

"Did you recognize that shifter that was dragged out of this office?"

"No, Alpha Heir, I did not."

"That is Alpha Heir Bronze to you, is that understood?"

"Yes."

"Yes, what?" I am going to lose my temper with this one in very short order, and I can see the surprise on Flint's face at his disrespect.

"Yes, I understand." He keeps looking over my left shoulder as though he is on some parade ground.

"Are you deliberately trying my patience or just as stupid as the body that was dragged out of here?" I stand and lean forward, my knuckles taking my weight on my desk.

"My apologies, Alpha Heir Bronze."

"You don't recognize the shifter that is teaching your son? How is that possible?" Flint's eyebrows shoot up and he sits slightly straighter in his seat. This does not go unnoticed by Coal's father.

"I've never met him, Alpha Heir Bronze." Miles swallows nervously.

"Never met the teacher... Or your son? Which is it?" I am seriously in danger of letting Titan loose on this shifter.

"The teacher, Alpha Heir Bronze." I can see by the fear in his eyes that he knows the next question before it's past my lips.

"When did you last see your son?" I say this slowly and quietly.

"I don't know, Alpha Heir Bronze." The sweat is running from his brow now and the fear is almost a physical thing emanating from him.

"I was going to lecture you on the correct behaviors of a responsible father, but I see that I would be wasting my time. You are disrespectful, selfish and a waste of my time and the pack's resources." I call out to the warrior that is positioned on duty outside the office door, and the door whips open. "Take this shifter with the last one. Same rules apply except this one abandoned his pup rather than striking him. Before he leaves the packland ensure that he rejects his mate. I will tell her to expect it. NO, wait! I'll tell her to reject him. Why should she suffer any pain of rejection? Miles, you will reject Eve in return or I will alpha command you to do so."

Once Miles has been escorted from the office I slump into my chair and rub my palm across my face. "All that shit and it's not even lunchtime, dammit!" Flint bursts out laughing and when I turn to look at him, I can't help but join in. The next ten minutes I spend explaining to Flint about Taria's failed kidnap attempt by the rogues, and answering his shocked questions.

When I get to the point where I describe her encounter with Savannah in the dining hall, I have great difficulty making him believe that Taria did in fact, snap Savannah's neck in front of all the diners.

"It's never going to be boring once you two are finally together, I'll say that," Flint states, shaking his head in disbelief.

"Funny, that's exactly what Tati said to Taria."

Chapter 19

TARIA

After I explained my expectations to my team, and seeing how they were so affected by being unable to get to me, and also being defeated by the home team warriors, I gave them the evening off. Being at the Wolfsfoot packhouse and having a protection detail from Alpha Gabriel, I felt safe enough that I could do so. Everywhere I went though, I saw either Wesley or Ember.

Having had a good night's sleep, I went for breakfast, where I call both Wesley and Ember to the table and have them join me. Alpha Gabriel and Luna Tati had to cry off from dining with me when something came up, but promised to catch up later.

Sitting and talking with Wesley and Ember gave me a feel for the Eclipse Pack, and I was pleasantly surprised when they told me how much the pack was looking forward to me becoming Luna. My attitude had been a definite red flag when they first heard about me, and I couldn't get them to elaborate on where this information had come from. The following gossip of what I was doing to become a good Luna, and the positive feedback they were gleaning, put everyone on my side, apparently. The news of my matchmaking with Dahlia and Silas had gone the rounds like wildfire, and I again wondered at their sources.

I voiced my concerns about having dispatched Savannah in such a public display, and they both beamed at me and couldn't have made it any clearer that Savannah had had that coming for some time, and not just because of her obsessive chasing of Bronze. She was not a liked shifter at any level, and no matter where she went, she caused drama and left chaos in her wake. Although I was at peace with my actions, I can't help feeling vindicated by their words.

Steering the conversation away from me, I start a whole new subject when I ask how Ember had obtained her bat. Listening to how she was supposedly failing at her warrior training, I think that Wesley and Ember are pulling my leg. No confidence and being the butt of jokes, and almost bullying, which does not sit well with the female I see before me. Getting the gift of the bat from Bronze seems to have given her instant confidence, and a way to channel the aggression that wouldn't come naturally. Hearing some of the stories about her training has us laughing loudly, and nearby tables smiling along with our laughter.

Discussing how many bats Ember now has, the different sizes and materials, shows that she has taken the idea and not only run with it, but turned it into a science. When she tells me how it has helped her form a friendship with a female called Hannah that works in the carpenter's shop, it brings up a whole new string of events.

Learning Hannah's story of her brother trying to force her into an arranged marriage, how she ran to escape it, also the fact that he was still trying to make it happen, I decide I'd like to meet her when I get to the Eclipse Pack.

"Oh, you don't have to wait till then," Ember beams. "We can meet her today, if you like. She works at the Eclipse Pack carpenter's shop here at Wolfsfoot. She stays over rather than travel every day. Alpha Heir Bronze tried to get her to stay at the Eclipse packlands until the Elijah threat was put to bed once and for all, but she wouldn't hear of it. I think she would have made her own bat if anyone had tried to disrupt her life any more than it already has been." Ember glows at the thought of having more than one female running around wielding a bat.

Looking around the dining hall, I see Wylder and Giselle. Calling them over, I advise them I plan to visit the carpenter's shop in the town. I require them to remain at the packhouse, as they will take over my protection detail when I return, so Wesley and Ember can get some rest.

I look again and see my Wolfsfoot protection detail dotted around different areas of the hall. None have anything to eat in front of them, so I guess that they are all still on duty. Approaching the one I know as Drake, I ask him if it would be okay for them to accompany me to the town to meet one of the Eclipse Pack carpenters. Seeing his eyes sparkle, I know he's asking his alpha if it's okay.

Getting an affirmative answer, I smile and head back to let Ember know we can go when she's ready. By the time we've cleared our trays, I look around and see that the protection detail is by the hall doorway waiting. Confirming with Drake that he has okayed the journey with Alpha Gabriel, we set off.

I have great difficulty trying to picture the bundle of energy that is Ember as a demure, frightened female. She has been in conversation with Drake quite a lot during our travels, and he seems to have had a few suggestions to offer where her warrior training is concerned. I need to delve into her training further as it's okay having the bat, but her wolf can't use one.

Arriving at the carpenter's shop, I wait until the shop has been given the all clear and then Ember and I walk in together. Seeing Ember, a female runs over and hugs her furiously. Trying to disentangle herself causes the female to step back, looking confused.

"Ember, whatever is the matter?"

"Hannah, I'm on Luna protection duty. You can't do that while I'm on duty!" Ember's eyes are wide with concern that she could be in trouble.

"You're such an idiot, Ember. You'll need to come up with something better than that if you think you're going to stop me giving you a hug in public." She goes to hug Ember again, but Ember steps back.

"You must be the Hannah that I've heard so much about. I am Luna Taria of the Eclipse pack." I use my soon-to-be-title to reinforce Ember's position.

"Luna? Alpha Heir Bronze's Taria? Oh, my Goddess. I'm so sorry, Luna Taria. Ember, I didn't know. Wait. How did you become one of the Luna's personal bodyguards?" Hannah looks so completely baffled that I suggest she take a breath, introduce me to the rest of the shifters here, and then let Ember explain.

Having met the other two carpenters at the shop, Cameron and Logan, they take great pride in showing me what they have made and have available for sale. Their work is of an excellent quality and the construction methods are all very traditional. The males puff out their chests as I praise their talents and when I compliment them on the exquisite detailing and scrollwork, they both point to Hannah.

"All the fancy stuff and the intricate carving is done by the marvelous Hannah. We can turn the stuff out and it will stand the test of time, but when it comes to getting people to buy it? That's all down to Hannah's exceptional skills." Cameron beams at Hannah and makes her blush.

Hannah gives a little curtsey before stating, "It's a team effort, Luna Taria. If they didn't produce such high-quality furniture, I'd have nothing to decorate. They sell themselves short too many times."

"Well, I think you're all doing a fantastic job together, and I look forward to commissioning some pieces when I'm settled in at the Eclipse Pack. You'll be able to add that to your shop title then. *Cabinet makers to the Luna*. How does that sound?"

"That would be awesome. We could have little brass plates made that we could attach to every piece of furniture we make." Logan has come up with an excellent idea there and I tell him so.

"Logan, that's nothing short of genius. As soon as I'm officially declared Luna of Eclipse, I'll expect you to see me and we'll get some pieces made for the alpha apartment. Get the brass plates organized and ready and I'll be the first to have them on furniture."

"Yes, Luna Taria, I'll get on to the brass plates immediately. Thank you for the honor of being your cabinet makers." He dips his head as do Hannah and Cameron. I almost buzz with excitement at having made their day.

Next, Ember insists that Hannah shows her how they are doing with the science of her bats. Taking me to a large cabinet at the back of the shop's display area, I see a detailed carving of several bats flying, with a full moon in the background. It has a very lifelike effect to the carvings and is almost picture quality. On closer inspection, what I thought was black paint turns out to be burn marks to make the bats black.

"Hannah, those graphics on the doors are out of this world. You are truly talented. It makes you believe that when you open the doors, bats will actually fly out." I am stunned at the quality and dedication it represents.

"The cabinet is full of bats, but they only fly in Ember's hands," says Hannah, opening the doors where there is a selection of Ember's bats displayed. Each one is totally stunning and without doing so consciously, I reach out and stroke one. They both laugh.

"Everyone does that when they first see the cabinet. No one has been able to resist it," Ember says, grinning. Eventually, having exhausted the topic of bats and their potential for calming situations, or solving them in a quick and violent way, we close the cabinet doors.

Stealing Hannah away from her work, we sit in their waiting room at the rear of the shop so I can get her opinion of what is going on with her brother, and why he thinks it's okay to sell her *off like a piece of furniture*.

"I don't have an answer for you, Luna Taria. I don't know where his head is with such an idea. We were never close as siblings, but we always behaved like brother and sister, I suppose. He's a year older than me though I never looked up to him as a sister should to an older brother. He was never there to stop a bully, never warned off any overly zealous suitors. I looked after myself whenever I needed to. It would never have entered my head that he would try to sell me as a piece of meat, just to raise his standing in the eyes of others. I would have thought if he'd been hanging around with a crowd of decent males that it would have had the opposite effect." She looks thoughtfully at Ember and me.

"I have to agree with you there, Hannah. Even in the Blood Pearl Pack's darkest days, before I was born, I don't think the males even then would have sold a female. Goddess knows they treated the females badly, but I have never heard of them selling them." I'm sure my momma would have told me if that had been happening. She told me everything to explain how she had ultimately challenged the alpha of that time to better the lives of the females, and selling she-wolves was never mentioned.

"So, how do we keep you safe from your brother, Elijah was it? I understand you not wanting this to run your life, but how do we make it go away. Short of sending a few shadow warriors to end his miserable life, that would be the simplest way." I grin at that last statement as it was meant in jest, but I'm horrified when Hannah replies.

"Yeah, do it. He's made my life a misery so why should he even have a life. If they can get me close enough, I'll even do the deed myself." Hannah wiggles her eyebrows at Ember. "Come with, and I'll borrow your bat for the coup de grâce."

When Ember and Hannah burst out laughing, I almost faint with relief. If we ever have a serious war to fight, I'm going to put these two together on the battlefield with any other like-minded she-wolves I come across, I think to myself.

Asking if there are any other Eclipse Pack businesses in town, I'm told there is a clothing shop as well. Dragging Ember away, we head over to the next business.

Arriving at the shop, I look at some of the fantastic designs on display in the window. Once again, this shows some genuine talent in the Eclipse Pack, and I can't wait to be a part of it all. Looking at some of the work gives me an idea.

Once again, I wait for the shop to be given the all clear before I enter. Thinking this may be taking things a bit too far, I think again before voicing my thoughts. I told Wesley that I expect him to be the best of the best and I see that this is what he is doing. How simple would it be for me to waltz into a building and find that it was an ambush? It's no different to being in the woods. We know already that the rogues have shifters in all the packs, so perhaps this is the way that protection details should be working.

Meeting Reagan, the seamstress, and Malakai, the tailor, I pass on my admiration for the creations on display. Seeing yet more stunning examples inside, I throw out my idea to them. A matching set of outfits for myself and Bronze for when we take over the pack together. Nothing gaudy or outrageous, but classy and elegant that shows we are united.

Malakai immediately has his design head on and starts throwing out his thoughts. The Eclipse Pack has an unofficial pack color of gray, so two outfits in the same color gray. Bronze and I could have suits. His would be a tailored three-piece suit, and I could have a female version. I like the idea immensely but will need to speak to Bronze before making any final decision. I'll get Reagan to take my measurements while I'm here, as there won't be time to come back before the ceremony takes place.

Thinking of the timescale, I ask if they have a private office I could use. I need to run this by Bronze if they are going to have any chance of getting the suits made, delivered and any final adjustments done.

Five minutes later, and it's agreed. Swearing them to secrecy, they are ecstatic that they are doing this. Malakai has Bronze's measurements already as he has made clothes for the Alpha Heir previously.

While I'm talking with Reagan, I see a one-piece suit that looks very sporty. "What is this worn for, Reagan? It looks like it would be very comfortable," I ask her.

"It was something I designed for the female warriors, mainly for training. I thought it would give them far more freedom of movement than regular sportswear, as the material is stretchy and flexible, but no one seemed to like it. Most thought it would be too revealing for a training session. I sold a couple of suits, but I was assured that they were only for indoor sports, if you get my drift."

"Well, I like them. I'll take two suits." Seeing the smile on her face makes me all warm and fuzzy. I do enjoy it when I do something for myself, but it also does something for others. "Also, Reagan, I need a word in private about another little project you can help me with." Spending a few minutes with her has my idea go from just that to a confirmed order. I look forward to that being delivered to me at the packhouse.

Making our way back to the Wolfsfoot packhouse, I get a chance to talk with Drake. I'm intrigued when he tells me he has a warrior from the Eclipse Pack visiting Wolfsfoot in a week or so for training and an assessment of her abilities. An Eclipse Pack warrior being assessed at Wolfsfoot surprises me but also that it is a female. Delving deeper, I find that Drake is not simply a warrior but a warrior trainer, and is in exceptionally high standing in that community.

Learning how he trained Luna Tati to become an accomplished warrior has me more than a little green with envy. Now, if I can persuade Alpha Gabriel to let Drake be part of my escort to the Eclipse Pack, I could pick his brains on the way and even sit in with the training, and learn a few more tricks. Oh, I can be so devious at times, I scare myself!

Chapter 20

BRONZE

I think it's a great idea. I like the way she thinks. Dressing alike at the ceremony and also forming the mate bond at that time is pure genius.

'I think the pack will love it, too, Titan. Sharing such an important moment with them will endear her to them even more. They certainly seem to have embraced everything they have heard about her so far.'

I wish we could have been there when she dispatched Savannah. I would have given all your teeth to have seen that.

'My teeth? Don't you mean your teeth?'

No. I can't live without my teeth. I need to be able to chew my rabbit meat. You could live on rabbit food!

Laughingly I reply, 'There are times when I think I could live without a wolf!'

Thinking of the mating bond reminds me I need to speak to Eve. Mind linking with her, I ask her to join me at the alpha office and when there's a knock at the door only seconds later, it takes me by surprise. Looking up, I'm even more surprised to see Xander of my inner council.

"Alpha Heir Bronze, can you spare a moment?"

"Of course I can. Come in. What can I do for you, Xander?" Gesturing for him to take a seat, he settles into a chair and looks apprehensive.

"I was wondering if I could ask your advice on something?"

"I'll help if I can. What's the problem?" I've never been asked for advice before, so I hope it's something simple, I think to myself.

"Well, it's relationship advice, I suppose you'd call it. I've never had a relationship yet and I'm drawn to someone that I can't approach due to her circumstances. I don't know if it's typical mating bond stuff as she is already mated. I'm so confused by it I don't know what I should do." He looks so confused, and I can see that this isn't just some passing fancy or childish infatuation. He looks completely lost.

"You're quite right that it doesn't sound like a typical mating bond if she's with another male. Does she feel the same?"

"Oh, my Goddess, she doesn't know I exist. I wouldn't dream of putting her in such a position as to tell her my feelings while she's with another male." He looks at me as though I were mad to even think of such a thing.

"I have to be honest with you, Xander, I've never heard of anything similar, but that doesn't mean it hasn't happened. Can you leave it with me and I'll do some discreet research to see where we stand? Do you at least know if the female is in a happy, stable relationship?" If she's not, I'm wondering if Xander is feeling protective of her or maybe just sorry for her.

His sad look tells me she isn't, before he answers, and I can also see his pain as he speaks. "She is not happy at all. I've watched from afar as she has become steadily less of her normal lovely self, and more and more miserable. She hides it well from others, but I see it. It isn't hidden from me, Alpha Heir Bronze."

"I have to ask, Xander. Who is the female?" I don't expect an answer and he doesn't disappoint me.

"No. Sorry. I cannot reveal who she is. That would not be an honorable thing to do."

"Leave it with me, Xander. I don't want to give you poor advice, so I need to discreetly look into this and see if we've encountered any similar situations in the past. I will see what can be done."

"Thank you, Alpha Heir Bronze. It feels better to have at least shared my problem. I will wait for any suggestion you may come back to me with." As Xander leaves the office, I sit there wondering how on earth I am going to find a solution to such a situation.

A knock at the door and I think to myself, is there no peace anymore? The guard opens the door at my bidding and in steps Eve. I'd forgotten that I'd called her here. Damn, that's why I'm not getting any peace, I think to myself. Maybe I should have a secretary and let them run my schedule.

Once she's seated, I look at her in more detail. She is clean, smart and respectable, but I think Madison hit the nail on the head. Things are a little less than satisfactory within her purse strings.

"Eve, I have a problem that I need help with, and you could be the answer to my prayer. Do you have any commitments ongoing at this time? Anything that could prevent you from helping me out?" I want this to be her decision to take it on rather than me having to order it.

"Alpha Heir Bronze, there would be nothing that could prevent me from helping you out. You have only to command me." Well, that went well, I think to myself.

"This isn't something that should be a command, Eve. I need a new schoolteacher and I need one fast. I also don't just want anyone to fill a vacancy. This needs to be someone that I can have one hundred and ten percent faith in to do right by the pups. Madison is doing a fantastic job with them, but I need someone else on that same level of commitment. I want that person to be you." I can see the confusion in her eyes and I know I'm going to have to tell her of Lincoln raising his hand to Coal.

"Where is Lincoln going to be, or will there be three of us teaching?" There it is, the stinger I knew was coming.

"I have relieved Lincoln of his position as of this morning. He will no longer have a part to play in the pack at all. He has been requested at the shifter council warrior training school." Taking a deep breath, I explain the situation that I walked into in the classroom and the subsequent removal of Lincoln, which also brings to mind the removal of her mate, Miles.

Eve takes the news of Lincoln's behavior better than I expect, I have to say. Knowing that the pups are back in safe hands is a relief and I can see Madison and Eve making the learning experience much better all round. I'm not sure how she will take the news of Miles' departure, though. I would have thought she would welcome him gone, to be honest.

Having Miles out of her life doesn't faze her in the least, in fact, I think she has welcomed it. When I get to the part about her having to reject him, that's when I meet resistance. There seems to be some form of stigma attached to rejecting a mate and I get the feeling that it is some form of familial thing about a female doing it. She's asked if Miles can do it, but I'm not having him off the hook that easily. Explaining to her I don't agree that she should be the one to feel the pain of rejection when she has done nothing wrong, takes some doing. In the end I give Eve a couple of days to think it over and then we'll talk again. I know one thing for sure though, if it comes down to it, I will make it an alpha order that she rejects that worthless shifter.

Next, going in search of my mother, the sum of all knowledge when it comes to feelings in our family, I'll put Xander's problem to her and see what she suggests. Asking my father about such things is as much use as having a chocolate fireguard.

'Mother? Where are you?'

'I'm outside in the new orchard, Bronze. Is everything okay?'

'Need some of your wisdom. I'll be there shortly.'

Heading to the orchard, I'm reminded once again of the lack of color we have going on. Finding my mother waiting for me, I'm reminded how beautiful she is when she smiles at me. Giving her a big hug, she seems surprised.

"Wow. It's been a long time since I had one of those," she gushes.

"Honestly? It can't be that long, surely?"

"You tell me the last time you gave me a hug, then? You've been so busy growing up, you forgot to keep hugging me, but it's okay. Every mother goes through it."

"Well, they shouldn't. Anytime you feel I've forgotten, you have my permission to remind me. By the same token, you look beautiful today. I guess I have not been complimenting you, either?" I smile at her and see her cheeks take on a little pink.

"Your father never goes more than a day without telling me, but I think his eyesight is fading, if I'm honest." Her laughter echoes through the trees. "Now, what can I help you with? It can't be anything serious or you'd be knocking on your father's door."

"Mother, that's not fair. I come to you for advice all the time, and this is a big thing." Explaining all about Xander's problem, she listens quietly, nodding occasionally.

"That's not as uncommon as you may think. Some of it is lust, envy, jealousy, but it sounds to me like the Goddess is trying to right a wrong mating."

"That can happen? I wasn't aware that the Goddess ever got a mating wrong?" I'm stunned by that revelation.

"It isn't necessarily that the Goddess has got it wrong, per se. Shifters change, personalities clash, their priorities don't align. Most grow together and the bond grows with them. Occasionally, a shifter can be too selfish or too stubborn to change. They may look at someone else's' priorities as unimportant or restrictive. It's usually the human in us and rarely do our wolves suffer these differences." Looking into my eyes, she must sense my unease. "I don't think you need worry on your and Taria's behalf, Bronze. I think the Goddess has this one nailed to perfection. I can't wait for you to take over the pack, as I only sense good things for you both. Your father has said the same to me about the fact you are both so well suited. As for Xander, let me make some enquiries. My spies may know something." She taps the side of her nose and I laugh at her amateur dramatics.

"Thank you. I appreciate it immensely." Giving her another hug, I leave her smiling and head off in search of Herb. Being in the orchard has reminded me of my need to speak with him.

Finding Herb deep in conversation with two others, I give him a few moments until he sees me waiting, and he quickly cuts it short and walks over to me.

"Alpha Heir Bronze, what can I do for you today?" As usual, he sounds very upbeat and enthusiastic.

"Quick question first of all. I'm not very green fingered, so this is just a question and not a criticism, okay? We don't seem to have much color going on. Is that a change of season thing, or are we so busy with the fruit and vegetables that we haven't got round to brightening the place up yet?" I watch as he digs through his trouser pockets and he pulls out some crumpled sheets of paper.

"We're in the middle of redesigning the gardens at the moment, so things do look a bit unloved. The vegetables we can't do anything with until after harvest, but I want more flower beds around the packhouse to greet guests with a riot of color and scents. I thought of having the Eclipse Pack written in flowers at the front, but that just doesn't cut it. It would be really cheesy and tacky." He pulls a face at the thought and I give him a brief nod of agreement on that.

"I haven't seen any requests coming through the Alpha's office for any gardening equipment or supplies lately. I hope that means you have everything and are not paying for it out of your own pocket?" Giving him a squint-eyed stare, he quickly lets me know that my father had already signed off on what he is currently using.

"Alpha Chet signed off on a huge order of stuff not too long ago, so we should be good for some time. A lot of what we grow, we can keep seeds or tubers and perpetuate our crops that way." He looks at me shyly and asks, "I hear a rumor that Luna Taria is interested in gardening. Is that right? I'd love her to give me an outsider's view of what the gardens look like."

"As soon as she's settled in, I will personally introduce you, and I'm positive that she will have feedback for you. I bet she'll want to go through that project folder of yours, too. I haven't forgotten it but feel that I've ignored my responsibility there."

"Not at all, Alpha Heir Bronze. I understand how busy you must be. Rest assured, if I needed you to see something or sign off on a major change, I would be beating down your door." His smile when he speaks of his work shows just how much he puts in of himself. If ever there was a shifter in the right role, Herb is it. Telling him so almost has him bursting with pride.

Chapter 21

TARIA

Having spoken to Tati about my idea for Drake staying over at Eclipse to train and then assess Adaline, she agreed that it would make perfect sense. She confirmed that he was going to be part of my escort, so when she put it to Gabriel, he agreed immediately. The journey to Eclipse was thankfully uneventful and with no rogue interference this time, I am feeling even more justified in my taking out Savannah.

You need to stop going there. Your actions were above reproach. Let it lie now.

'I can't help it. I've never killed anyone before and it's not like she was a rabbit for food!'

Eeww! I wouldn't want her in my mouth. The thought alone makes me want to vomit. Seriously though, I'd be more concerned if you hadn't had any doubts.

I frown as I respond, 'I don't see myself as a cold-blooded killer type, somehow.'

Neither do I, more of the smiling assassin type.

Maya thinks she's a comedian. 'OH! That's so not true. An assassin, indeed.'

You were smiling right up to the point her vertebrae snapped. I am so proud of the way you did it, too. No messing around. No taking time to think of any consequences. She made a threat, and you countered with direct action. That was a future issue resolved right there.

'If one person calls me the smiling assassin, I'll know it came from you.'

Arriving at the Eclipse Pack border, I'm greeted with reverence and although that was to be expected, the number of smiles and head tilts makes me feel very welcome. Knowing that I won't be able to meet with Bronze until tomorrow's ceremony, I'm escorted directly to Alpha Chet and Luna Sage at their private residence, away from the packhouse.

As we approach a beautiful cottage, I see a couple standing at the door, but more surprisingly, I see Wesley at the gate. I never noticed he was missing from my escort, so he must have gone ahead to announce my imminent arrival and also check security. I like that and make a mental note that he has taken on board everything we discussed.

Mate! Mate! I smell our mate! Maya is bouncing around like a puppy seeing his first rabbit.

'Of course you can smell him. These are his parents. Calm down and behave in front of them.'

Before I reach the gate, Luna Sage can't contain herself any longer and launches herself down the garden path and straight into my open arms. I see no other options, other than to defend myself, and fighting with the luna on her own doorstep would probably be considered the height of bad manners in any pack. As I doubt that she has any ill will towards me, I hug her back as she takes me in a surprisingly fierce grip.

"Oh, Taria. We are so pleased you're finally here. Come inside and let's get better acquainted. I always wanted a daughter. Not that I didn't want Bronze, I love him to pieces, but another female in the household was always a dream of mine. I've got so much to share with you and so little time."

"What do you mean, so little time? I've only just got here." I'm totally confused by that.

"We're due at the Shifter Council in just a few days and I want to be sure I've done all I can to get you settled in before then."

Alpha Chet steps up and also gives me a hug. "Welcome Taria. Both to our home and to the Eclipse pack. Forgive my Luna. She has been looking forward to this day for a very long time." He looks at her and I see the love in his eyes. I can only hope that Bronze will look at me the same way in years to come.

Speaking with Drake and the rest of the Wolfsfoot escort, I thank them for their protection and release them from any further commitment to me. Drake, of course, is staying to do the training and assessment of Adaline, and once the ceremony and bonding are completed tomorrow, I want to be part of that too.

Joining Alpha Chet and Luna Sage in their cottage, they show me my room and then we retire to the living room. Luna Sage is talking at one hundred miles an hour, and after only a minute or so, Alpha Chet steps over to her and gives her a gentle kiss on the lips. She looks at him adoringly and then speaks again. "I'm talking too fast, aren't I?"

"Yes, my love. Poor Taria's eyes are as wide as an owl's and I'm sure she hasn't been able to digest a third of what you've said so far. Take a breath and start again. I'm going to make us all a drink." Giving her another kiss, he leaves her all starry-eyed and smiling as he leaves the room.

"He knows that kissing me always stops me in my tracks," Luna Sage tells me. "I sometimes do it on purpose just for the hell of it. Now. I'll start again, but if I'm talking too fast, just stop me. I do get overexcited sometimes."

"I'll just put my hand up, if that's okay?" I say laughing and wonder if I could make the kiss thing work with Bronze?

We spend time talking about anything and everything. I am going to miss them both when they leave, as I feel a connection to them that is warm and comforting. I know things have to move forward, so accept that I will not have them here in the pack, but I will keep in touch with them on a weekly basis.

"I think that's enough for now, don't you?" Alpha Chet interrupts politely. "It's been two hours and poor Taria must be on information overload by now. Let's think about having our evening meal, shall we? I've had Ash prepare a cold buffet for us and the Luna's protection detail. I made sure that the Wolfsfoot team had a good meal before they got ready to leave and had plenty to take with them. I spoke with Alpha Gabriel and they can take their time on the way back, so they'll have enough for a decent meal in the forest later and a hearty breakfast tomorrow."

Two hours? Where did that time go I think to myself? Following Alpha Chet through to the rear garden, I see tables laid out with a variety of foods. Various meat platters, salad bowls, breads, and fruit. It looks amazing.

"Your chef has done you proud, Alpha Chet. Everything looks wonderful." I can't wait to get a plate and taste it.

Almost as good as a freshly killed rabbit. Almost! I hear Maya mumble.

It doesn't take long to demolish my first plate of food and go back for more. My second plate doesn't have anything that I had eaten on my first, either. There is such a variety and I'm loving it.

Seeing Luna Sage watching me, I stop and look guilty. "I must appear very greedy, Luna Sage. I apologize. All the extra training and running around here and there has made my appetite into a monster. I eat more than I ever have, but haven't gained an ounce in weight." I watch sheepishly for her reaction.

"You go for it, Taria. I envy you your youthful metabolism. I can put weight on just by planting a lettuce seed, never mind eating anything. Between you and Bronze, I'm sure we'll have some very healthy new generation pups." Luna Sage gives me an outrageous wink and I blush furiously.

Seeing Wesley at the edge of the garden, I call him over with a gesture.

"Luna Taria. What can I do for you?" I know he is my Gamma, and it's his job to protect me, but he always speaks in such a way that I feel he is so much more. It's difficult to explain and especially as I have known him for so short a time. If I didn't know better, I'd say it was an unhealthy infatuation, but it's not like that. It is the typical

Luna and Gamma relationship. It's just that as yet I'm not used to it.

"I want all of you to take turns at getting something to eat. You first, and don't eat too fast, you have time. Enjoy a plate of this wonderful food while we're in a safe environment. You are doing me proud. I want you to know that and that I appreciate it."

"Thank you, Luna Taria. I will pass that on to the team." His eyes glow as I see him mind link with the team. I will be able to do that tomorrow once I'm accepted into the pack.

Hearing Alpha Chet speak Drake's name, I look around and see him talking with Drake and a couple of pack members. Being nosey, I walk over and Alpha Chet introduces me to Dixon, the current Chief Warrior, and Adaline, who is to be assessed by Drake as Dixon's successor.

"I'm pleased to meet you both. I've been looking forward to having a conversation with each of you for some time. Dixon, we need to talk about my personal bodyguard as a matter of urgency. I can't have someone on my team that isn't classed as a warrior, so how do we get around that?" I tilt my head as I look at him and see some confusion. "I want Ember qualified as a warrior and if we have to create a new warrior class or 'warrior bat test', then so be it."

"Ember is part of your personal guard?" Dixon exclaims. "When did that happen, and by whose authority?"

"While we were at the Wolfsfoot Pack, and by my authority. Why are you so surprised? Has she not demonstrated enough ability, courage and strength of character that you could believe she can hold that position?"

"She has become quite advanced with her bat, however, should she become disarmed, my concern is that she would be overpowered easily," Dixon responds.

"Very well. So, what have you done to address your concern?" I look him in the eye and wait for his response. Seeing nothing forthcoming, I turn to Adaline. "Should you become Chief Warrior Dixon's successor, what do you propose to implement to aid in Ember's skills to protect me?"

"I would work with her wolf, River, to ensure that should she ever lose her bat in combat, she would be able to shift seamlessly and let her wolf takeover. I'm sure that her wolf has the same determination to succeed that Ember has shown since she came into possession of her bat. River would be my immediate focus. Secondary would be Ember's combat skills without her bat. I'm sure Chief Warrior Dixon would have come up with a plan to aid Ember in defense of his Luna, had he not been so surprised by her sudden promotion to your personal guard." Adaline looks toward Dixon, who is recovering from my unexpected enquiry.

"Luna Taria," he mutters, "forgive my surprise, but what drove your decision to place your life in Ember's hands? I agree that her abilities with her bat are exceptional, and I have been working with her personally to further her skills, but to put them into a real-life scenario could be risking your life to a stick in the hands of an angry female." Sounding genuinely worried.

I shake my head at him. "Chief Warrior Dixon, you need have no worries on that score. That angry female and her stick defeated four Wolfsfoot Pack warriors soundly, and held off several more, while the rest of my protection detail were held captive. She was nothing short of hell on wheels when it came to the crunch, and you would have been proud to be her tutor had you seen her." Once again gesturing for Wesley to join us, who I notice has waited to have his meal after the rest of his team has had theirs.

"Wesley, please take time out to give Dixon and Adaline here your opinion of the fight that took place in the Wolfsfoot Pack packhouse when you arrived as my escort. Leave nothing out and speak freely, especially on your thoughts as to Ember being on my personal protection detail." I listen carefully as he describes how everything went belly up so quickly on their arrival, and the fact that they were refused outright to be able to communicate their arrival to me.

Watching Dixon's reaction to Wesley's narrative, I am reminded of Silas and his perception of Dahlia. I think he suffers from a similar case of seeing Ember as she was and not what she has become. Adaline, however, looks less surprised and more impressed.

"Adaline, would you take over the training of Ember and River, please?" Looking again to Dixon, I say, "This is no reflection on you. Chief Warrior, I think you have done a very thorough job, but as I have become Ember's mentor and you are going to be changing roles in the near future, I'd like to have a sense of stability in her training."

"Luna Taria, I am not certain to receive the promotion to Chief Warrior. I have a lot to do before Alpha Heir Bronze makes that decision." Adaline looks at me nervously.

"I doubt very much that you want my first memories of you to be that you failed me," I state.

"That would not be acceptable, Luna Taria. I would not want to disappoint you in the least."

"I am sure that when we train with Drake, you will impress him greatly, and convince Alpha Heir Bronze that you are the only suitable candidate." Smiling at her, I see her pride causing her to stand taller and straighter.

Grinning at her mischievously, then I ask, "And exactly how fast and how high can you climb a tree?"

Chapter 22

BRONZE

That has to have been the worst night's sleep I've had in a long time, or should I say, the lack of. Knowing that Taria is here but not being able to see, or speak to her, before today's ceremony has been the most difficult thing I have ever had to go through.

'And most of last night's lack of sleep is down to you, Titan. Thank you very much.'

Is not my fault. You should not have let mate arrive until ceremony. Her scent is everywhere and is driving me insane.

'We are both wanting our mate, but one of us has a one-track mind,' I reply.

We need heirs. I'm sure Maya feels the same, and why wouldn't she when she sees what she's getting as a mate.

'I have never known a wolf to be so confident as you can be. If you get any more egotistical, I'll have to have the doors widened so you can get your head through. I sincerely hope Maya has you jumping through hoops before she lets you get your way with her.'

Unlikely. Titan sits and gives a regal tilt of his head, as though dismissing such a ridiculous thought.

Putting my focus back on the day's upcoming events, I take a shower and wear some casual clothes while I wait for my father. He's bringing breakfast to the room and we'll go over the schedule for the day once more. Not that I need to, as it's already been burned into my brain by him, and Flint, so many times already.

The door opens and my father steps in with Flint following. A kitchen assistant follows with a trolley containing enough food to last a week, never mind breakfast. I quickly reel off the schedule for the day and they look at each other before bursting into laughter.

"Well. It's obvious we don't need to go over that again, then. Are you ready for the day's events, son?" My father begins taking items from the breakfast trolley and Flint soon follows suit.

"I'll be glad when the day is over and things get back to normal," I breathe a sigh and grab some food myself.

"Your life will never be normal again, my friend," Flint smirks as he says this while chewing on a piece of meat. "As if taking over the pack isn't a big enough change, you're taking a mate, too. I'm not sure which is going to create the biggest change overall."

"Having Taria by my side will help with the running of the pack, I'm sure. Didn't you find Mother's advice and counsel helpful, Father?" Waiting for him to finish chewing, he swallows and looks a little guilty.

"I have to be honest, Bronze. Your mother was always a behind the scenes kinda gal. She did more than she ever got credit for, and usually before I even asked for her help with anything. I remember many years ago, there was what could only be described as a crime spree, a strange thing in a pack of shifters. Things were being stolen at an alarming rate and although we all suspected the same shifter, we had no evidence to act on. When there were murmurs going around the pack that I wasn't in control, the said shifter disappeared and the thefts stopped. It wasn't until several months later that your mother hinted that she had had a hand in it. To say I was shocked would be an understatement." Raising his eyebrows, he takes another bite of his breakfast.

"Mother arranged for someone to disappear? I can't believe it, Father. You're making it up," I shake my head at him. I'm not gullible enough to fall for that one.

"He didn't just disappear, and there was more than one involved. Sage asked for my help when I was visiting the pack and we took care of the problem." Flint looks at my father rather sheepishly. "I'm sorry, Chet, but she swore me to secrecy, and if I hadn't helped, she was going to do it alone. If anything had happened to her, I would never have been able to live with myself. As it happened, I need never have worried. She was nothing short of awesome. Needless to say, she took no prisoners and told them she was not having such low life's causing her mate to look bad in the eyes of others. I'll never forget that night as long as I live."

"No wonder she wasn't in the least bothered by Taria dealing with Savannah," I state to the room in general.

"I always thought it was some of the warriors that had banded together and taken matters into their own hands at her instigation. I never imagined that she would have been physically involved." I see a look on my father's face that can only be described as pride.

"It seems, Father, we have similar tastes in feisty females." I can't help but grin as I look at Flint's very guilty expression at having kept such a secret from his good friend.

Finally, it is time to dress for the handover ceremony. Wearing the suit, supplied by Taria and the tailor's shop, it feels remarkably comfortable and I have to admit, I look darn good. If Taria's suit makes her look anywhere this good, and I don't doubt it will for a moment, she is going to take my breath away.

Walking through the packhouse to where the ceremony will be held outside, I have never felt so nervous. I don't think it is the handover that is causing it, it is seeing Taria again after so long.

The staging area that has been set up for the pack handover ceremony looks surprisingly austere. I'm not sure what I was expecting, but it was certainly not something as impersonal as this. My mother certainly hasn't had her hand in this, I think to myself.

The pack is present other than essential duties, such as the border guards, and they all watch as my father takes his place on the stage with Flint. I can't help but scan the crowd for any sign of Taria, but find none. I would have been surprised if she had been here as our mating bond may have caused issues with our concentration on the handover.

You are wrong. Mate is here. She is present somewhere watching the proceedings. She would not miss your ascension but has cleverly masked her scent, so I can hardly tell. Concentrate on the task at hand. Let me worry about our mate.

Listening to my father and Flint give their speeches, I wonder if my voice will be as steady and confident as theirs. I still can't see any sign of Taria anywhere...

Stop looking for mate! She doesn't want to be seen until she is ready to make her entrance. Don't spoil this for her. It will be how the Pack remembers her for years to come. Focus on your highlight of the day. You are becoming the Alpha of your pack. She is becoming Luna of a pack new to her and also a mate at the same time. This will be the biggest day of her life, except for meeting me and having pups, of course.

'Don't make me laugh now, Titan!'

My father ends his speech and both he and Flint beckon me forward. Taking my place, the blood oath is completed and the pack becomes mine. As the pack's new Alpha, I give my acceptance speech in a clear voice that carries well. It isn't as long as their speeches were, but I hope that the content shows the pack that I am dedicated to them and their future. As soon as I'm finished, there is a roar of cheers and I'm taken from the stage to be congratulated by the pack.

I'm kept busy with handshakes and backslaps for what seems like hours, but is in reality only a few minutes. When I turn back to the stage where I will await Taria, I stop and stare, dumbstruck.

The transformation is nothing short of miraculous. Center stage is an archway covered in roses of many pastel shades. The floor is strewn with colored flower petals on top of a red carpet that covers the bare wood flooring of minutes ago. A line of pack members are walking by the stage and placing gifts at the front. I am nothing short of speechless.

Through all this, I see Mother standing proudly with a huge smile directed at me. She gestures for me to join her and I make my way past yet more pack members, eager to congratulate their new Alpha.

Approaching my mother, I hold out my arms to hug her, but she holds back in front of the pack. Stepping in close, I scoop her into a hug and be damned with what anyone thinks. The pack erupts with cheering and when she sees this, she hugs me back.

Taking my place at the center of the stage, I make a small speech to the standing pack announcing the arrival of my mate and our imminent bonding. The pack remains silent and I'm unsure if they don't like my speech or are just awaiting Taria's appearance. As one, they all take their seats except for a small group at the back by the center aisle. They remain standing and all are wearing a dark cloak. Throwing off their cloaks, all but one, I see Wesley, Ember and two warriors standing in a uniform I don't recognize. The final cloak falls to the floor and Taria, my Taria, stands there resplendent in her tailored suit.

As she walks towards me, the pack members gasp as she passes them. Her suit is the same as mine, but cut in a feminine way that enhances every curve of her form. She looks nothing short of spectacular and I watch her approach with her guards in their own gray uniforms, looking as regal as anything I've ever seen.

The pack is in an uproar as they watch their future Luna take her place by my side beneath the arch. Standing slightly away from me, she gives her own speech that tells of the way she has been greeted by the pack, and that she will do everything she can to be the Luna they deserve and to follow on in Luna Sage's footsteps. Announcing that they are monumental steps to follow has my mother shedding a tear.

I step forward and complete the blood oath which brings Taria forward in the pack's hierarchy and bonds her as my Luna. We still have the official mating to complete but that we will do behind closed doors.

Taria turns to the pack and pledges to do her best for the pack from this moment forward until her Luna reign ends, which brings a loud cheer forth from the pack.

Presenting my mate as their Luna, I begin the process of sharing the pack's mental status with Taria. Trying to do it in such a way that it doesn't overwhelm her, I smile when she tells me to stop treating her like a child and get on with it. She takes the whole thing in her stride and I see her eyes glow as her wolf helps her.

Speaking to the pack with a mind link, she calls for a pack run and I hear yet another cheer as the pack agrees. Stepping away from me, she removes her jacket, then unbuttons her blouse. Thinking that she is going to strip naked, I'm about to stop her when I see a blue bodysuit show itself. When she is standing there in the suit, Ember stands by her in a similar gray one. They look amazing.

Taking my hand, she calls for all those that are able to shift to do so and join us in the run. As soon as Maya appears, Titan growls a deep and meaningful growl in her direction, then howls to start the run. Hearing the pack howl as one is an indescribable feeling, and we all take off for the forest. Wesley, Ember, and the two warriors surround us and I can't help but grin as I watch Ember's wolf, River's pride at being her Luna's personal guard.

Chapter 23

TARIA

Arriving back at the packhouse after the run, I feel exhilarated. Retrieving my suit from the stage where I'd dropped it, I get dressed and cover the blue bodysuit. I'm not in the least embarrassed by the snug fit of the suit, but as I'm going to be mingling with the pack, I feel the gray suit would be far more appropriate. It will also allow Bronze to concentrate on matters other than my curves. Ember has had no such concerns and is thoroughly enjoying the male attention that her bodysuit is attracting.

Titan has done nothing but preen since he met Maya, and to her credit, she is playing very hard to get. She wants to mate as badly as Titan, I can tell, but she is making him work for the privilege, that's for sure.

Bronze has my arm and is walking me around the festivities, introducing me to everyone. He isn't preening like Titan, though he does look very proud of himself. I myself have to admit to being more than a little smug as to how I made such a grand entrance and won over the pack. Walking arm in arm with my mate has me wearing the biggest grin possible.

Seeing how much effort has gone into the food for the garden party following the ceremonies, I'm astounded. The preparation alone must have been staggering. Mentioning this to Bronze, he steers me toward a female who is watching the tables that contain the vast array of dishes.

"Luna Taria, please meet Cook Ash. Although I'm afraid that the title of cook seriously underrates her abilities. Cook Ash, your new Luna, Luna Taria."

"At your service, Luna Taria," Cook Ash tips her head in respect and I immediately get a good feeling from this female.

"Chef Ash, you have excelled with such a magnificent feast. You are to be congratulated on this achievement." I wait to see if she notices the change of title.

"Thank you, Luna Taria, but it is cook, not chef. I have had no formal training to grant me that title."

"To produce food to this standard and to not have had any formal training, that alone, in my eyes, entitles you to be called a chef. From now on, you will be referred to as Chef Ash and will receive any pack gratuities that go along with that position." I see the conflict in her eyes and wait to see what she has to say.

"There is not, nor has there ever been, a pack chef's position, my luna, but thank you for the thought. It means a lot to me to just have that recognition," Chef Ash blushes furiously.

Turning to Bronze, I raise my eyebrows and I see him smile first at me, then he turns to Chef Ash, saying, "As of this moment, there is a requirement within the pack to fill a vacancy for a newly created position for a chef. Cook Ash, I believe you fit the criteria for the role. You are duly appointed as pack chef. Congratulations on your promotion." Offering his hand, she shakes it and looks like she is going to burst into tears.

Offering her hand to me, I brush it aside and as she looks at me, horrified that I would refuse, I grab her to me in a hug. "Well done, Chef Ash, and may I also add my congratulations on your promotion. Not before time, I may add," giving Bronze a mock glare, but know it's not particularly his doing.

Once Bronze is satisfied that he has paraded me enough, we join everyone else in partaking of the sumptuous feast. Sitting to one side, we eat and pack-watch. It would have been the icing on the cake if my Momma and Pops could have been here to see this, but I understand that with the rogues causing so many issues, they couldn't be away from the pack.

Once we've eaten, I ask Bronze if he will give me a tour of the grounds. Holding hands, which brings the mate tingles to the fore, we slip away and the first thing I'm drawn to are the kitchen gardens. They are certainly full of healthy plants, and there is an array of different herbs. I notice that there are other plants mixed in the beds too, and this reminds me of a conversation I had with Dahlia about something she called companion gardening. Different plants grow well when in proximity to others, and some keep bugs and harmful insects away. Someone here obviously knows their stuff, too.

Passing newly turned flower beds, I see fresh shoots appearing and can only imagine that they will be a riot of color when everything is in bloom. Walking past vegetable beds, they look like they have been tended by an OCD gardener as there isn't a weed in sight. Nothing appears to have been eaten by slugs or snails either, which is very unusual. There is always that one plant that gets demolished by the evil demons that leave their silver trails all over.

Entering an orchard, I see a circular bench surrounding the trunk of a large apple tree. It looks new and as we approach, there is a male sitting on the bench, his back to us. As we approach, Bronze speaks out.

"Not enjoying the festivities, Herb?"

The male jumps to his feet, spilling some food from a plate that he had on his lap. "Oh, Alpha Bronze, Luna Taria. I was present for the ceremonies and grabbed some of Cook Ash's lovely food, but I'm not a crowd person, so I came to enjoy my new bench and the solitude in the orchard."

"You mean Chef Ash. She's just accepted a promotion, I'm happy to say." Bronze grins, enjoying the fact that he has done a good deed so early in his new leadership.

"Well, she certainly deserves the title. She never lets us down, no matter the occasion. When I treat my team to a picnic, she does us proud every time. I don't know where she gets her inspiration, I'm sure."

"Judging by what I've seen of the gardens so far, I'd say you visit the same library. Your herb garden looks amazing and so do the vegetable beds. Your orchard seat is so much better than just a standard bench, too. You've impressed me and it's my first day as Luna." I step forward and offer my hand, which he takes and rather than shake, he bends and touches his lips to the back of it. I feel Titan growl rather than hear him and I turn to look at Bronze. "You two need to calm yourself. I think Herb and I are going to get along famously. I like him, and his olde worlde style, too."

"If you have a spare moment at some time, my Luna, I would love to share my vision for the future of the Eclipse Pack gardens with you." His eyes sparkle with enthusiasm, and I find it quite infectious.

"That would be my pleasure, Herb. We are going to be firm friends of the earth, I can see that." Watching his face light up, I give him a beaming smile.

"Herb, you should show Luna Taria your project folder. I have been remiss in not having made the time to study it with you." Bronze looks at me and continues, "Since being the head gardener, Herb has made so many improvements and in such a short space of time, it's been incredible. What Chef Ash is to food is what Herb is to gardening."

"I look forward to seeing your projects and perhaps being a part of some of them." I can see Bronze wants me away from Herb, and I smile inwardly at his jealousy. Taking our leave, we stroll off and Herb resumes what's left of his food as he sits on his bench below the branches of his apple tree.

Titan, what is Herb's wolf called? Maya asks this in such an innocent voice, but I almost can't breathe as I wait for his response. I also see Bronze miss a step in his stride as she asks.

You do not need to know his wolf's name! That is not something you need to be concerned with!

Seeing Maya in my mind as she sits there with a smirk on her face, I can't hold it any longer and I burst out laughing. Grabbing Bronze's arm to stop myself collapsing to the floor, I have tears running down my cheeks.

"I can see you and your wolf are going to keep me and my wolf on our toes." Bronze grins at me and I see Titan flash in his eyes.

"Life will never be boring, that's for sure." I stare into his eyes and almost melt as he leans down and tenderly kisses my lips. Placing my hand on the back of his neck, I pull him into a deeper and more passionate kiss. Breaking the kiss only when we have to breathe, we look at each other and can see the longing we both have.

"This is something we need to explore further when we are alone tonight. If I can keep a tight enough rein on Titan that is. He has only had thoughts of Maya for some time now." Bronze rolls his eyes as he speaks.

"I think he can wait his turn, don't you?" I say this with a smile and walk slightly in front and with what I hope is a sexy wiggle of my ass. Getting a slap tells me it was.

Reaching the nursery, I see someone in there. "Didn't you close the nursery today for the ceremonies?" I ask Bronze, surprised that he wouldn't.

"Of course. Why would I not have everyone possible attend the handover and the introduction of my Luna?" Heading into the building, I see two enormous eyes staring at me on the doors. Once in the hallway I see more eyes on me. They look like they are following my every move.

"Those eyes are a little spooky for a nursery, don't you think?" I whisper to Bronze as we head to the classroom where we had seen movement.

"There's a story behind those eyes. I'll tell you later." I swear he giggles as he says it.

Opening the door, we see two females working at a desk, but what catches my eye is the pup that is scraping at something on the back wall of the classroom. I can't believe two adults are sitting there while a pup scrapes and cleans the walls. Before I get a chance to say anything, both females jump to their feet and smile at Bronze and me as though this was an everyday occurrence.

"Good afternoon, Eve, Madison. How are things today?" What is going on here, I think to myself.

"Alpha Bronze. Luna Taria. Congratulations to you both."

"Is there a particular reason that you have not closed the school today, as I instructed?" Bronze does not sound at all put out that these two have ignored what would amount to an alpha order.

"The school is indeed closed, as you instructed. All pupils have been given the day off to join in the pack festivities." The one that I take to be the youngest informs us.

"And yet, Madison, here you and Eve are. At school." He tips his head in a questioning manner and raises his eyebrows.

"I was supposed to be here with Coal, just the two of us," says the one I now know as Eve. "When Madison found out that I was going to take advantage of the closure to help reprogram some of Coal's thought processes, she refused to let me sit here alone."

"And how is the reprogramming coming along?" Bronze looks towards the pup and then back to Eve.

"Oh, I'm confident that there will be no more defacing of pack walls or buildings in the future by the time I've finished with his restart button. The program will be reinstalled to the correct parameters." She smiles sweetly, but at the same time, it's darn scary if you ask me.

"How are classes coming along in the day-to-day scheme of things with the class? Have we seen any improvement in the pup's learning and general attitude to school?" I find this whole thing quite bizarre and can't wait to hear about it when we leave. I'm sure there's a story to be told, but I can't for the life of me get a handle on it.

Both females positively bounce with enthusiasm as they rush to tell us how much better things are since that ass has been gone. They reel off some of the activities that have been introduced and how the pup's grades have gone through the roof. I take particular notice when I hear that there is a weekend gardening activity that all the pups willingly attend.

"Very good, ladies. It sounds like you're doing an excellent job. Remember, if there's anything you need, see me or Luna Taria here. We will support you fully with your endeavors." Turning to the pup, Bronze calls out to him, "Coal. Don't miss the eyes in the mouse hole in the hallway, will you?"

A very sulky pup answers, "No sir, Alpha Bronze. I'm sure my momma will make sure I don't miss any."

"Carry on, soon-to-be-a-warrior Coal," Bronze watches as his words sink in and the pup positively beams at him.

"Yes sir, Alpha Bronze," he calls out in his best official warrior type voice, and goes back to work with a renewed vigor.

Bronze looks at the two females and winks at them. Winks? Eve looks at Bronze as though he just hung the moon and then at the pup. Seeing the pride there, it has to be her son. Only a momma could look at a pup that way.

Walking away from the nursery and back towards the festivities that we can clearly hear as we get nearer, Bronze explains about Coal, some of his antics, and how Eve is bringing him up alone. When he describes the day he caught Lincoln about to hit Coal, I see Titan's eyes blaze and think how lucky that teacher was that day when Bronze held him back. I'm not in the least concerned when I hear that he was sent to the Shifter Council warrior training school.

The story of Coal's father, his poor behavior and also being sent to the training school, has my blood boiling when I think of how Eve is doing such a good job bringing up that pup on her own. I must speak to Flint when I get a chance and see what's happening with those two. I wonder if there's any way to make their life more difficult than it already is?

Chapter 24

BRONZE

The festivities show no signs of drawing to a close and as much as I enjoy seeing the pack so at ease and enjoying themselves, I do have other priorities that need my attention. Top of the list is sitting beside me in her gray suit and she looks amazing. The blue bodysuit she has beneath that, however, is causing me much more physical discomfort than mental. What's more, I'm sure she is fully aware of my condition.

Turning to look at me, she gives me a smile that is both innocent but pure lust at the same time. Oh yes. She knows exactly what she is doing to me and my wolf. Titan hasn't stopped pacing since we kissed and Maya has been talking to him without me knowing what she has been saying.

"Bronze, it's been a very long day for me, what with all the excitement of the two ceremonies. Would you mind if I retired to my room and got a shower and a good night's rest?" Her eyes tell me that rest is the furthest thing on her mind right now.

"I don't mind at all, with the exception of going to *your* room. We are now living in the alpha suite. My parents moved their belongings to the cottage last night and this morning, my rooms were transferred to our suite."

"I'll get my immediate needs then and see you there." Taria stands and I see a few furtive glances and knowing looks from those around us.

"I think you'll find everything of yours is already in the alpha suite, too. I had them moved there after the ceremonies." I give her what I hope is an innocent grin, but I'm sure by the look she gives me in return, it comes out the complete opposite.

"In that case, perhaps you'd give me a few minutes to allow me to freshen up before you join me. After all, we wouldn't want you to arrive in, let's say, five minutes and catch me in the midst of a shower, now would we?"

What was previously just an uncomfortable condition now becomes unbearable, and I can see Taria is fully aware of that fact. Taking off her jacket, she drapes it across my lap, bends to give me a chaste kiss on the lips and then whispers, "Five minutes, my love. Any more and I will be out of the shower, dried, in a nightdress and asleep."

Watching as she walks away, I have to make a conscious effort to close my mouth and prevent any drool slipping down my chin. Her walk could grace any catwalk and it's all I can do not to run after her, scoop her up and run to the alpha suite.

Now you know how I feel! That Maya is going to be the death of me by teasing and tempting, I swear to the Goddess.

'I never expected either of them to have such an intoxicating effect on us, Titan. Taria has had me at a disadvantage all day, and the worst thing is, she's known it! Life will never be boring with those two around.'

That's a fact. Four minutes left!

Seeing my mother approach, I cringe as I know she will expect a hug and I so do not want her close to me right now. Having her feel *that* pressing against her is the worst thing that could ever happen. Taking a seat beside me, she congratulates me on Chef Ash's promotion and then talks about how the day has been for her and father.

Three minutes!

"If you'll excuse me, Mother, I need to see if Taria has everything she needs for the night."

"Well done, Son. You lasted longer than your father did. He joined me before I'd crossed the dance floor on our first night and all but dragged me upstairs. I was suitably outraged by his behavior until the alpha suite door slammed shut behind us. Go! At least you can walk straight now and can give me a hug!"

"Mother, you are all a son could ask for, and more." Standing together, I give her a hug and then darn near run across the room to a chorus of cheering and ribald comments. Waving to the pack, I rush upstairs to the alpha suite.

Stopping outside the door, I take a moment to catch my breath and gain some composure. Titan is almost howling at me to *get on with it!* Walking calmly into the main room, I see a trail of clothes leading to the bedroom. Walking by a shoe, then another, I hear the shower running. A blouse is by the bedroom door, quickly followed by gray pants near the bathroom.

Walking into the bathroom, I'm expecting to see the blue bodysuit, but am not prepared for the way in which it is displayed. Instead of it being strewn across the floor as I expected, it is still very much attached to Taria. She is standing in the shower, facing away from me and her wet hair streaming down her back. If it was at all possible, the bodysuit clings to her shapely form even more when wet than it did before. It envelopes her even more tightly to enhance every muscle and curve of her exquisite body.

As I step closer to the shower, Taria turns, and I'm sure she heard the growl escape from my chest. Seeing the view from the front has me suppressing the howl that Titan wants to bring forth. Stepping into the shower, I grab her and pull her to me. As I wrap my arms around her, she throws her arms behind my neck and her legs around my waist.

As her head is now slightly above me, I look up and slam my lips to hers. Feeling her respond, I push her against the wall and feel the water soaking through my clothes. Breaking from the kiss, I keep her against the wall as I try to get my jacket and shirt off. Sensing my urgency, I see Taria's fingers become her wolf's claws and she literally shreds my upper clothes to rags.

This drives me further insane with lust, and all I can hear are Titan and Maya screaming in my mind. *BITE! BITE! BITE!*

Looking at Taria, I can tell she is experiencing the same emotions.

"Do it! Do it now!" She whispers in such a hoarse voice that without another thought, I grab her hair, pull her head back, and bite her neck in the most perfect of marking spots. The scream that she emits could have been heard all over the pack lands. We hear the pack howl in our minds and at least some in the packhouse must have heard her.

Not caring in the least, she looks me in the eye and we press on with our mating. Before I can rip her bodysuit from her perfect curves, she pushes me away and starts to undress herself. Just the act of withholding my desire lifts us both to another level of lust. She never breaks eye contact as she slips from the suit and then watches as I remove the last of my clothes.

Taking her in my arms again, she lifts herself so she can wrap her legs around me. As though this was part of some long practiced dance, my manhood slips into her and she sighs as it does so. Burying her head into my neck, I feel her bite me and can't help but thrust myself deep into her until we are fully joined. Holding her there, she lifts her head and stares into my eyes. I see Maya in them as they sparkle, and I'm sure that Titan is showing in mine, too.

As much as I want to take things slowly and ensure that we are both pleasured, I feel Taria's muscles squeezing me and I realize that this is not what she wants. She starts to slide up and down my shaft and it isn't long before I can resist no longer. Withdrawing to the last possible contact, and then slamming into her, we begin to race each other to the finish.

Feeling her rhythm, I slow slightly to match it and as soon as I do, she reaches her climax. Her muscles grip me tightly and I feel them rippling and drawing my seed from me. The growl that starts deep in my chest echoes around the bathroom as I fill her and pull her tightly to me.

We stay there, joined and spent, until I lift my head from her neck and stare into those deep, magnificent eyes.

"I think I owe you a new suit, my lover." She mutters as she looks at the remains of my shirt and jacket.

"It did not go unnoticed that you were a tad more careful with yours, my darling, but I'm not complaining. I am more than happy to watch you slip out of that bodysuit on a regular basis." I give a little growl as I remember the vision. "Perhaps we should get a different colored one for each day of the week?"

"Surely, good sir, you would become bored after a short time of a daily performance?" Her eyes are laughing, but the rest of her speaks to me differently.

"I'm confident that it can be more than once daily, and even at differing times, m'lady. Shall we retire to the bedroom, continue our exercise and see where it leads us?" Still carrying her with her legs around me, I take her to the bed, where we do indeed continue until we are both satisfied and can do no more but hold each other in slumber.

Waking first, the sunlight streaming through the window is bathing Taria in its golden light and her hair shines as it spills across her pillow. Raising myself on to my elbow so I can look down on her, I marvel at how we mated last night. Considering it was all new to both of us, we certainly didn't shy away from pleasing each other. She is certainly beautiful both inside and out.

"Not seen enough, yet?" Her voice startles me out of my reverie, and her hands slowly push the sheet down to her waist. This starts another hour of pleasure giving and receiving, much to Titan's disgust, as he is impatient for his time with Maya.

When we finally show our faces in the dining hall for a late breakfast, there are many knowing smiles, but thankfully no comments. Taria strolls through the hall, showing her strength by giving everyone an enormous smile and having not a care in the world that some of those present may have heard her as we consummated our union.

I had asked if she would like to have breakfast in the suite rather than face those that had heard us, but she was adamant that if they had heard, there was nothing that could be done about it. She wasn't in the least bit shy that we had been good for each other and some were aware of that fact.

Our first official task of the day was to meet the Inner circle that I had appointed. They were due to meet us in the alpha office, but I had a little surprise for Taria first. Once our breakfast was finished and we had replenished some of the tremendous amount of energy we had expended in the night, I took her hand and we walked into the main hall of the packhouse. Almost opposite the alpha office is a door with a warrior blocking it, standing at attention, just as the one standing at the alpha door.

"Is that what I think it is?" Taria asked, and I could see the excitement in her eyes.

"I want to show you where we keep the pack's most treasured items and how we look after them." I see her try to hide her disappointment and I try to hide my smile.

"Wesley has many duties as gamma, as you are aware, and guarding our treasure is one of his foremost priorities. Isn't that so, Gamma Wesley?"

"It is so, Alpha Bronze. I will not let you or the pack down. I will give my life before I let anything happen to our treasure." Wesley plays his part to perfection and as he steps to one side, he reveals the plaque on the door reading, 'Luna Office.'

Watching as she sees the plaque, her hands cover her mouth. Reaching out, she runs her fingers over the plaque and looks at me with glassy eyes.

"It was hand carved by Herb. He wanted to do something personal for the new Luna and when I mentioned growing some flowers for your office, he came back with this instead. He will still have some plants for you as well, though."

"It's outstanding. I love it. I can see Herb being one of *my* inner circle before long. Wesley, Ember, Herb and Chef Ash. Sounds like a force to be reckoned with. What do you say to that, eh, Wes?" Taria punches Wesley on his bicep as he blushes at her informal use of his name. I've never, in all the time I've known him, ever heard anyone call him Wes.

Opening the door for her, Wesley waves us through the door. The room looks stunning and has a beautiful polished desk set near the enormous fireplace but away from the window. Taking time to study the layout, it has been done tactfully but in a very security focused way. It is the first time I've seen the finished project, and I have to admit to a certain level of jealousy.

The alpha office is a very nice space to work in, but this is something else. I feel my mother's hand in this, but also many others. The chairs are all leather but look incredibly comfortable. There is an executive chair behind the desk that you could get lost in. On the desk is a name plaque, also obviously done by Herb, stating 'Luna Taria Blueblood, Eclipse Pack'. She picks it up and holds it to her chest.

"I'll treasure this forever. It's the first time I've seen my new name!" Watching her eyes, I see the tears forming and hold her to me.

Looking around the room, she gushes as she sees everything that has been done to make the room not only an official luna office but those things that make it personal to being her, Taria's, office.

Reluctantly leaving her office as we now have to meet my Inner circle, as she passes Wesley, she stops in front of him, pops up onto her tiptoes and gives him a peck on the cheek. "Thank you for everything and please pass that on to all those involved for me." If he hadn't been willing to die for her before, he was now. I could see it in every fiber of his being.

Approaching the alpha office, my warrior lets me know that the inner circle has all arrived and are waiting. Entering the office, I see them all stand from around the conference table. I notice also that they have left the chair by my right hand empty for Taria to use. That simple show of respect goes a long way with me, and I nod to each of them as I walk around the table.

Once seated, I take a moment to introduce everyone formally to Taria. Adaline, Eve, Xander and Dixon are all very friendly and I don't sense any type of nervous undercurrent from anyone. It isn't a meeting to discuss anything specific, more of an informal introduction as to what can be expected in the future. Letting them chat a few moments amongst themselves, almost as a brainstorming session, to see what comes out of it, I look around my office.

"I'll get Wesley to order one for you, if you like." Taria's quiet comment makes me smile.

"I don't know what you're talking about, I'm sure," I reply, trying to sound sincere.

"Very well. You can carry on relying on the kitchen for a thermos of coffee. I much prefer to make mine fresh and from my own shiny new coffee pod machine." Her giggle has everyone looking at us, but she carries on without missing a beat. "Does anyone have any spare staff hours that they can devote to Herb, the head gardener?

He has been doing some amazing stuff that will benefit us all in the long run and I'm sure that he can utilize any spare muscle or time that we can support him with. Eve and Madison have got the pups involved on the weekend to do seed planting and seedling repotting. If he can find the pups something to do, I'm sure he will be grateful for any adult help. I'll be taking an extra interest in the gardens, and Herb has a project folder that he wants to go through with me. If anyone here feels that I can help or support them in anything, please don't hesitate to come and see me. I have an office across the hall and I will be operating on an open door policy, so don't think you'll have to make an appointment to see me. If I'm available at the time, I'll be happy to see you. If I'm not, I'll arrange something with you."

Everyone seems to be opening up and having a warm response to Taria, which I'm pleased about. I didn't doubt for a minute that she'd fit in, but there's always that one percent that makes you nervous.

Once I'm satisfied that we've achieved what I wanted from today I call an end to the meeting and look forward to getting my luna's opinion of everyone, although she has met some already.

"I like them all. They seem to be keen to do right by you and none of them look like they are here to kiss your ass."

"Well, I asked for an honest opinion," I laugh as her words sink in.

"I wouldn't speak like that in front of anyone else, my lover, but you surely know I'll speak my mind when we're alone?" Taria waits for my reaction, in case I think she is too brutally forthright, I'm sure.

"My darling, I respect your open dialogue when we're alone and know without a doubt that you wouldn't speak out of turn in a formal setting. I'm glad that you share my thoughts on them, though. I wouldn't want an ass kisser within ten miles of me.

Slipping herself onto my lap, she whispers, "Well, you won't hear me say that about you! Have we got anymore official duties to perform now, or can I tempt you back to our suite for some unofficial duties?"

Walking as sedately as we can through the packhouse we make our way to our suite and are very active with unofficial business the rest of the afternoon.

Chapter 25

HERB

Having met Luna Taria, I found her absolutely charming. I was taken with her openness and her genuine interest in anything garden related. I'm going to check through my project folder and make sure it is fully up-to-date before I show it to her. I know Alpha Bronze hadn't been that interested, he has enough to be doing if I'm honest, but I was mildly put out that he never made the time to even look at it.

Everything is coming on well with the extra help that I have been given. Anyone that has qualified for pack punishment has been diverted to me rather than Chef Ash and her kitchen, which I am very grateful for. I have been able to dedicate more time to supervision, which has paid dividends rather than have my head down, ass up working on some of the simple menial tasks. Head down, ass up! That was a term my father used to use. Why I've suddenly come up with that, I don't know.

My father would have been in his element working with the pups. He loved planting seeds and then repotting the seedlings, and seeing the pups' faces when their seeds began to sprout would have made him so happy. It was the beginnings of life itself, he used to say. Obviously where I got my love of everything green, I'm sure. Mother always wanted more flowers. She always said he didn't grow her enough flowers and yet, never a week went by without her having vases of flowers in the house. We never went hungry for vegetables either. I don't know how he did it when we had such a small garden. Every inch always had something growing, and we'd be harvesting something throughout the year.

Heading back to my workshop, I cast my critical eye over each of the beds as I pass, and to my surprise, I only pick up the absolute minimum of issues. Things are certainly going well. Walking into my workshop, I head over and sit at my bench. I use this for virtually everything from drawing designs, eating lunch, potting, mixing my different composts, even keeping my folder updated.

Taking my folder from the shelf above the bench, I start at the beginning and flick slowly through it. It still astounds me that so much has changed and such a high percentage of improvements have succeeded. I'm pleasantly surprised to find that the folder doesn't need anything added, and is showing all the latest ideas.

Thinking over what my schedule is for the day, I could easily make time to stop by the Luna's office and see if she has a few minutes to spare herself. I'm sure that she could give me some more suggestions for things that I haven't thought of yet.

Entering the packhouse, I see Ember at the Luna's door. She scares the hell out of me, I don't mind admitting. Before she got that damn bat from Alpha Bronze, she was always such a sweet thing that I always smiled when I saw her. If I'd been her fated mate then, I'd have been over the moon. Now, though, I'd run a mile if she looked at me and said, 'Mate!'

Approaching slowly, she watches me and I feel like a mouse being toyed with by a cat. "Hello, Herb. Come to see the Luna?" My folder flies from my hands and I jump a mile. Diving to the floor, I scrabble around for my folder, and the few sheets of paper that have fallen out.

"Erm, yes, Warrior Ember. I have, yes, come to see Luna Taria. Is that okay?" I stutter and must sound like a completely petrified lunatic.

"Herb, what's got into you lately? You're always on edge. Is something wrong? If you're being bullied or are frightened of something or somebody, you just have to tell me and I'll put them straight." Slapping her bat into her palm has me nearly peeing my pants and I jump again, dropping my folder.

"No, nothing's wrong. I'm fine, everything is fine. No worries, no problems. Everything is just peachy. Can I go now?"

"Go? Go where? You just got here to see the Luna. Are you sure you're okay?" Ember bends down to help me pick up the folder and loose papers, and I just stare at her.

"I'm not okay. You scare me." I blurt it out and then look at her, horrified at my own admission.

"What? I scare you? Why on earth would I scare you? What have I ever done to make you afraid of me?" She looks at me with a look of shock on her face.

"You two, come inside at once." Luna Taria is standing at the door to the office and points toward her desk. "Come in and sit down, the pair of you."

"Luna Taria, I can't leave your door unattended," Ember states, still looking at me with wide eyes.

"That's an order, Warrior Ember, not an invitation," the Luna calls to the warrior at the alpha's door, instructing him to get someone to watch her door immediately.

Before I sit, I start to babble an apology to the Luna making sure she knows that it was all my fault and that Ember had done nothing wrong.

"Herb, do shut up and stop stuttering. Ember, sit down and stop worrying about the door for just a minute." Taking her seat behind the desk, she calmly looks at us both. "Right. Ember. Herb isn't so much scared of you as he fears your bat. Practically all the males in the pack are scared of your bat, and I'm not surprised. Whenever your name is mentioned, the bat gets a mention, too. From what I can gather, you used to be a shy little thing that became a fire breathing beast when Bronze gave you that bat. Perhaps we can work on softening your reputation somewhat." Looking at Ember, I see the recognition sinking in.

"I'm sorry, Ember. I know you would never hurt me, but I made the mistake of watching you train a few times with Dixon, and you're just so fierce nowadays compared to before." Seeing Ember's eyes brimming with tears, I hate myself for causing them. Reaching over, I place my hand on hers and give it a gentle squeeze.

"Right, now that we've got this settled, Ember, take the rest of your shift off and get some rest. I'll send Herb to find you once I'm done with him, and you two can get your friendship back on track. Go! No arguments," Luna Taria sends her off and checks to see who is on door duty. She doesn't seem surprised when she learns that Gamma Wesley is there.

"I'm sorry for causing all that drama, Luna Taria. It wasn't Ember's fault. All she did was speak to me and I just fell to pieces."

"The Goddess should have made you fated mates. You would be perfect for each other, but who knows why these things do or don't happen. Is that your project folder?"

As soon as I start to show her my folder, I become a different person. My confidence is back and Ember is forgotten, for the time being, at least. Going over the many projects I notice that Luna Taria asks insightful questions and has many wonderful suggestions. The more we talk, the more I'm taken with our new Luna.

When she tells me of Blackshadow Pack's walled garden, I'm totally hooked on having one ourselves. Ideas are thrown back and forwards between us, and eventually we have a rough plan that we agree on for the layout. Our packhouse doesn't have the ballroom that Blackshadow Pack has, which leads out to their walled garden, but we do have the ability to add one to the side of the packhouse with space to create the walled garden from that.

"Herb, what should we call the walled garden? Any ideas?" Luna Taria has a glint in her eye, so she must have thought of something already.

"No, Luna Taria. I think you have an idea, though. Am I right?"

"While talking with Alpha Bronze, he mentioned wanting to reward someone for doing a good job and it just struck me that maybe he could name the walled garden after them. You could make a name plaque too, like these you made for me. I haven't said thank you for them either, that reminds me."

"Gamma Wesley passed on your gratitude for them. I'm glad that they pleased you. I wanted to do more than just some potted plants and flowers to make you feel welcome." It was a pleasant surprise when Wesley found me and passed on the Luna's thanks face to face. He could have mind-linked me, but he wanted to express the pleasure that Luna Taria showed when she saw them.

"So, we have a name, but we will keep it quiet until the garden is ready for unveiling. We need it done as soon as possible. Draw up the full plans and list of materials, manpower, etc. I'll get it signed off and we'll make it happen. We are going to be one hell of a team, Herb. Let's show the pack what we're made of." Laughing, I high five the Luna and then look at her horrified as I realize what I've just done.

"You just high-fived me? And I responded. It's a good job there's just the two of us in the office or Bronze may have had your head on the garden wall!" Seeing her laugh, I take a deep breath and promise myself to try to be less enthusiastic in the future. Leaving in good spirits, I go in search of Ember.

DRAKE

Having spent an hour in the training ring with Adaline, I'm confident that she can be the Chief Warrior that Alpha Bronze would expect. I'm a little surprised at just how good she is, to be honest. If it wasn't for my size and strength, she could have bested me on more than one occasion. For someone so young and with no experience of an actual battle, she has shown exceptional skill and tactical knowledge. I wouldn't have any problem going into a life-or-death situation with her either at my side or having my back.

When we went to the forest to begin her advanced training and stamina building, I noticed how she was evaluating the surrounding trees. My penchant for tree climbing has obviously preceded me, or she has done her homework, one or the other. When I explain what I expect when it comes to the tree climb, I see the corners of her mouth lift and know then that she has been practicing. I feel a little of Luna Tati's handiwork here and I believe that is confirmed when I shout go, and see her fingers immediately become wolf's claws as she leaps for the trunk.

To give her credit where it's due, she has certainly been putting in some hours of training as she achieves a creditable time and shows no signs of being out of breath. Well, I think we'll just put that to the test a little more forcefully than a normal training session.

I'm interrupted when Luna Taria joins us and I see her infamous bat warrior alongside her. Nodding to them, I wait and see what develops.

"Instructor Drake, how are things coming along with Adaline?"

"Luna Taria, please call me Drake. I'm not one for titles myself and my past is best kept to a low profile at times." I nod respectfully to her, and she smiles in return.

"I was not aware that you had a past that you didn't want known, so my apologies, Drake, if I spoke out of turn." She looks at me with a new light and I see the unasked questions in her eyes.

"It is merely a warrior's past, yet some may still live that would seek revenge for their family or comrades lost in otherwise long forgotten battles." I have no doubt that there are some still out there that would hurt my Caroline or our pups if they could find me.

"I was wondering, Drake, if my disobedient warrior and I could join Adaline's training session?"

"You have a disobedient warrior? I trust that is said in jest and not something that should be of genuine concern, Luna Taria?"

"I gave her some free time, but her *dedication* to duty apparently translates free time to *dereliction* of duty. So, I have a shadow for the afternoon." The smile that passes between them speaks of a high degree of respect for each other.

"I may test the skills of your famous bat warrior before the day is out and see if her reputation is valid. Perhaps we could learn a few things from each other. I used to be quite proficient with similar weapons in my days of service." I see something flicker across the face of the female warrior and wonder if I have offended her in some way. "It is of no importance, but I have not come across a skilled weapons fighter in a very long time. I would take it as a personal favor just to spar with someone again."

Having regained her breath from the tree climbing, Adaline approaches. "If I may, Ember, this would be a once in a lifetime opportunity to gain some valuable experience and instruction. If I were in your position, I would grab the offer with both hands." Adaline looks at Ember and is gently nodding encouragement. "I am learning so much from Drake, things that I would never have thought of and no one else has ever mentioned. I mean, tree climbing for a wolf shifter? Honestly? Yet it builds speed, dexterity and stamina all in one simple exercise. And I can call my claws forward at will. Who knew that would be such a useful skill to master!"

Ember looks from Adaline to Luna Taria and I see the indecision in her eyes. Luna Taria puts her hands on Ember's shoulders and raises her chin as she speaks to her. "Ember. I told you that I would be your mentor and that I would do everything I could to help you. Drake can teach you things that no other shifter ever could. I think that the decision, although ultimately yours to make, is an opportunity you should not pass on. If it were anyone else, I would order them to do it, but I respect you more than that. You need to decide quickly, though, as I want to do some tree climbing with Adaline before we have to get back to the packhouse."

Leaving them alone for a few moments, I step into the forest and go in search of a suitable branch to make myself a staff. I know that she will train with me now, as Luna Taria made the decision for her in a subtle and caring way. Luna Taria is very good at what she does, I must say.

Finding a suitable branch doesn't take long and I soon have it stripped down to a training staff. Walking back, I see Ember warming up and I too do some stretches and prepare myself as I step into the training ring.

Ember steps forward, and I take my stance. As soon as I'm ready, Ember launches her first attack, which surprises me with its speed and accuracy. I was expecting more thought going into her attacks and less ferocity.

After only a few short maneuvers, I am defending more than I would expect to be from someone who has had no formal training. Taking the initiative, I begin to take the fight to her and find it difficult to find a way past her defenses.

It's only when I begin to push her that I sense that she is holding back. Pressing home my attacks now, I see her beginning to counter some of my moves with exceptional skill. She manages to score an occasional hit, and they are not light training taps either, which is my own fault for pushing so hard.

Seeing her flinch as one of my staff strokes catches her, I foolishly drop my guard and the next thing I know, I'm on the floor and I see stars. Looking up from the ground, I see Ember grinning, and I know she played me perfectly into that move.

Holding out her hand, she helps me to my feet and asks if I am okay.

"A little embarrassed that I was so easily fooled into such a move, but you fight extraordinarily well for someone with no formal training in weapons."

"Chief Warrior Dixon has been sparring with me and recommended some books for me to study. My love of my bat led me to study above and beyond what most would probably do. It gives me such a feeling that I can't begin to describe when I fight with it." Ember is bubbling with excitement as she speaks.

"I can help you for the short time I am here, if Luna Taria can spare you to join Adaline and I while we train. Is that something that can be arranged, Luna Taria?" I'm already sure of the answer before she confirms it, and I can't help the smile as I think how much I am going to enjoy training these two warriors. It doesn't enter my head to think of them as females.

"Right…now that you two are sorted, how about my tree climbing?" Luna Taria calls out as she heads for the tree line. "Last one to the top serves dinner to the pack!"

Chapter 26

TARIA

Laid in bed beside Bronze, my muscles ache, and not just from our mutual exercise over the last hour or two. Climbing the trees with Adaline and Ember was great fun, though I could only beat those two when I cheated. They were up and down the trees like squirrels. Drake found my attempts to win hilarious and even when he gave me a 'Luna's head start' they would catch me easily.

"I know I am fit, Bronze, but compared to those two, I might as well be a hippo climbing those trees. You should see them go!"

"My darling, I'm sure that there are many others out there that can't hold a candle to your tree climbing abilities. Hippo or otherwise." His comment earns him an elbow in the ribs and I smirk as the air rushes from him.

"Be careful, my love, this hippo may sit on you."

"I would certainly have no objections to that." Grabbing me, he swings me on top of him, but I continue rolling and slip from the bed. "Hippos perform better in the water, so do you care to join me in the shower?"

An hour later and back in bed, we discuss Adaline's appointment to the chief warrior position.

"What made you have Drake assess Adaline for the position? Surely not because she was female alone?" I had been meaning to ask since I was at the Wolfsfoot Pack, but it kept slipping my mind.

"She began her warrior training and immediately showed an amazing aptitude for it. I was impressed greatly, and so was Dixon. We knew we had something special there and when I created the training position especially for her, she made it her own from day one. Her idea for the rucksacks and toy pups was nothing short of genius."

"Rucksacks and toy pups? That you will have to explain further." Propping myself on one elbow, I look down at him as he explains it to me. Hearing how competitive all the females became has me laughing until I cry.

"Seriously, my darling, their attitude went from not interested to death before dishonor in seconds. You've never seen such brutality over a stuffed toy in your entire life. Male warriors wouldn't go in the ring if the rucksack was in there with a female." I'm sure there was some exaggeration in his story, but I got the message that Adaline could be creative and get the job done.

"Having Drake do the assessment was to protect Adaline from some of the jealousy and backbiting, that the promotion would surely bring. Others would see themselves as better qualified, longer serving warriors, more experienced. This way, she would have a weapon in her arsenal that no other Eclipse warrior would have."

"The seal of approval from an outsourced trainer. That's pure genius, Bronze."

"Better than that, my darling. You may not know it, but Drake is a legend, as both a warrior and a trainer. He plays down his reputation, being the modest shifter that he is, but he has been involved in battles, rescues and some say, even secret operations. Even shadow warriors have been known to defer to his knowledge and experience." Bronze speaks with a reverence that I have only ever heard him use before when he speaks of his father.

"Drake mentioned something to me in passing today about his warrior past," Before I say more Bronze sits upright, looking shocked.

"He must think extremely highly of you, Taria. He never speaks of it to anyone. He has made council members apologize for merely mentioning his past."

"Don't be jealous of Drake as well as Herb, my love. I couldn't cope with every male I speak to causing you to become a green-eyed monster."

"Envy maybe of Drake. To be held in high regard by such a shifter as he, is something to aspire to. Even alphas can be guilty of a little hero worship, you know," Bronze replies.

Laughing at the look he gives, thinking it somehow depicts hero worship, I have to laugh. "That, my love, makes you look like you're suffering from gas! I have my hero. I need no other."

"And who, may I ask, m'lady, has that place of honor within your heart?" Bronze asks in what I think, he thinks, is his regal voice and with his brightest smile.

"Why, brave sir, it can be none but the brave and righteous receptor of my love. The good Sir Titan, of course." Watching his eyes flash with Titan, Bronze grabs me and scoops me from the bed, walks me back to the bathroom and as he puts me down below the shower head, he flicks it on at the coldest setting. Squealing at full volume as the cold-water hits my warm skin, I expect Ember or Wesley to burst through the door at any moment. Bronze rushes out of the bathroom as Maya bursts out without me being able to stop her, and stands below the cold shower until her coat is plastered to her skin, then runs into the bedroom.

As Bronze is laying on the bed he has no time when Maya leaps onto the bed on top of him before she shakes her coat for all she is worth. Hearing him squeal too, has me laughing on the bedroom floor as Maya shifts back.

Didn't see that coming, did he? I giggle.

Waking in the morning, we shower yet again and this time in a warm spray. Sitting in the dining hall later, having breakfast, I watch as Xander wanders in. This reminds me of the inner council meeting we had.

"Bronze, what is the issue between Xander and Eve?" I watch as Xander picks at the food on offer and places next to nothing on his plate before finding an empty table and sitting alone.

"I'm not aware of an issue between Xander and Eve. What makes you say that?" Putting down his cutlery, he looks to where my eyes are pointing. "He has never had any issues with anyone, as far as I know."

"Well, there is definitely an issue between them and I think it comes from Xander. I sense nothing from Eve, although there is certainly sadness in her demeanor, not surprising when you consider what she went through with that male she had."

"That reminds me. She has to reject him as her mate. I told her she had to do it as I wouldn't allow her to suffer the pain from him severing the bond."

"Make it an Alpha order and do it quickly. I think you'll find that you'll make two lives much happier with that one order. I'm sure that there will be a resolution to Xander's behavior and Eve's sadness, if you do it." I look at Bronze and I see him make a connection.

"Of course. I was so blind." Seeing him concentrate on the Alpha order, he takes only a few seconds. "Xander came to see me and asked my advice on a relationship issue. He felt drawn to a female, but she was in a bond. He wouldn't divulge anymore than that and I didn't make the connection to Eve. I think you may have some Goddess in you, you know that? First that couple in the Blackshadow Pack, now Xander and Eve." Bronze wiggles his eyebrows at me, and honestly it looks ridiculous from an Alpha.

"Well, let's not get carried away with the Goddess stuff just yet. How about we wait and see what develops?" I don't know how long it could take for a mating bond to form, especially as it could either be a second chance, or have to be a chosen mate.

Leaving the dining hall, we are nothing short of accosted by Luna Sage, who grabs my free arm, and apologizing to Bronze, she quickly drags me away to my Luna office.

"I have so much to show you and so little time, Taria. Come sit by me." Still dragging me by the arm, she sits me at the conference table where I see piles of paperwork in neat stacks. I look at them and she must read my face as she smiles.

"Don't worry, Taria, it's not as bad as it seems. Some of it is just sort of reference stuff in case you need it later. Let me go through it quickly and we can discard any piles that we don't need right away." Managing only a feeble smile, I prepare myself for what is probably going to be a long dreary slog.

Luna Sage starts to run through page after page of information, and far from being bored, I find it interesting. She has recipes galore, and although I'll probably never need to cook anything in my life, I'm already thinking of Chef Ash. I could get her to prepare some of Bronze's childhood meals for special occasions, or perhaps I'd have a go myself. I'm quite sure that I'd have to defer to Chef Ash in the end, though. Never having boiled an egg, I don't see myself creating a meal reasonably similar to something his mother used to make.

When she's done with the recipes, she takes another pile of papers, and this time there are mainly photographs with some descriptive pages attached.

"These are all places that are on the Eclipse Pack lands. You'll no doubt get to see them all in your own time but it took me far too long, and because of that I didn't get to enjoy them nearly as much as I would have liked. This will give you the head start I wish I'd had."

Flipping through some of the photographs, I see beautiful woodland scenes, waterfalls, creeks, sunrises and sunsets. "I could spend years walking the pack lands and never stumble across half of this stunning scenery. Thank you, Luna Sage. I will treasure these and try to visit them all."

"You are Luna now, Taria. I'm going to be Council Member Sage," She smiles at me and I can't help but think she's going to be an outstanding council member.

We spend another hour at the table before there is a knock and Bronze peers around the door. "Mother, I need to steal my Luna away from you. You're taking up too much of my precious time that I could be spending with her." Grinning, he steps in, closes the door and walks over to us. Standing behind us, he rests a hand on one of our shoulders and makes a tremendous fuss of doing an eye roll.

"No. Not the dreaded Luna Sage lists of everything in the world. I'm sorry Taria, I should have protected you from the dreaded lists. Mother has a passion for them, as you now see."

"You need to take me to all these wonderful places in the pack lands. There are some stunning locations that we just have to see for ourselves," I show him some of the photographs and I see that he hasn't seen some of them himself.

"It would be something to tell our pups, wouldn't it? Where each of them was conceived." He wiggles his eyebrows again. I have to stop him from doing that or he'll do it in front of the wrong people and they'll think that the Alpha has gone mad.

"Just like his father. May the Goddess help you, Taria. She didn't do much for me, though!"

Chapter 27

BRONZE

The last few days, my new life as both Alpha and as a mate, has been quite a whirlwind. Even though my father had taken a step back before my official take over, I hadn't understood how much he was still doing. The admin alone takes more time than I realized. He popped his head into the office earlier and just grinned when he saw how much paperwork I was trying to wade through. He never said anything, laughed, and left.

It's been quite a conscious effort not to rush my alpha duties, too, so I can spend more time with Taria. I think she understood that sooner than I did, as she has been coming to the office with mugs of coffee, from her new machine I don't doubt, and just hanging out while I've been busy.

The Goddess has excelled with our fated mates. Maya has become the missing link from my existence that I never even knew was missing. I have always felt whole as a being, but I know now that I have only been waiting for Maya to arrive.

'Wow. That is very deep coming from one who only measured life in time spent chasing rabbits.'

You may scoff, but I know that is also how you feel. You have been a different shifter since Taria arrived. You have also been very considerate of my and Maya's needs. That in itself was a pleasant surprise.

'Just a minute, there. I have never been inconsiderate to you. When have I not taken you into account? I even asked for your input for my inner council, did I not?'

I didn't say you were 'inconsiderate.' I said you had been 'very considerate.' I was thanking you, in my own way.

'Oh, okay. I took it you meant something completely different.'

Knocking on the door ends that conversation and I call for whoever it is to enter. Eve walks inside and I gesture for her to take a seat at the desk, giving her a smile. I'm confident I know what is coming and I've been preparing myself for it.

"Alpha Bronze, I have rejected Miles as my mate, as you ordered."

That is not what I was expecting. I hadn't felt the order completed and was expecting an argument over it. That was something I could not have tolerated or overlooked, not for Eve or anyone. An alpha order is nothing short of law and must be obeyed. Some can fight against it, but it is ultimately obeyed by the very essence of the shifter.

"I would think that would be something of a relief, considering he did nothing to help you or your son. Being tied to someone so useless, Eve, was not allowing you to be the shifter you could be. I know that you can be so much more than you have been seeing yourself."

"Alpha Bronze, I was brought up in the belief that you mated for life, in good or bad. It is hard for me to see past that." Eve looks like she is going to be in tears shortly.

"*In good or bad* does not relate to the partner or relationship. It means fighting through *good or bad times* together. Miles chose to be a bad mate. It was a conscious decision by a male to ignore his responsibilities to his female and, even more importantly, to ignore a life he created, his son, Coal. Males and females have failed bonds. That's an unfortunate part of life. Choosing to ignore his responsibilities as a parent is unforgiveable. You could have been utterly awful to Miles and I would still have insisted that he be the best parent he could be. You were a good mate to him. You have not been to the pack and asked for help with bringing up your pup. You have been the best mother any pup could ask for. If you weren't, you would not sit as a member of my council. It is that strength of devotion and purpose that has put you there. I am not the only one to see it."

Seeing the tears run down her cheeks, I mind link Xander to come at once to the alpha office. I know he is not on border patrol today, so hope he is somewhere near the packhouse. I also tell the warrior on guard to let him know that Eve is present and upset. I don't want him arriving and having a confrontation with me because he thinks I'm the cause of her tears. If Taria and I are correct and he's going to be Eve's next mate, he will be protective of her.

It's only a couple of minutes when I hear a knock and this time the warrior opens the door to allow Xander to enter as he is expected. Xander's attention is completely focused on Eve as he walks directly to her and kneels by her side. Without a word, he takes her hands in his and looks into her eyes.

"What can I do to help?" He speaks so few words, and yet they speak volumes in their heartfelt tone. Eve stands and pulls Xander to his feet as she rises. Putting her arms around him she rests her head on his chest and sobs.

Walking quietly to the door, I stop and look back. Xander looks at me and gives a gentle tilt of his head. Leaving the office, I instruct the warrior on guard that no one enters until they have left.

Crossing the hall, I go to my Luna's office and knock before entering. Seeing Taria look up from behind her desk, I grin and give a mock bow. "Our matchmaking skills have no bounds, my darling. I have just left the good maid Eve, in the strong and caring arms of Sir Knight Xander."

"Oh, come hither, good sir, and spill thy beans promptly." Jumping up, she bounds around the desk and launches herself into my arms. "How did that come about? And so quickly, too."

Sitting in one of the chairs, with Taria comfortably ensconced in my lap, I give her the brief story and, surprisingly, get reprimanded because it is so brief.

Feigning my horror at being scolded, I point out to Taria, "I would have thought you'd be ecstatic that it happened so fast? I was half expecting a long, drawn out game of cat and mouse before they finally got together. They are both quite shy and reserved in normal day-to-day life, so this has been quite bold for them."

"I am ecstatic," she says unconvincingly, "but was hoping for something a bit more romantic and perhaps a bit more drama. Maybe Xander could have stormed to the Shifter Council warrior training school and made an example of Miles. That would have been both romantic and dramatic."

Laughing at her idea, I reply, "And probably got himself into some serious trouble at the same time. Eve has gone through enough drama, don't you think? An attentive and supportive approach from a male could go a long way to giving Eve and Coal better lives. It will be interesting to see how Coal develops with a male to guide him."

"My romantic side can get carried away occasionally, can't it?"

"Don't ever try to suppress it. It's a very endearing character, and it shows just how much you care about those around you." Giving her a long, lingering kiss, I feel myself getting aroused and decide it's time I went back to some of my official duties again.

"Before you dash off, Alpha Bronze. I have a surprise for you in the alpha suite. It can wait until later, but you can't go there without me. I forbid it." Seeing the laughter playing across her face, I have to smile.

"You forbid the Alpha to enter the alpha suite, is that what you're saying, Luna?" I ask her.

"It does sound a bit pretentious when you say it that way, I suppose." She says as scrunches her nose up and tips her head on one side. "Please don't go to the alpha suite without me, oh most powerful leader and key holder of my locked heart. Is that better?"

"Much. I'll wait for you to grace my presence when I retire to my suite." Watching as she sticks her tongue out at me has me laughing as I leave her to resume my next task.

Seeing my warrior nod from across the hall, I know my office is empty, so I make my way back. I sincerely hope that Eve and Xander work out, as I think they would be good for each other.

Once I'm settled behind my desk again, I run through my mental to do list.

Take Maya hunting again should be priority number one.

'You've been for runs and for hunts. You'll get plenty of opportunity for more.'

We need more time together to mate. She wants pups but is not doing the things we need to do to have them.

'Oh, please, that is so not true. You have mated as much with Maya as I have with Taria. Don't be so greedy or she may decide that you are too demanding and cut off your wolfy desires altogether.'

Humph! Wolf needs are more frequent than human needs.

I can't help but laugh as he throws himself down at the back of my mind in a tantrum of self-pity with his back to me, refusing to look through my eyes.

Taking my phone, I place a call to Alpha Lyle at the Spirit Walker Pack. We haven't spoken in a few days and I need to see how things are over there.

"Hello, Alpha Bronze. I was only thinking of you and Luna Taria this morning. How's mated life suiting you both?" Lyle sounds confident and full of life. I was half expecting a frazzled and frustrated Alpha.

"Everything is first class. We couldn't be happier. You sound remarkably well. I was expecting you to be rushed off your feet."

"It's absolutely manic here, to be honest. The rogues seem to be testing the border somewhere different daily. I don't know where he's getting the bodies from. As fast as we kill them, he sends more. I think he has a secret cloning factory and is turning them out on some production line. Our losses are light you wouldn't think we're at war with anyone," Alpha Lyle's voice is almost joyful as he tells me this, and I have to agree when it comes to the question of where Arric is getting his forces from.

"Our warriors are trained far superior to anything he has, but even so, he can't continue taking losses without there being an end to his army at some point. I don't see what can be gained by throwing his forces at any border if he isn't even weakening defenses." I think Alpha Lyle has to be missing something within their tactics. Not just Alpha Lyle, but perhaps Alpha Gerry of the Blood Pearl pack is also missing a vital clue.

"If you have any spare warriors, I can always use a few more. I can step some of mine down from the patrol rota so they can get some extra rest." Alpha Lyle sounds hopeful and I mention bringing Taria for a visit and maybe bringing some warriors with me. I could probably spare a dozen or so, maybe some of the females with their rucksacks and toys would like a change. I think they'd be up for the challenge.

"We could come over for a few days, and I could leave some warriors with you when we return. How does that sound? I'm sure Taria would be up for a visit, she was disappointed that she couldn't make it before." I know Taria would relish the chance to visit and meet Alpha Lyle. I'll have to warn him about her matchmaking abilities, though. He is still single, after all.

"I'll speak with Alpha Gabe and Luna Tati and we can stop over at the Wolfsfoot Pack to break up the journey each way. Look forward to seeing you soon, then."

"They'll both enjoy the company, I'm sure. I'll see you soon then, Alpha Bronze."

One task completed and another created. I'll have to get Dixon and Adaline to sort me out some warriors to travel with, and some to leave there for a while. I'll do that now while it's fresh in my mind.

Leaving the office yet again, I almost crash into Dixon as he comes out of the dining hall.

"Sorry, Alpha Bronze, I was thinking instead of looking." Dixon looks shocked that he almost walked into someone, let alone his Alpha.

"You saved me a hunt. I was just coming to find you and Adaline. Do you know where she is, by any chance?"

"You have to be joking, Alpha Bronze, right? Where has she been every hour for the last few days? Adaline, Ember and Luna Taria have had a monopoly on Drake since he arrived in the pack lands. No one can get within fifty feet of him without having to battle through them first. I swear by the time he leaves, those three will be Shadow Warrior qualified. I'm scared to death to do any more weapons training with Ember. Thank the Goddess that Luna Taria gave that task to Adaline as soon as she arrived. Have you watched Ember recently?"

"Well, let's see what he's got Ember and Adaline doing, shall we? Luna Taria was busy in her office a few minutes ago, so we only have to battle the two of them. As Alpha, I get to fight Adaline!"

"That is so not fair, especially as you're the one that created the whole bat monster in the first place. I said that on the day you turned up with it and she immediately went from shy mouse to raging dragon. Do you recall how she marched into the training ring and offered to take on all challengers?" Dixon shakes his head as he remembers the day.

"It's because of that, I'm claiming my Alpha right NOT to fight Ember!" Laughing, we head for the training area and our fates. As we approach, we can hear wood on wood and it makes us both cringe. When we can see the training ring, we see Adaline and Ember battling it out, only this time, Adaline has a bat and Ember has a staff. Listening to the two weapons collide with such force has both Dixon and I wincing. If one of those blows lands, there will be at minimum some broken bones.

Drake appears by our side as if from thin air. "Neither one has landed a blow as yet, and it is not from holding back. They are both excellent with either weapon. I made the mistake of letting Ember get my guard down once, and I paid the price. Since then, I have not held back either and have only injured her twice in all our sparring. I hear, Alpha Bronze, that you are responsible for the bat?"

"You shouldn't put too much faith in rumors, Drake. However, this time, the rumors are true. I thought having the bat would boost her confidence in training. She was always being beaten in her classes and even when the females that were training with her left her an opening, she didn't see it. I gave her the bat and told her she should protect the pups if we were ever under attack. My attempt to boost her confidence took an unexpected turn and created the bat warrior you see today." I look at the sparring and wince at the ferocity with which they are training. Once again, I dread to think how much damage any one of those blows could cause.

"Adaline! Ember! I call a truce. I need to speak to you." I watch as they step back and give each other a bow, then walk towards me. As they walk, I can't help but hear them arguing over who won that session. "Nobody won. I declare it a draw between two superb warriors. You should be proud of yourselves and thankful that one of you isn't dead or fatally wounded. I think you need to reduce the amount of anger in your training."

They look at each other in total confusion and they both speak at the same time. "That was just a fun session, Alpha Bronze."

Adaline continues, "There was no anger, Alpha Bronze. Anger defeats the point of the training as it reduces focus and increases recklessness. I would stop any training session where a warrior tends towards anger, step in myself so I could make the point clearly and painfully."

"And have you had to make your point at any time?" I ask, almost dreading the answer.

"I have indeed, Alpha Bronze. Three times to date. All male border warriors who didn't believe that a female should be considered for the Chief Warrior position. I believe their opinion changed after they had spent time at the infirmary."

I can't help the laughter that bursts from me as I look at the innocent and almost angelic look on Adaline's face as she tells me this. Realizing that she is completely serious, I try to make it sound like a coughing fit rather than laughter. "Well, good for you, and should this continue, I will be more than happy to have words with the entire border force, if necessary."

"I appreciate the offer, but that would only confirm their belief if I had to resort to asking the Alpha for help."

"No, Adaline, you misunderstand my intention. If it were to continue, those warriors would not only be questioning their Alpha's authority but also his judgement. I will not stand idly by while that happens. I would willingly meet them in the training ring myself and deem it as a challenge to my leadership of the pack. You carry on as you are as I have every faith in your ability as my Chief Warrior. Dixon, as of this moment, you're fired. Report to me in future as Delta Dixon. That has a ring to it, don't you think, Drake?"

"Indeed, it does. Delta Dixon. If he could sing, it could be a stage name for his next career." Drake smiles at his humorous comment and the rest of us look at him as if he has grown two heads.

"Drake! You just cracked a joke. Do you need to sit down? Should we take you to the infirmary?" Dixon shows his mock concern and reaches an arm around Drake's shoulders as though to support him.

"No, but you might if you carry on. Adaline, may I be the first to congratulate you on usurping this male from his obviously inherited position of Chief Warrior. How he got there in the first place baffles me, but the pack will now flourish under your skillful and pleasant leadership." Shrugging Dixon's arm from around his shoulders, "Dixon, congratulations on being sacked and also in your appointment to Delta, chief of all that is paperwork. Rotas, personnel reports, investigations, statements, more reports..." Drake walks away, still muttering about different aspects of any paper task he can think of.

When he sees Luna Taria approaching, he bursts into song, surprising all of us with how good his voice is. She stops and stares as he gets closer, thoroughly confused by what is happening before her. Bowing outrageously to her, Drake announces in a voice loud enough that we can all clearly hear him, "Luna Taria. May I present myself to you as the wandering minstrel that shall be forever known as...DELTA DRAKE!!"

Dixon launches himself after Drake and Drake runs away, still singing loudly. We are all laughing hysterically as Taria reaches us and looks at us all as if we are mad.

"Come, my Luna. Take me to our suite and show me the surprise you have for me. Chief Warrior Adaline, congratulations on your recent appointment. I will look forward to the infirmary reports from this day forward. Ember, you are without doubt the most accomplished bat warrior the Eclipse pack has ever, or will ever have. Now, if you will excuse us, I have a surprise awaiting me."

Leaving two females, mouths hanging open, I take Taria's hand and we head off to the alpha suite. When we reach the doors to our suite, Taria is almost bouncing with excitement, making me wonder exactly what is waiting behind the door.

"I can't wait to see your face when you see these," Taria opens the door and I step in. Seeing absolutely nothing different or out of place, I'm not sure how I should react.

"You don't like it! How can you not like it? Isn't it just so awesome?"

"I'm sorry, my darling, but what am I missing?" I feel an idiot right now. She is so excited and I can't see what it's all about.

"The dining table. Isn't it awesome? They have gone above and beyond." Following her eyes, I finally see that the table is not our usual one.

"Oh my. That is beautiful." The table is slightly lighter than the old one, but that is where the similarity ends. This one is larger and has an amazing amount of detail carved into it. There are now eight chairs and two captain chairs, all beautifully detailed as well. "I wasn't expecting that. It's beautiful. We'll have to start taking meals here now. We can't let it go to waste, can we?"

"There's more. Come to the bedroom." Taria's enthusiasm is infectious and I almost drag her there.

An enormous four-poster bed now dominates the room and has drapes at each corner. At the foot of the bed, there is a trunk in matching wood and design. Two wardrobes and a chest of drawers all stand along a wall and complete the majestic effect of the room.

"My parents will be jealous when they see these. The room was pleasant before, but this is just out of this world. How did you get it all done so fast?"

"It's amazing what dropping the Alpha's name can accomplish. I think the promise of a fat bonus may have clinched it, though, if I'm honest." Taria is positively glowing as she watches me appreciate the craftsmanship that has gone into the woodwork. "Oh, and our shop in Wolfsfoot town is now officially 'cabinet makers to the Luna.' What do you think of that?"

"Taria, I don't know how you got all this done in such a short time. You amaze me." I am truly amazed that she could get such intricate work done in so short a time.

"Ah, well, now there's the thing. I had to charm a few people and even bully one of them, gentle bullying, of course. The bed was commissioned by a customer who was delighted to wait for another to be built when I told him he would know that his next Alpha was conceived in a bed he had originally commissioned. This he found so amusing that he gave us the bed as a wedding present. I just had Hannah work her magic on it. I took the liberty of showing the original buyer the finished bed and he has upgraded his original order to something similar. The wardrobes were built ready for sale but I had them altered to fit the bed design, and the drawers were commissioned by a miserable old witch that wasn't going to part with them until I told her that unless she let me buy them off her, I would have her transferred to the packhouse to be my personal assistant to all things social. She couldn't hand them over quick enough at the thought of having to attend crowded social events."

"I wasn't aware we attended any crowded social events, my darling." I wonder what those are going to be?

"I know that. You know that. She doesn't know that!"

Chapter 28

TARIA

Having spoken with Alpha Gabe and Luna Tati, we're on our way to a stopover at the Wolfsfoot Pack to break up our journey to visit Alpha Lyle at the Spirit Walker Pack. I can't wait to tell them at the carpenter's shop how well received the furniture was. The bed doesn't creak at any of the gymnastics that go on there, though that bit of information doesn't need to be divulged.

Ember is excited to be seeing her friend Hannah again, although it hasn't been that long, to be fair. Bronze mentioned his concern for Hannah as there hasn't been much news coming through about her brother Elijah. Not having any siblings, I don't know what a typical brother and sister relationship looks like. I'm fairly certain that it wouldn't include selling your sister, though, surely.

Xander and Eve have been seeing a lot of each other, but there has been no mention of mates from them or anyone that knows them. I had a sly chat with Madison, who told me that Xander has been picking Coal up from the nursery occasionally. She also said that Coal has been noticeably calmer of late, but still is full of life himself. I had to get her to clarify that statement as it seemed a bit conflicting.

Madison said that Coal was still as energetic as always, but that his attitude was calmer. He wasn't full of mischief, but was channeling his exuberance into his learning, and even helping some of the other pups.

All in all, the Eclipse Pack seemed to have very little drama going on. Whether this was down to exceptional leadership skills, or the fact that all the rogue dramas were centered on the other packs, was yet to be seen.

Stopping off for a break and some food, Wesley found us a lovely spot. As I sat with Bronze we looked out over the beautiful scenery, I realized why Wesley had picked the spot. There was a wide-open view for a couple of miles and no cover for anyone to hide in. Far from being the beauty spot I first imagined, it was the best defensible position for miles around, too.

"You're becoming quite the warrior Luna, you know that, don't you?" I hadn't been aware of Bronze watching me so closely and reading my thoughts.

"Watching how closely Wesley and Ember take their job so seriously, I am learning more than I realize, I think. Maya is rubbing off on me, too. I am more in tune with my wolf-side than I believe I have ever been. Though don't tell Titan that! He'll be unbearable if he thinks I'm developing their sexual appetites." I can't help but laugh when I see Titan flash in Bronze's eyes.

Lunchtime over and we're back on the move, shifting between wolf and human, we are making excellent time. We have no stragglers, and everyone appears to be coping well with the pace that Wesley has set. I am very impressed with my Gamma and he is living up to everything I expected of him.

Ember looks like she is out for a Sunday stroll, but I notice how she misses nothing that goes on around her. One of the warriors strayed from his pack position twice, and on the third time she tripped him deliberately, bringing him to the attention of the others. One weak link could cause the death of one or all of us, and I can see him being brought to the attention of Adaline on our return, if Wesley or Ember don't deal with him first, that is. The rest of the run is uneventful and our wayward warrior manages to steer clear of Ember's radar.

Arriving in Wolfsfoot Town, Wesley gives Ember the rest of the evening off and I agree to meet her at the carpenter's shop in the morning. Bronze and I meet with Alpha Gabe and Luna Tati, and plan for a pleasant evening of catch-up. Wesley, too, gets the night off, as we can be sure that Alpha Gabe and Luna Tati have enough security in place that he can have a night to recharge his batteries, ready for the next leg of the journey to the Spirit Walker Pack.

Our evening goes well, and it's easy to see how Alpha Gabe and Luna Tati have become comfortable with each other. That doesn't mean that they take each other for granted or do their own things, more that they seem to sense what the other is thinking or what they need. I can only hope that mine and Bronze's relationship develops into such a close knit bond. I can't see why it shouldn't.

Breakfast over and I take Bronze into the town to see the carpenter's shop. I'm sure that they are all expecting us, and are nervous to see their Alpha's reaction to their work. Wesley seems to be on high alert this morning and I'm going to sit down with him and find out what's going on. His heightened sense is rubbing off on me, and I'm looking for any sign of trouble from every direction.

When a mob charge at us from a shop doorway I grab one and before I can strike him, Bronze has my attacker away from me. "Taria. It's just a bunch of kids running out of the diner. What's the matter?" Bronze obviously hasn't picked up on the tension, or has some prior knowledge, perhaps.

"Wesley! Come here." I watch as he approaches, still looking around at everything and everyone. "What's going on, Wesley? Why are you so hyped up?"

"It's nothing, Luna. Everything is fine." He isn't even looking at me as he answers.

"Gamma Wesley. You will address me as Luna Taria, not just Luna. You will give me the truth right now or I will have you removed as my Gamma this instant. Do I make myself clear?" Wesley's eyes pop open and I see him begin to come back to some form of himself. "What is wrong, Wesley? Your nervousness is affecting me and I almost killed a teen because of it. Speak, now."

"I heard a rumor that Elijah may be in the area, but it is unconfirmed. My gut tells me it is true, but that is all. If he is near, then there may be other rogues, too." He stands before me at attention.

"And you did not share this with your Alpha or Luna? To say I am shocked that you would keep such information to yourself is an understatement, at best. I am bitterly disappointed in your decision process, Wesley. We could have made alternative arrangements had we known, and could also have told our hosts of this danger to themselves and their pack. Instead of that, here we are in the middle of the town and open to any sort of attack."

Bronze takes the opportunity of me stopping for breath to step in. "The poor decision making was mine Luna Taria, not Gamma Wesley's. He told me of his suspicions and I informed Alpha Gabe. We didn't tell anyone else in case it was leaked or anyone behaved differently. I was not expecting you to pick up on the tension. I apologize, and this will not happen again. It was not that you couldn't be trusted, or that there was any doubt in your abilities, just that we wanted as few as possible to be aware. Alpha Gabriel has warriors in and around the town on high alert should we find Elijah or any other intruders." Bronze has his hands on my shoulders and is looking deeply into my eyes. If he could sense the hurt and anger I currently feel, he would be running for the hills.

"I understand, Alpha Bronze. Let us discuss this at a later, more appropriate time." Turning away from Bronze, I look directly at Wesley. "You are the Gamma, Wesley. As such, you report directly to the Luna as your Alpha has ordered. Your Alpha will always be your ultimate leader, but you report to me as the new Luna of the pack, and as your Alpha wanted. Am I making myself *perfectly* clear?" I look between Alpha Bronze and Gamma Wesley. Wesley, to his credit, does not look to Bronze before answering.

"Perfectly clear, Luna Taria."

"Alpha Bronze, it appears to have slipped your mind that only yesterday, you referred to me as a warrior Luna?" I look at him with raised eyebrows and a smile so he can see that my tension is slipping away.

"Yes, it would appear I had forgotten that. I will not let it slip my mind again. I should have included you in the information and planning, my apologies. Although you are, as I said, a warrior Luna, I will always be the one who has the last word on our defenses and security. I don't doubt that the good intentions of Alpha Gabe are being similarly straightened out by his Luna, too."

Taking his hand, he squeezes mine, and I squeeze back. Disaster averted, and no one injured, thank goodness. I would have been devastated if I'd hurt an innocent teen. I do understand why Bronze stated the security issue, and I know I am second under him.

As we approach the carpenter's shop, we become aware of shouting and suddenly a body comes crashing through the front window of the carpenter's shop. The male jumps up and, seeing us, he runs away as fast as he can. Wesley is at my side, and Bronze signals for two of the warriors to join him, and he rushes into the shop. Moments later, he returns, and the two warriors have a struggling male between them.

Hannah is begging Bronze to spare the male and I can guess that this must be her brother, Elijah. Ember walks out of the shop and has blood all over her clothes and her bat. My look must tell her what I'm wondering. "None of it is mine, Luna Taria. This coward brought three more males with him to kidnap his little sister. If she hadn't intervened, he'd be just as dead as those two inside."

Looking from Elijah to Hannah, I can see that she doesn't want her brother harmed, but I can't say I get the same vibe from him. I don't think he cares about anyone but himself, even standing there held by two warriors, I see him scheming.

"Hannah, this has got to stop. We cannot keep looking over our shoulder all the time, and we cannot allow rogues to wander in and out of each other's pack lands because of some family bond."

"I understand, Luna Taria, but he's still my brother." Hannah's eyes are pleading and I can see that Bronze is also torn with the decision, having known Hannah longer than me. I see him mind linking with someone and although I'm not included in the link, I'm confident that he is speaking to Alpha Gabe.

Bronze looks at Hannah and then at Elijah. "You are going to be given one chance, and one chance only, to give up this ridiculous quest of yours to sell your sister, a member of my pack now. She lives under the banner of the Eclipse Pack and, as such, my protection. Do you give your oath that if you are released, you will return to your own pack lands and leave Hannah in peace to live her life as she wishes?"

"I will leave her be." Elijah looks at his sister as he says the words, but I know they are false. Everything that I can read about his manner and body language screams falsehood.

"Alpha Gabriel has agreed to give you this chance. You have invaded his pack lands to attempt this kidnapping, and he wants you to know that you are never to set foot on these lands again. You will be shown no mercy if you ever cross his borders again. Is that clear?" Bronze has eyes of steel as he speaks and watches Elijah.

"I understand, completely." Elijah is trying not to grin, and Bronze is trying not to show how angry he is.

Four Wolfsfoot pack warriors appear and take Elijah into their custody. As they walk away, I see the swagger returning to Elijah and I sincerely hope he puts a foot wrong before he reaches the border and the Wolfsfoot warriors kill him.

Hannah thanks her Alpha and then me before walking back into the shop, and beginning the process of clearing up. I look at Ember and she has a faraway look in her eyes.

"I should have killed him when I had the chance, Luna Taria, but how could I justify killing my friend's brother as she pleaded for his life? That decision will come back to haunt me, I know it." Ember will take time to come to terms with this, I think to myself. I hope Elijah doesn't come back and hurt his sister, because that will be something I don't think Ember would ever forgive herself for.

"Warrior Ember, I am giving you a Luna command. If you ever see Elijah again, you are to terminate him immediately. Any repercussions from that action will lie squarely at my door and I will bear any consequences of my order. If we come across him again, it can only be because he has broken his oath." Placing my hand on her shoulder, I feel some of the tension ease and her muscles slowly unwinding. "Is that order okay with you, Bronze?" To which Bronze gives me a small nod of agreement.

"Thank you, Luna Taria. It will be as you order." Ember walks away, but only as far as the door and takes a guard's stance. I look at Bronze, who has been talking with Cameron and Logan, no doubt praising them on the wardrobes, drawers, trunk, and bed.

Once we have left the carpenter shop, we call at the clothes shop and thank Malakai and Reagan for the wedding suits. Bronze also thanks Reagan for the training suits and I'm confident that there will be a package arriving at the alpha suite in the not-too-distant future.

Chapter 29

LYLE

After hearing about all the drama that Alpha Bronze and Luna Taria went through at the Wolfsfoot Pack, I hope their visit here is a little more sedate. I have enough going on myself without having anything else brought to my door.

It was evening when Alpha Bronze and Luna Taria arrived and we enjoyed a meal together while they told me of Elijah and his plan to sell his sister. That is such a low moral standing that I just cannot envisage any Spirit Walker pack member sinking to. Having said that, I don't think any Alpha of any pack would expect to have a traitor in their midst, but I'm sure we must all have them.

My interest is piqued by this bat warrior, Ember, of Taria's, too. Apart from the fact that Ember looks stunning, the whole bat warrior thing has me intrigued. When Alpha Bronze explained how it all came about, I was laughing so hard I almost upended the table we were eating at.

If I wasn't so set on finding my fated mate, I could quite easily have approached Ember as a chosen mate. I'm not convinced that there isn't some mutual interest going on there either. Perhaps I should use the bat as a way of getting her into the training ring with me?

Listen to yourself. You've obviously been alone too long.

'I was just thinking out loud, nothing more.'

I wouldn't think too 'out loud' if I were you. If you're wrong and she takes offence, I bet she could cool your ardor with that stick of hers in short order.

'It's not a stick, it's a bat. Apparently, it's a very efficient weapon in her hands.'

Well, if you decide to ever test its efficiency, just be sure to know that you'll be on your own when you do. I'm having no part of her stick, branch, bat, or whatever the heck else it comes under.

'I bet if she threw it, you'd chase it and bring it back, tail wagging!'

That is the most disgusting, underhanded, degrading, insulting thing you have ever said to me! You think I'm a dog, indeed! I've a good mind to ask the Goddess to put me with someone far more worthy and understanding of my talents and abilities.

'No one else would put up with you like I do, Hunter. We are perfect for each other, and you know it.'

That's as may be, but wait till you find your fated mate. I'll tell her all the things you've just said. You lecher!

My thoughts are interrupted by a mind link from the border warriors. It seems there is a buildup of rogues yet again. I find all these 'hit and die' tactics more than a little baffling. They are gaining absolutely nothing from them.

Mind linking with Chief Warrior Glen, I'm not surprised when I find he has already dispatched more warriors. We set up a staging area for reinforcements closer to the border so we don't have to have such long traveling times. It has proved invaluable with all the regular skirmishes. Perhaps this is one of the things that Arric has not yet realized. Maybe he is testing our response times, thinking we are still traveling from the packhouse grounds. Interesting.

Luna Taria has asked to see what our gardens are like, so we are all going to have a tour of the grounds later, and see what suggestions she has, if any, for improvements. We don't have a head gardener as such, so I'm sure that will be one of her recommendations. I have someone in mind who is one of our regular garden team but have always balked at making the position permanent for her, as her name is Blossom. I think it's my inner child that has prevented me so far.

It wasn't your inner child that was thinking of Ember!

'You intrude my thoughts at some of the most inopportune moments, you know that, don't you?'

As you said, we are perfect for each other.

'I may have been exaggerating, slightly.'

A knock at the door halts our banter and after having called 'Enter', the door swings open and Earl Stone Shadow, my Beta, walks in.

"Alpha Lyle, I have received some information that you should hear immediately." The seriousness of his tone and the look on his face tells me I'm not going to like what he has to say.

"Take a seat and let's hear it."

"The rogues know of the Eclipse Luna's visit to our pack and may try a kidnap attempt." He looks at me as though I would be shocked at this news.

"I'm not surprised they would know of the visit, but I'm surprised they would consider a move such as a kidnap. They haven't won a single skirmish, so how could they possibly hope to penetrate far enough into the pack lands and grab a well-protected visitor? Especially someone like a Luna?" Sitting back in my chair, I steeple my fingers as I give this some thought.

Mind linking with Alpha Bronze, I ask him and Luna Taria to join me in the alpha office. I need to let them know of this potential threat and give them the choice of going back to the Wolfsfoot Pack earlier than planned.

A tap at the door announces Alpha Bronze and Luna Taria's arrival. Standing to greet them, Beta Earl drags a third chair in front of my desk and we all sit.

"My Beta, Earl, has heard of a possible attempt to kidnap Luna Taria while she is here. It seems that they are desperate for your company, Luna Taria. This would be their second attempt, that we know of," Lyle shakes his head. "I must apologize that this should happen during your visit here."

"Alpha Lyle, don't apologize. I am becoming used to it. I have your dedicated warrior team, and my own excellent team at my disposal and with Alpha Bronze also in attendance with his personal warriors, I don't see how they could possibly succeed." Taking a moment to consider the threat, Taria looks at Bronze. "How many warriors do you think they would commit to such a plan?"

"Realistically, they would want to be stealthy, so as few as ten, if they were shadow warrior class. With the level of skill, they seem to display, I would guess there are more likely to be forty. How they would get forty warriors into position, this far into Spirit Walker pack lands, though, is something else entirely." Alpha Bronze looks at me for my thoughts.

"Honestly, their warrior skills are nothing short of atrocious. I could send a troop of pups and they would come back with Arric as their prisoner." Luna Taria looks me in the eye and I can see she has a suggestion but is holding back. "You have the look about you that suggests you are the cat that got the cream. What are you thinking, Luna Taria?"

"What if we let their forty warriors enter your lands and attempt the kidnapping? We could kill thirty of them, take ten prisoners and get as much information as we can from them before killing them too? Forty is also a good round number to help diminish his forces."

Earl looks at Luna Taria as though she has gone mad. Bronze is nodding his head as though he thinks it's a good idea and I just have to laugh at the serious look on Taria's face.

"You cannot be serious, Luna Taria? You would suggest that we allow a large force to penetrate the pack lands and hang you out as bait? What are you thinking?" Beat Earl cannot contain himself and is totally aghast at the thought.

"Yes, Beta Earl, I am serious," Luna Taria tells him. Then Alpha Bronze adds, "I think it's a brilliant idea. Earl goes out of here and tells everyone that Taria was so full of herself that she thought the idea of a kidnap attempt preposterous. Alpha Lyle adjusts his patrol warrior's rota to leave a suitable gap in the defenses and hey-ho. Forty rogues in the bag and all the intelligence gathering you could wish for."

"I'm not sure I would be so quick to use my Luna as bait, but the plan has merit, I must say." I look around and only see a negative face on Earl.

"Ha! When you find your mate, you'll have as much faith in her as I have in mine, I'm sure." Alpha Bronze looks positively glowing with pride, and I hope he's right on that score.

"Earl, let's get on with it. Have Chief Warrior Glen come to the office, and I'll brief him on the plan. Let it be known that Alpha Bronze and Luna Taria are going home in two days' time. That will speed up their planning and probably encourage more mistakes."

It takes less than an hour to have everything organized and all we have to do now is sit back and wait for them to take the bait. We use the garden walk as the perfect time to have the kidnap attempt and subtly broadcast the event throughout the pack. The rest of the day passes with some visitor inspections around the various buildings as expected during a state visit by another pack.

Breakfast comes around quickly and once we've made a big impression of being up and about, we announce our intention of walking the gardens after lunch, starting at the furthest point from the packhouse, which is our pond. It is closer to the tree line than any other feature and would be the logical choice for an ambush by a large force.

I had my warriors hidden further into the woods last night and they have already reported that rogue warriors have been slipping in since dawn. The trap is ready to be sprung.

Walking towards the pond, it's difficult not to laugh at the absurdity of the rogue's attempt. My warriors counted fifty rogues and reported that a herd of elephants would have made less noise if they'd been eating from every tree as they went by.

Once we have reached the pond, we wait around so long that we genuinely run out of things to talk about. Luna Taria looks as though she is ready to bolt into the trees and drag them out when finally they make their move. Gamma Wesley and Alpha Bronze immediately stand by Taria while the tornado that is bat warrior Ember goes straight to offense.

I'm fairly certain that my warriors have agreed on a safe zone of fifteen feet from Ember as no one goes anywhere near her or to her aid. As soon as the rogues leave the safety of the trees, she is on them and they don't last more than a few seconds on their feet.

It is comical to watch as my warriors have formed a wedge or funnel for the rogues as they leave the cover of the trees. Several take on my warriors, but it seems the rest have a death wish and rush at Ember, probably thinking if they can get the bat from her they will be able to take her out.

Putting a halt to the slaughter, I call my warriors to gather the living and escort them back to the packhouse. They can be detained in one of our outbuildings and interrogated at will. At first count, Ember and her bat have accounted for half the attacking force. I can't help but grin as I watch her clean her bat on the clothes of a dead rogue and then grin at her Luna when Luna Taria cheers.

When Ember approaches me, I can't deny that I'm not a little disturbed when she asks if she can torture the prisoners! When I point out that we don't torture our prisoners, she apologizes for her poor choice of words and states that she meant interrogate them. Giving her my blessing, I think I may have dodged a bat myself there by not having her as a mate of any kind!

When the interrogations are over, it appears that Arric wants Luna Taria so badly because he failed to get Luna Aurora as his Luna, or Queen, as he still insists that he is going to be King of the pack lands.

My suspicions are also confirmed that there are rogue spies in all the packs. What does surprise me, however, is when one of the rogues lets slip that they even have information coming from the Shifter Council. I must inform Flint of that, though we couldn't confirm if it was the council or the council warriors that were relaying the information.

Chapter 30

BRONZE

Speaking with Alpha Gabe in his office, I can't help but vent my anger and frustration over this rogue leader, Arric. I refuse to dignify him with a title. Twice now, we have foiled kidnap attempts on Taria.

Who does he think he is, that he can just take any she wolf that he takes a shine to? This time he is trying to take my female. My Luna. My mate. It's only Taria's show of complete indifference to the whole thing, and her ability to take care of herself, when needed, that is stopping me from taking a small force and ending this Arric character once and for all.

I'm reasonably certain that the Shifter Council would frown on such behavior as well. Although if I get irate enough to follow through on the idea, I'm sure that I wouldn't give a care as to what they did or didn't think on the matter.

Having arrived back at Wolfsfoot Pack by mid-afternoon, I have been thinking since we dealt with the rogue force sent to kidnap my Taria, my Luna, I spirited myself and Alpha Gabe away so I could vent my feelings and get it off my chest.

He hasn't said a word, just sat and let me vent, giving me an occasional nod or frown. I realize that he is just appeasing my mood, but I'm also grateful for it, too. Having finally run out of steam, I stop pacing and I throw myself into a chair.

"I can understand how you must be feeling. If someone was threatening Tati, I would be the same. I don't recall ever hearing of anyone that has tried to do what this idiot is doing. It would take an enormous force to overwhelm all the packs and even then, I'm not sure that everyone would bow to him."

"I would take any survivors and become rogue before I bowed to him, Alpha Gabe. I would fight to the death and take him with me." My temper is rising again and when I see Alpha Gabe trying to hide a smirk, I can't help but grin. "Okay. That's enough for the moment. I'll put it in a pigeonhole for now, or until he tries again. If he does try again, though, I swear the gloves will be off."

"Let's go find our Lunas and get something to eat. You must be starving after expending so much energy, cursing the name of Arric so vehemently," Alpha Gabe stands and leads the way out of his office, and we go in search of Taria and Tati.

After enjoying a substantial lunch, during which we compared Flick, Spirit Walker Pack's cook to our own Chef Ash, we told Alpha Gabe and Luna Tati how we had upgraded the cook position to that of chef. This was in recognition of how Ash had consistently gone above and beyond her duties or responsibilities. Luna Tati thought that was a great idea and dragged Taria off to the kitchen to promote Flick.

Seeing Alpha Gabe's eyes change slightly, I know he is receiving a mind link message, then he states, "Flint is trying to contact us, and I mean us, not just me. He must know you're still here."

Letting our Lunas know that we will be in the office when they are done with Flick, we head to the alpha office and Alpha Gabe puts a call through to Flint.

"Flint speaking," His voice comes across short and sharp, so he must be under some stress. He does not normally answer a call so brusquely.

"Hello, Flint, this is Alpha Gabe. I have you on speaker as Bronze is with me too. What can we do for you?"

"Ah, Gabe. I didn't look to see who the caller was, sorry. I'm glad I've caught you both. It will save me saying everything twice. I'm sure Bronze has been bending your ear about another attempt to kidnap his Luna?"

"He has mentioned it in passing, just a casual word or two," Alpha Gabe answers, then grins at me.

"I'd be very surprised, Bronze, if you haven't been ranting in Gabe's ear since you arrived there. I would not be happy if I were you. Anyway, the rogues that were captured spoke very freely to an Eclipse interrogator, so I'm told. Not too sure why Lyle didn't have one of his own interrogators do it," Flint muses.

"I can clear up that little mystery, Flint," I interject. "You remember Ember, Taria's personal bodyguard with the bat? She asked for the opportunity, and Alpha Lyle graciously allowed her to do the questioning. She has quite the reputation among not only our packs, but apparently, among the rogues, too. They sang like canaries after she hit the first prisoner with her famous bat."

"No, no, no. You mustn't tell me those things. I cannot know of any torture taking place, even if it is of rogue prisoners," Flint's voice takes on an edge of panic.

"Flint, no one mentioned torture. One of them lunged at her and she subdued him in self-defense. You mustn't read too much into things." I grin at Alpha Gabe as Taria has already told the story of Ember's persuasive measures with great gusto, and there was certainly no lunging or self-defense involved.

"Ember is indeed becoming quite a legend in her own lifetime, isn't she? Alpha Lyle mentioned some of her positive attributes during our conversation. He was quite taken with her, by all accounts."

"Yes, Flint. Taria and I got that impression and we didn't think it was all one sided either. Ember paid considerable attention whenever Alpha Lyle was present. I think it was unfortunate that there was no mate spark there. That could have been quite the union if there had been." Those two could have produced quite a litter of strong-willed pups had the Goddess seen fit to pair them I think to myself.

"Well, back to my reason for this call. She uncovered that the rogues not only had spies in all the packs, but that they had spies in the Shifter Council. I have Roul looking into the council warriors to see if he can uncover anything from that perspective. Looking into the Council itself, I find it hard to believe that one of us would be capable of such betrayal." Flint is trying, but failing, to sound convincing.

"Well, we don't have to look too far back in Council history to find betrayal, do we, Flint? I don't mean that as an insult, just that with the Alpha Torrence and then the Eve Planter scenarios, you've had your share of drama. I wouldn't for one moment think that any of your newest recruits would be the spy. Merry, however, could be a good spy catcher. She can be very sly and sneaky at times, so I'm told." Alpha Gabe is only speaking what I'm sure any of us pack Alpha's would be thinking. "There may not even be a Council spy. It could be Arric spreading misinformation to try to 'divide and conquer.' Though I admit that Arric being that clever sort of negates the idea, but it could have come from one of his subordinates. They can't all be as stupid as him."

"I hadn't thought of that approach, Gabe, so I'm glad that you called me back." Flint sounds relieved, and it's not often that we Alphas give him some mental relief. Quite the opposite, in fact.

"Looking at it objectively, Flint, if there was a spy, would it be Merry or Lykos? Not a chance. Neither would it be Roman or Cinder Walker. Chet and Sage haven't even arrived there yet, so they are out. That only leaves Porter, Ulmer and yourself. You are not the spy. We wouldn't be having this conversation if you were. Ulmer? I think he's shamed himself enough that we can discount him doing anything like this. Porter? You know him better than any of us, so would you have any doubt about his loyalty? That's a question only you can answer. I'd put my money on it being a council warrior if I were the betting type." Having thought it through as I speak, I'm one hundred percent convinced of the warrior theory.

"It would have to be a high-ranking council warrior though, to pass on any valuable information," Flint theorizes, "Though we have nothing of any value to pass on. We are not involved in any of the border disputes."

"No, but you are sending reinforcements to two packs. That could be valuable information. Or one of those warriors could be passing information that they glean from their deployment to a pack? Who wouldn't trust a council warrior with some juicy gossip? They could almost be above reproach at pack level."

"I think you could be onto something there, Bronze. I'll let Roul know of this new theory, but I believe he'll be ahead of me on this.

He's much more distrustful of others than I am. Well, keep your Lunas safe from Arric and his hairbrained scheme of taking one as a mate. I'll be in touch should I or Roul find anything."

Before either myself or Alpha Gabe have a chance to say goodbye, the line is dead and Flint is gone. Looking at each other, I can see the cogs are turning in the same direction. Who, in our own packs, could be a spy or, more accurately, a traitor?

Leaving early the next morning, we make good time returning to the Eclipse Pack lands. As we travel, I have a moment of inspiration and mind link with Gamma Wesley. Stopping for one of our breaks, I openly task Wesley with deviating our return route to foil any kidnap attempt that may be in the wind.

A couple of hours later, Wesley announces that we are approaching a likely spot for a short break. Slowing us all to a walk, he leaves the cover of the treeline just in front of us and returns once he is satisfied it is safe for us to leave the safety of the forest.

Quietly observing Taria as we walk out into the open alone, she stops and presses her hands to her mouth. The view before us takes your breath away. There is a beautiful clear pool surrounded by lush greenery and accessed by a small sandy beach. The thing that makes it spectacular, though, is the waterfall that cascades from a high cliff where the river is hidden by more lush greenery. It looks as though the water is cascading from the trees and bushes and not from a river at all.

"Oh, Bronze. This is one of the places in Luna Sage's photos. It is even more beautiful than the picture gives it credit for. The water magically appears from the trees and just look at the rainbow! Oh my, it is spectacular. Thank you for showing me this."

"It was one of my more inspirational moments, I admit. Of the many places in the photos, this is one of the most breathtaking." I have my arm around Taria's waist and she leans into me, gazing over the view before us.

We spend an hour in and around the pool, but with so many warriors present on protection detail, we have to keep a sense of decorum, so there aren't any pups conceived here today.

Regrettably having to leave before we get to see the sunset, we agree that at some point in the future, we will return and perhaps spend a few days here. Arriving back at the packhouse late, and after dark, we make our way directly to the alpha suite, where we make up for our inability to be more hands on at the waterfall.

Chapter 31

TARIA

Waking up first for a change, I take great pleasure in waking Bronze and dragging him into the shower. I think dragging may not be the correct term as once I got him out of the bed and suggested it, it became more of a race! An hour later and we're dressed, ready to go for breakfast.

"Have we got anything scheduled for today, duty wise, or have we got the day to ourselves, my love?"

"I have one or two things scheduled for us today, my darling, but nothing duty wise unless something comes up." Bronze told me he had become accustomed to our little terms of endearment when we're alone and wondered if it's the same among all mated couples? I thought perhaps the older generation would be more prone to such things.

"Oh, and what one or two things may they be, if I'm so bold to enquire?"

"Well, m'lady. I ain't telling, see. It's what we commoners call a secret, so's you'll just have to wait and see." Knuckling his forehead like some old sailor from days of old, has me laughing.

"I don't know where you come up with some of this stuff, I'm sure, but I like it when you surprise me and make me laugh." Gripping his arm, we walk into the dining hall, still wearing huge smiles. It does not go unnoticed by those already eating, and we see many of them smile at us as we walk by.

Once we have our trays loaded with food, we look for a table to sit at. I say loaded because we have used a lot of energy with traveling and not a small amount showering, so have a fearsome hunger. As we look around, we both see Xander looking at us, and it's fairly obvious that he wants us to join him, Eve, and Coal at their table.

He is not so presumptuous as to openly invite us in front of the pack, but Bronze is sensitive enough to save Xander such embarrassment, so approaches and asks if we may join them.

Both Xander and Eve stand as we take our seats and Coal barely glances up from his food. When Xander coughs gently, Coal realizes his mistake and is on his feet in seconds.

"Sorry Luna Taria. Sorry Alpha Bronze," he mutters, but he does make eye contact, which shows he is genuine in his apology.

Once we're all seated, Xander points out to Coal that he should recognize the Alpha first, before anyone else in his apology.

Coal makes a face that suggests he's sucking on a lemon. "But Poppa, the Luna is a lady, so I thought ladies came first with my manners?"

"You're quite right in normal circumstances, son, but the Alpha being present makes things not normal." Listening to how Xander explains this to Coal, I see him being an outstanding role model for the pup. Seeing the glow of pride on Eve's face also tells a story, but I'm not sure who she is more proud of, her son or her new mate.

"Alpha Bronze, we'd like to thank you for what you have done for Eve and Coal. Having her reject her mate was difficult for her, but it opened the way for us to become chosen mates. I'm quite sure that had we waited, the Goddess would have got around to making us second chance mates, although I've never had a first! I'd like to thank you personally for giving me the opportunity to be a mate and a father to such a wonderful female and her pup." Coal stops eating as he hears this and positively beams at his poppa.

"Well, Xander, to be honest with you, it wasn't all me. Luna Taria recognized it first and pushed me into making Eve reject that useless...I mean, her mate. I was looking into the thing that you had asked me about, but Luna Taria was way ahead of me when it came to matters of the heart. You're not her first success, and I doubt you'll be her last." Eve gave Xander a quizzical look when Bronze said he was looking into something, so I hope he hasn't overstepped a mark there.

"You make a wonderful family, the three of you. I'm sure if you were to become four, that would be even more perfect. I think Coal would be a great older brother for a baby boy or girl," I say, and see Eve blush.

"Ewww. A girl brother! It would have to be a boy brother! I wouldn't know what to do with a girl." Coal's reaction has us all in hysterics. When we can get our breath, it's Xander that once again, is the voice of reason.

"Let me tell you something about a little sister, Coal. They look at their big brother as if he is a hero. A brother that takes care of his sister is like a God in the world of family, second only to her Poppa. Little brothers can be good fun but also can be terrors. You never know which from one day to the next. If you're blessed with a sibling, it won't matter whether it's a boy or a girl. At some point, they will worm their way into your heart and grow on you."

"A sibling? Oh my. A boy or girl was bad enough, but a sibling as well? I think we should just stay as a family of three and be done with it." Coal plops his head onto the table in a show of despair.

Taking their leave, Xander gathers his new family, and thanking us again, walks away.

Bronze turns to me and wraps his arm around my shoulders, and whispers in my ear, "If I'm half the father that Xander is proving to be to Coal, I'll be more than happy."

"If I wasn't confident that you'll be the best father ever to our pups, we wouldn't be spending so much time in the shower," I whisper back.

Feeling him puff his chest out with pride at my words, I suggest we get on with his scheduled duties before he drags me back to our shower in the alpha suite, which I'm sure is already crossing his mind.

Walking out of the packhouse, Bronze turns me away from the direction I was going to take to see how the gardens are coming along and I find myself heading for the training area. As we get in sight of the training ring, I see two she-wolves going at each other, with reckless abandon.

As we get closer, I recognize Adaline's wolf, Star and Ember's wolf, River. River is certainly coming out second best at the moment, that's for sure. When we are seen to be watching, Adaline calls a halt to their training, they shift to human form and then walk over to us.

"Good Morning Alpha Bronze, Luna Taria. River is picking things up very quickly with her wolf fighting. I don't think it will be long before she will be as confident in her abilities as Ember now is. I wish I could get to the bottom of their original lack of confidence, but it's like looking for rocking horse poop, trying to get either one to open up." Adaline punches Ember on the shoulder and gets a raspberry blown at her for her trouble.

"If River gets half the confidence Ember has now, she won't need to worry, Adaline." Bronze turns to Ember. "If I'd known that giving you that bat would've made such a positive impact on your life, I wish I'd thought of it sooner. I am extremely proud of the warrior you have become, Ember, and I know that when you are with my Luna, I need not fear for her safety."

Ember blushes furiously as she tries to stammer out a thank you to Bronze. I can't help but smile at her reaction. "Ember, I don't think I've ever seen you so flustered before. Well, except when we were at Spirit Walker Pack and Alpha Lyle was around, eh?"

"Oh, Luna Taria! He was such a hunk of man and wolf meat. He made both River and me drool. I will never forgive the Goddess for not giving him to me, but he became just like a brother so quickly. I could have forgiven myself for committing incest with that Alpha!" Realizing how carried away she has become, she looks at us all, squeals, and runs back to the training ring, calling for Star to join them as she returns to River's form.

All three of us can't help but bend over with the laughter that bursts out at her embarrassment. Star returns and heads for the training ring and Bronze takes my hand and leads me away, saying, "Taria, never tell her that Alpha Lyle had similar feelings or you'll lose your bat warrior to the Spirit Walker Pack in a flash."

Walking back towards the packhouse, but by a different path, I'm astonished to see building work going on. Looking at Bronze with a frown, he laughs at my expression.

"You didn't seriously believe you could get away with doing something on the sly in my own pack, did you? Herb came to me so excited about your ideas that he couldn't see past the fact that he was betraying a trust. Herb has only one loyalty, and that's to his garden. He was mortified when I reminded him it was supposed to be a secret between the two of you."

"How did you know it was a secret between me and Herb, may I ask?" I hope he hasn't got spies watching my every move like Arric supposedly has.

"It wasn't difficult to work out. It is exactly the sort of thing you would do for someone and so selfless, too. I wish I had your natural talent for appreciating people the way you do." Leaning over, he kisses my forehead and, for some reason, this simple act has me gushing like a little girl.

"You don't do so bad yourself, Alpha!" Squeezing his hand we intercept Herb who, upon seeing me, looks like he's about to bolt.

"Herb, you traitor. What happened to secrets between a Luna and her favorite head gardener?" I give him a mock stern look as we approach, but change it to a smile when he looks like he may pee his pants.

"Oh, Luna Taria, I'm so sorry. I was just so excited and I was trying to get it done as a surprise for you before you returned from your trip. It wasn't until I asked Alpha Bronze for the extra manpower, and explained why that he pointed out my blunder. Please forgive me, it was blurted out with all the best intentions."

"Your forgiven. It looks like more than we originally planned, though. Have you enhanced the design somewhat?"

"My day is just getting worse. Yes, I did indeed tweak it a little. I included a larger pond and fountain, a lawned area for intimate picnics, an orchard with miniature fruit trees. In my defense, Alpha Bronze signed off on everything!" Herb throws an accusatory look at his alpha, who holds up his hands in surrender.

"I most certainly did sign everything off. I think it was a tremendous idea, from the original idea to the enhanced ultimate plan. I think Madison will be over the moon to have something so spectacular dedicated in her honor." Bronze smirks, as he knows he has just put another nail in Herb's virtual coffin.

"HERB! You even gave up the reason for it? I just can't trust you ever again. I may even demote you to the lowliest weeder in the pack for this grievous insult to our friendship."

"Wait until you see the plaque I've made, Luna Taria. It exceeds all my other efforts at…I'm going to shut up now and go do some weeding." Herb looks at me and tries a half-hearted smile.

Laughing along with Bronze, we encourage Herb to walk us through his ultimate goal for the area, and I have to say I am impressed with his vision. It really is so much more than the original plan and the tweaks are actually minimal but with dramatic effect.

Herb soon forgets that I'm pretending to be angry with him as his one passion takes over and he floods us with what flowers and shrubs will bloom, where and when. His vision for a year round garden of color is astounding.

Chapter 32

BRONZE

Talking to Flint, I find it hard to believe what he's telling me, if I'm being honest. He has called to update me on his, and Roul's investigation into a potential spy within the council ranks. They've ruled out a council member, which was always a tenuous idea, at best. What they have come back with, though, I think is pretty absurd.

"Our information is from an excellent source, Alpha Bronze," Flint's use of my title has the hairs on the back of my neck bristling.

"Shifter Councilman Flint. Quite frankly, I don't care if your excellent source is the Goddess Selene herself. Miles has not been at the council warrior training school long enough to have been supplying council information to that moron, Arric. If you and Roul can't see that, then so be it. You will have a leak far longer than necessary if you believe such garbage. I strongly suggest you think again as to how much of an excellent source, your excellent source actually is." I'm trying not to lose my temper with this information that I'm being fed, but I'm starting to lose the battle with my temper.

Hearing a gentle, rhythmic tapping on my door, I breathe a sigh of relief and call 'enter'. Recognizing Taria's knock, I wave her to me as she walks in. Pointing to the phone as she is about to speak, she realizes I'm on speaker phone. I tap my knee and she looks surprised that I want her on my lap while on a call.

Flint waffles on about his source yet again and I hit the mute button, quickly explain what he is trying to convince me of, and then put the microphone back on. Taria listens for a couple of minutes and then interrupts Councilman Flint.

"Excuse me, Councilman Flint, I have just arrived so haven't heard everything that's been discussed so far but I have a few questions, if I may be so bold?"

"Ah, Luna Taria, of course you may."

"You're talking about a potential informant within your ranks, correct?" She sounds positively sickly sweet, but from where I'm sitting, I can see the steel in her eyes. A pity Councilman Flint can't, I think to myself as I wait for her to drop the bombshell that she is obviously preparing.

"Yes, indeed, Luna Taria."

"Flint, why are we using titles? We don't generally use them for private conversations. Can we dispense with the banal formalities, please?" Ouch, first point to Taria.

"Yes, we should, Taria. I'm not sure why we are doing so." Flint is on a back foot already in this conversation, and I relax a little as I grin at his discomfort.

"We aren't, you are. Now my next question, what information are you confident has been leaked? Not what you think or suppose. What information are you 100 percent confident has been leaked to this rogue leader, Arric?" Taria winks at me and ruffles my hair.

What the? Only my mother has ever ruffled my hair, and that was many years ago!

Flint is now a little more flustered, and it's very clear that he doesn't have that information to hand.

"If you don't have a grasp of even that amount of minor detail, how can you presume that there is, in fact, a leak, Flint?" Taria is squirming in my lap, and is fully aware of the effect she is having on me. She is obviously enjoying both her verbal and physical actions right now.

"Luna Taria…" Flint begins but gets no further.

"No, Flint, we are not doing that title thing. You are frustrated, I can tell that. You are finding this whole subject of a Shifter Council spy distasteful, just as much as all the pack Alphas, and we Lunas, are frustrated at Arric having spies within our packs. If we don't stand firm as a united front he wins. It is just that simple." I am glad Taria arrived when she did, as I would have probably slammed the phone down by now. "Who are you suggesting as the spy? Have you come up with a suspect yet?"

"You are correct in assuming that I find the whole thing distasteful, Taria. It is, however, a necessary evil that we investigate the matter. We have identified Miles, a council warrior that came from the Eclipse pack, as the spy."

"Miles? Council Warrior Miles? How in the Goddess Selene's name has Miles qualified as a council warrior already? He hasn't been there long enough to complete your selection process, surely? And is he exempt from the training program altogether? He was a warrior here at Eclipse, but he was not an elite class warrior by a long shot. Perhaps he will be a Shadow Warrior next week?"

Although this all sounds sarcastic, Taria makes it appear as though she is merely pointing out the obvious without making it offensive. "Someone there is clouding your judgement, Flint, and not only yours but your investigator's, too. They are pulling the wool over your eyes and I suggest you take a step back and re-evaluate the information you have been fed. If you can verify exactly what information has been passed to Arric, I guarantee that it will be before Miles was at GrandRose mountain with the council. I'll hand you back to Bronze, I have to go do some Luna chores. Have a good day, Flint."

"Erm, Taria. Thank you. I appreciate your tact in bringing me back to earth. Some was a bit brutal, but I appreciate it."

"Anytime, Flint. It's what we females do best. Corral you males and let you think it was your idea. You really should get yourself a female, you know. We enhance your lives and make you feel whole. Ask Bronze, when I've left the office, of course."

Giving her a hearty slap on her backside as she hops off my lap, she lets out a squeal and then pouts at me. As she leaves the office, I have to smirk as she rubs her behind where it must smart. I know my hand is tingling as I caught her harder than I had intended.

"Are you there, Bronze?" Flint's voice brings me back to our call.

"Yes, Flint. I'm still here." I feel a lot calmer now and am prepared to carry on the conversation, as long as he doesn't start with the title stuff again.

"That's not the first time I've become a bit combative when I've been frustrated. Bruno, my wolf, has pointed it out on more than one occasion. I guess he thought you could handle it, as he kept quiet. I'm sorry about that."

"I should apologize, too. I was getting irate fairly quickly as well. Two powerful males, eh? Not always a good combination when we're defending our own side." That's as far as an apology as I'm going with this, I think to myself. He started it! Laughing at my own childishness, I think it best to call it quits.

"If there's nothing else, Flint, I must get on with running my pack."

"Good bye Bronze. You have done well having Taria as your mate and Luna. Bye." Flint ends the call and I guess that is about as big a compliment as anyone could wish for. Both myself and Taria should be pleased with that. I'll tell her later, if I remember. Maybe I won't. I'll never hear the end of it!

Maya would live on that for weeks. I wouldn't tell them if I were you.

'No, you could be right. Maybe I can compliment her in another way.'

HA! Now that's what I call wolf thinking. I'll convert you yet.

'Taria is converting me very nicely, thank you. She doesn't need any help.'

Leaving the alpha office, I notice the worn sign on the door. I'll have to commission a new one from Herb, I think to myself. Alpha Office. I've always found it amusing that so many people refer to it as the Alpha's Office. Technically, I suppose it is correct either way, but it was the Alpha office first and foremost because it was the most important office when packs began to use a packhouse. I also know that referring it to the Alpha's office also makes it sound like some private domain of whoever is alpha at the time. An inner sanctum of secrets and important decisions. It is that, but only on very rare occasions. For the most part, it is a place where boring admin is completed and day-to-day decisions such as signing off on supplies for the kitchen, gardens, warrior rotas, and even Chef Ash's menus for the coming weeks, though I never have found those boring.

Knocking on the Luna office door, I wait a second and hear a call of 'enter, Alpha Bronze.' Taria recognizes my knock as I do hers. Walking into the office, I halt when I see Gamma Wesley standing before the desk, not seated. Hm, interesting, I think to myself.

"Shall I come back later?" I ask, as I don't want to step on any toes here. I know that as Alpha, I can just park my backside and be part of whatever is going on, but I like to think I'm above such pettiness.

"Not at all, I was just about to ask if you could join us. I was going to go over Gamma Wesley's record as my Gamma with him and it would be useful to have your input too." Taria returns to her chair behind her desk and I note with a touch of amusement that she leaves Wesley standing. I know she is playing with him because if there was to be any form of punishment, it could only come from me, the Alpha, in a situation like this.

Pulling a chair to Taria's side of the desk, I too sit down and then wait for her to begin.

Listening to her formal tone and the use of everyone's title, I can understand why Wesley has sweat running down him. She has said nothing as yet, that should have him worried as it has all been complimentary. It all comes down to waiting for the BUT that she is hinting at.

After a few minutes of this torture, she looks at him with such a look of pity that I almost break. "Have you nothing to say for yourself, Gamma Wesley?"

As his mouth begins to move to form any words at all, she shuts him down. "I think it is best that you don't, as you could very well ruin what has so far been the best day of your life. Alpha Bronze, have you anything you'd like to add?"

"Nope, I think Luna Taria, you have been accurate in your assessment of his performance in the role to date. I'll leave you to conclude." I am so close to laughing right now that I have to cough to hide it.

"Gamma Wesley, it is the decision of your Luna, me that is, that so far you have not only performed admirably as my Gamma, but that you have gone far beyond what would be expected of someone in your position. You have given your free time to enhance my protection detail, you have spent your own time training members of my team, including Ember, for which I know you suffered several injuries." Taking a moment, she looks him up and down as if he were on a parade ground undergoing an inspection. "You will recall our first official conversation when I gave you my expectations of you and your role. I am pleased to say that you have met all those expectations, and then some. Now, do you have anything you'd like to say?"

"I have no words, Luna Taria, other than my life is yours to command as you see fit." He looks as though he is going to explode, he is so pumped with pride.

"I have your loyalty, and your friendship, Wesley, I do not wish to command your life. That is something that you need to do, and I suggest you need a mate in it too. A male such as yourself has a lot to offer a female and it should not go unappreciated. I can always help if you need a push in any direction."

"We are all well aware of your prowess in the matchmaking arena, Luna Taria. Rest assured, that if I feel the need for any advice or aid in that direction, I will come to you first." Wesley almost spits that out in haste, but I don't think Taria has picked that up.

"I am commissioning a house built on the grounds, one that I feel is not only suitable for my Gamma, but that is suitable for my friend and any family he may have in the future. I won't hear a word about it, it is a gift and you cannot refuse. If you try, I will simply make it a Luna order, so let that be an end to it." Walking around the desk she approaches Wesley, and he clearly doesn't know what to do.

"Give her a big hug and then get out of here before she thinks of something else." I shake my head at him as he looks so bewildered.

Not only does he give her a big hug, but he kisses her on the top of her head. Titan is on his feet in my mind in a flash and watches for anymore contact. Wesley puts Taria down, gives her an exaggerated bow, and then leaves the office.

"You can be so cruel at times, my darling. I've never seen him so frightened by anything in his life than he was of your words. I think I'll just have to stay in your good books, won't I?"

"That's easily done, my love. Take me to another of your mother's special places and you'll be halfway there."

Chapter 33

TARIA

Having just returned from another of the special places that Luna Sage, Bronze's mother had left us in her photos, I feel invigorated. It was simply a clearing, a glade if you will, only an hour or so from the packhouse, and this time we were early enough to see a sunrise. Again, it was beautiful in its simplicity.

Lounging in the alpha suite, we are taking a little personal time before we have Bronze's parents here for a visit. When I last spoke to them, I got the distinct impression that they were already bored and that the slower pace of council life wasn't as fulfilling as it had been enticing. I could see former Alpha Chet settling into council mode far easier than former Luna Sage. She has always been involved in at least one ongoing project and to suddenly be sitting on a porch in a rocking chair, so to speak, must be difficult for her.

I've been in secret meetings with Chef Ash at every opportunity and practicing my cookery skills using one of Luna Sage's recipes. It has turned out surprisingly well, and I'm confident that when I present the meal at our alpha suite dining table, our first meal there will be a memorable one.

I am happy eating rabbits, thank you.

'You have never tried my cooking, so how can you even say that?'

I have seen how you humans mess with your food. You chop out all the good bits, mess with what's left so you don't have any big bits to chew on, and then put it on fire until all the goodness is burned out of it. You're disgusting when it comes to food. I can't bring myself to watch you barbarians eat.

Hearing Bronze calling to me in a mind link, I immediately head for the alpha office. Walking in without knocking, as he told me to do in the link, I see an angry Bronze behind his desk.

"What's happened, Bronze? What's wrong?"

"We made a mistake allowing Elijah to go free. He killed one of Alpha Gabe's warriors at the border and escaped. An innocent shifter died because of our decision. We showed him mercy, and this is what happens. I have told Alpha Gabe that we will do everything we can to support any family that the warrior has. He has been gracious in the fact that he stated that no one holds us responsible, but I hold us accountable." Taking a deep breath, he tries to get his anger under control, but I can see by his flashing eyes that Titan is not helping the situation.

Maya speaks to Titan. *Titan. You need to calm down and then help Bronze to become calm. He cannot make rational decisions when you are both so angry and letting it cloud his judgement. We know it was because of one of our pack members that we made the decision, but ultimately, the death of the warrior lies squarely with Elijah. We need to focus on what we do about him in a calm manner.*

That is easy for you to say, Maya. As Alpha, the decision was ultimately ours and the death is on our conscience.

Don't be so selfish. I won't have it. We are Alpha and Luna of the pack together! It weighs on both of us equally. Never forget that. Maya is calm in her speech, but the impact on Titan is not lost. He quietens down and I see Bronze's eyes clear.

"Bronze, what would you like to happen now?" I already know half the answer. "Other than finding him and ripping him apart yourself, I mean."

"I would like to hand him over to the Wolfsfoot Pack so they could conduct their own retribution as a pack," I'm surprised by his answer.

"I was thinking more along the lines of sending out a hit squad to just end his miserable life. I bet we wouldn't be short of volunteers for that task, either." I know one bat wielding warrior that would be first in line, I think to myself.

"I'm sure that one bat wielding warrior would be happy to go alone and she would be more than capable of being successful. It's only the trail of other bodies along the way that prevents me from saying 'yes'." His look tells me he has already considered that course of action.

"Ember will take it hard and personal when she finds out what has happened. She was regretting her decision to let him live for the sake of her friend, and I'm not sure that the friendship will survive this." Ember is cut from sterner cloth than Hannah. Hannah's sibling love will probably override the atrocity that Elijah has committed, just as she seems to forgive that he has been trying to kidnap and then sell her, too.

"I will take Gamma Wesley and Ember for a walk into the forest and explain what has happened. She can let out her anger in seclusion, and beat a tree to death with her bat rather than some poor warrior in the training ring."

Taking my leave, I go in search of them both and am lucky when I see them sat together in the dining hall. As I stand at the entrance, Gamma Wesley must sense my presence, and possibly also my mood, as he looks up, staring directly into my eyes. Touching Ember's shoulder, they both jump up and, leaving their table in disarray they hurry over. As soon as they approach, I turn and walk out of the packhouse without giving them a chance to ask what's wrong.

Walking into the forest, I stop when I feel we have enough privacy for me to inform them of the Elijah incident. As I speak, I keep all my attention on Ember, maintaining eye contact throughout. Rather than the anger I was expecting to burst forth, I see only sadness in her eyes.

"You were expecting this news, Ember," I say, and wait for her response. Several seconds pass before she answers.

"Yes, Luna Taria, I was. I have been steeling myself for this news since we spoke about it last. My anger I can contain and channel it when I next meet him. He will not be so fortunate again, as to walk away. I am sad that this is the end of my friendship with Hannah. She will try to make an excuse for him and that I cannot swallow. I presume that you won't be sending me after him?" Seeing me shake my head and my wistful smile, she continues, "No, I thought not. If you change your mind, I would only require the company of a Shadow Warrior and we could have it done in short order and very thoroughly, too."

"Both Alpha Bronze and myself have the confidence to know that it would be so, but as yet, have made no final decision, other than we are not dispatching our favorite bat warrior on the mission."

"Ha, that's a false compliment if I ever heard one! I'm your only bat warrior, my Luna." Ember's laugh makes me believe that she is taking this better than I expected, until her next words.

"Wesley. Let's have an hour in the training ring, just the two of us. What do you say?" Ember tilts her head on one side as she watches for his reaction.

Wesley fakes a look of horror, takes a step away, and puts his hands in front of himself as if to keep Ember away from him. "Not this side of hell freezing over, am I getting into any form of training with you for the next week. Do I seriously look like I have a death wish? No, no, no. Definitely not. No how, no way am I getting in the ring with you."

"I take it that's a no then? A little dramatic too, don't you think, Luna Taria? Are you sure you want a pup for a gamma?" Ember is goading Wesley to get him in the ring, but I can see he's not falling for it.

"Say what you like, I'll even yap like a pup, but I am not training with you. I value my life and any future relationship I may have too much to risk losing my masculinity to your damn bat, and that's final!" Wesley folds his arms across his chest as I suppose is a gesture of his defiance.

Ember and I burst out laughing at the look he gives us. I'm amazed that she has taken this so well, but there's a nagging doubt in my mind that she's putting on a front for me.

I don't believe she is. River has said that she has been talking about Elijah with her human and they were expecting him to return, if nothing else. They are both prepared to end that shifter, no matter what form that may take to do it. Maya's words soothe my worries, but they don't disappear totally.

Walking slowly back to the packhouse, I happen to glance over my shoulder and see Wesley's arm across Ember's shoulders. It doesn't look in the least romantic but does smack of brotherly concern.

Back at the packhouse, I see Herb scurrying away from the alpha office. I wonder what that little snake in the grass is up to now, I think to myself. Arriving at the office door, I see a new plaque on the door. 'Alpha Office' is displayed in a larger font and on a fancy background, too. It looks twice the size of the old one, as well. I sense a bit of professional jealousy here, but I'm not getting into a 'my plaque's bigger than your plaque' scenario. Oh no, I'm not. I won't be drawn in.

Diverting to chase down Herb, I run through the packhouse and see him in the kitchen garden. When he sees me, he takes off, and the chase is on. When Ember, who has followed me out with Wesley, shouts for him to stop, he trips in his haste to follow her order and is looking up in abject terror at her from his prone position.

"Herb, we need to talk about plaques!" Nodding vigorously, he listens to my instructions and looks relieved that he isn't in trouble with me, or more importantly, with Ember! He still has that fear of her despite their earlier chat.

Back in the alpha office, resplendent with its new door plaque, I'm surprised by the presence of the newly appointed councilors, Chet and Sage. I wasn't expecting them until tomorrow. Oh well, I can dazzle them with my culinary excellence a day early. Once the greetings are over and we've had a brief catch up, I make my excuses and slip off to the kitchen and my conspirator, Chef Ash.

Arriving in my new favorite place, I search out Chef, only to discover that she isn't due in for another few hours. Oh well. As I've made this dish several times now, under her supervision, I'm confident of my ability to 'go it alone'.

Cracking on with all my preparation, it doesn't take long to have my ingredients ready. Everything is portioned and laid out in order as required. Meat is prepared, fried off and put in the oven. Stage one complete. I am so pumped with excitement that stage two soon follows. Getting my timing right, stage three gets underway, and my confidence keeps growing. This is going to be an awesome meal in an awesome setting.

Nipping out of the kitchen while everything is under control, I let Bronze in on my surprise. He seems more than a little apprehensive when I tell him I'm cooking the evening meal and that we will christen our fabulous dining set. When he learns that I've been working alongside Chef Ash, he seems much happier, so I don't spoil it by telling him that today I'm flying solo.

Returning to my little piece of heaven, I check everything is going well and have a taste test, just as Chef Ash showed me. Realizing that it's missing something, I rush around the kitchen grabbing a few jars and bottles. A sprinkle here, a splash there, and another couple of sprinkles and I'm about done.

Grabbing some kitchen staff, I give them my orders of how to plate everything and when to begin serving. Seeing one of them raise their eyebrows at my jar and bottle selection, I ask them, a bit sharply, if there is a problem. Quickly shaking their head, as they know I've been working with Chef, I let them carry on and I waltz happily away to announce my upcoming culinary prowess.

We have all sat around the table and I have announced to my captive audience what meal I have prepared from Sage's recipes. They too seem a little awed by my boldness until Bronze tells them that Chef Ash has been on second chef duties. Not knowing what he's talking about, I assume that's why she wasn't in the kitchen today, but off somewhere doing something for Bronze.

The food arrives and is placed reverently by the kitchen staff before each diner. Noticing a pungent smell, I wonder what it can be. Everyone else looks from their plate to me, then Bronze and back to their plate.

"Don't be shy, enjoy." I take up my knife and fork and cut a delightful piece of meat and almost shovel it in with excitement and not a little pride. Seeing that I don't keel over dead must embolden my other diners, and they all begin to eat. Everything seems to go well for the first few bites, when suddenly my throat begins to get warm, warmer and then suddenly becomes a volcano of hot lava that continues down my chest at an incredible rate, burning everything in its path at a thousand degrees.

Throwing down the cutlery, I look around and see everyone else beginning to suffer the same symptoms as myself. Before I can grab a glass of water, Maya bursts forth and starts vomiting the few swallows of the meal that I have taken. Looking around, I see Titan, Shaman, Chet's wolf and Midnight, Sage's wolf, all doing the same.

Once Maya is sure that there is none of the offending food left in our stomach she shifts and I'm left sat on the floor near a pool of my own vomit.

Seeing each of the others slowly shift back, too, I look at each one and I'm just so ashamed of what I've done. Getting to my feet, I don't know which way to run so I can hide my embarrassment when I feel an arm reach around my shoulders and pull me to a chest. It shudders violently and I think that they are sobbing in pain until I hear laughter.

Pushing myself from the fierce grip, I see it is Chet that has grabbed me and is laughing so hard that he has tears running freely down his cheeks. Looking at Bronze and Sage, I see them laughing hard, too.

"I don't know what you're laughing at! I almost poisoned the ones I love most in the entire world. I'm so ashamed." I stamp my feet in temper and this just results in more peels of laughter echoing around the room. "Stop it! Stop this at once, I tell you!"

Chef Ash then dashes into the room, stops dead in her tracks, takes in the scene and also starts to laugh. Before I can get any angrier, Bronze pulls me to him, kisses my head and hugs me for all he's worth.

"Taria, it's fine, everything is fine. No harm done." He still has tears running down his face as he shudders with laughter. "I think you may have overdone the spices a bit, that's all."

"But it tasted fine. Chef Ash, I tasted it, just like you showed me. I did it all, just as you showed me."

"You got over confident, my Luna, that's all. I spoke to the kitchen staff, and they said that after you had tasted it, you ran around the kitchen muttering it needed a little kick. Unfortunately, the little kick you added wasn't so little. You used the hottest chilies and sauces that we have." Wiping away her own tears, she continues, "I was trying to get here before you started to eat as the kitchen staff were worried that you'd got a little overzealous with the extras."

"I'm never cooking again. That's it, I'm done, finished, kaput. Never again. You will feed me and mine for the rest of our lives, Chef Ash. I refuse to even set foot in your kitchen ever again. I don't care if the place is on fire and I'm the only one available, I won't spit on it. I AM DONE!"

With everyone still laughing, I can't help but join in, but I am still so done with cooking.

Chapter 34

BRONZE

The morning after our family meal and I still keep having a little chuckle, which is not going down well with Taria. I can't help it though as I recall all our wolves ejecting the hot food from our stomachs. They sure didn't like it and acted far faster than our human selves could.

Flint has announced that as my parents have come to visit anyway, the rest of the council was going to have an impromptu visit now that I was settled in as Alpha. I think they are just being nosey and seeing how my Luna and I are getting on. They've timed their visit with the grand opening of the new walled garden, which is coincidental, but they can see that things are progressing nicely under the new leadership.

My parents were doing an excellent job with the pack, but as with all changes of administration, it is good to have fresh eyes and a new perspective on things. I'm looking forward to the new garden and the new ballroom we had built to complement it. We poached the idea from another packhouse, but hey, it's a good idea, so why not.

I've declared a day off from all pack activities, except border patrol, of course, and I'll make it up to anyone that misses the festivities in some other way. Chef Ash went into excitement overdrive when I told her, and immediately called her team together and asked for their input for themes for the food. Taria has kept to her word for the last few hours and hasn't even been in the dining hall again, never mind the kitchen. I'm sure, given time, Chef Ash will convince her to have another go at cooking something. If that's going to happen, I'll have to stop these giggles that keep popping up every time I see the look on Taria's face as we all... See! I need to get it out of my head once and for all.

Heading out into the surrounding gardens, I take a few deep breaths and catch the scent of a few newly opened blooms. If the gardens all smell as exotic as Herb is planning, this is just a taste of what's to come and honestly, I can't wait. Walking by the training area, I see quite a crowd gathered.

As I approach, a path opens between them as they recognize their Alpha walking amongst them. Nearing the training ring, I see Ember with four other females and four males, all with a copy of her bat. Not sure that I can stand by and watch as eight of my warriors get hospitalized for the benefit of Ember's training, I'm about to call a halt when Ember wields her bat in an intricate move and they all copy her exactly. I watch this for five minutes, and then they begin sparring with each other.

Adaline walks among them and corrects some stances and the way some hold their bat. Ember is doing the same with others and I realize that it is in fact the eight that are training. Seeing me, Adaline comes over and explains the purpose of it all.

"Alpha Bronze, welcome. Ember and I were talking, and she happened to mention that when she 'interrogated' the rogues, there was some mention of her bat. Everyone apparently is aware of the 'bat warrior' and her ferocious nature in battle. We gave this some thought and came up with differing points of view that both had merit. My concern was 'what if someone else armed their warriors?' How would our warriors cope with that? Hence, we began training them in self-defense techniques against that eventuality." Looking at me with obvious pride in the idea, I nod at her as I think she is on to something here. "Ember, on the other hand, Alpha, came up with a different train of thought. What if we trained more with the bat as a sort of berserker force? You know, shock troops, as it were. If our foes are afraid of one female bat warrior, how would they react if they saw a dozen coming at them waving bats? It could be enough to weaken an enemy's resolve or even break their lines."

"I think you are both brilliant. That is pure genius on both ideas. Carry on with what you're both doing and if you need anything, don't hesitate to speak with me or Luna Taria. I'll tell her of your actions, and I'm sure she'll be as enthusiastic as I am." Thanking Adaline and waving to Ember as she glances over, I start to walk away.

Adaline rushes over to Ember and no doubt tells her of our conversation because Ember squeals and then runs on the spot with excitement. She stops suddenly when she sees me watching and laughing at her antics.

Knowing that the other Shifter Council members will arrive shortly, I make my way to the walled garden and seek out Herb. Finding him dashing around like a lunatic, I wonder what has gone wrong and if we will be opening the garden after all.

"Herb, stand still and take a deep breath. What's happened? What is wrong?"

"Happened? Wrong? Why? What are you saying, Alpha Bronze?" Herb throws the words back at me.

"Why are you rushing around in a panic?" I talk slowly and precisely to try to get the words to register with him.

"I'm not panicking. I'm ticking off all the last minute jobs that needed doing. Everything is exactly as it should be. What makes you think I'm panicking?"

"Very well. If you're happy, I'm happy. The Shifter Council members will be here shortly, and then we'll start the grand opening. I'll see you in a little while." Starting to walk away, I hear his panicked voice return.

"Shifter Council members. Oh my! We need more seats. Nathan, Ezra! More seats, we need more seats." Herb dashes off once again.

Arriving back at the packhouse, I almost fall to the floor as I see a new plaque outside the Luna office. It is made from a tree trunk that has been cut from a tree that was at least five feet across. The lettering is huge and flows like Taria's own handwriting. 'Luna Office' stands in letters twelve inches tall. I know what's going on here. This is one-up-man ship at the next level.

Laughing, I walk into the office and see Taria's huge grin. "Well, Alpha Bronze. What do you think of my new plaque? Two can play at that game, eh?"

"I think it's hilarious, however the Shifter Council are due at any minute and I can't have that sat there for the world to see."

"Oh my god. I'm sorry, let's get the darn thing in here out of sight, quickly." Taria rushes by me and I'm not sure what she thinks she's going to do with it on her own. It's huge.

As I walk out to help with the move, I have to jump to one side as she balances it upright on its edge and rolls it by me, almost squashing my feet.

"Gangway. Coming through." Like a tornado she wheels it past and then I hear a crash as it falls onto its flat side in her office.

Walking back in, I see she has her hands on her knees and is panting for all she's worth. "You didn't tell me they were coming today. Oh my stars. I would have died if I'd embarrassed you in front of the council."

"I'm sure they would have had enough of a sense of humor when it was explained to them." Taking her in my arms, I give her a hug and kiss the top of her head. "Life will never be boring, will it, my darling?"

"Hmm. I think you can do better than that, my love." Hopping into my arms, she kisses me deep and long. "That's more like how an alpha should kiss his luna!" Laughing, she drops to the floor just as there is a knock on the door.

"Enter," she calls out and as we turn, we see Flint poke his head in.

"Flint! Come in. We've been expecting you. Are all the members here too?" I walk towards him and grasp his hand in a firm shake.

"Yes, we all made it. You're the closest pack to Grand Rose Mountain, so it wasn't too much of a problem. You both look full of mischief, I hope I haven't interrupted anything?" Flint looks at us suspiciously but with a glint in his eye.

"Not what you're thinking, no." Giving him a quick explanation of the plaque scenario, he looks at the huge wooden plaque on the floor and bursts out laughing. "Oh, that is priceless. I love the way it is so outrageously enormous, too. That, my dear Bronze, is going to take some beating."

"No. This round, I concede graciously, but the war has only just begun, so I can afford to lose one battle." We all laugh and then head out to greet the rest of the council members.

Greetings out of the way, rooms allocated for the overnight stay and all the usual pleasantries taken care of, it is soon time to host the grand opening of our new garden. Getting everyone seated in the newly built ballroom, I congratulate our construction team on the recent addition and announce that we will, at some point in the pack's future, host a mating ball. At which time, we will invite the other packs to attend and hopefully enjoy several mating bonds being formed.

Beginning by mentioning the team that has been working tirelessly to create our new outdoor feature of the walled garden, I thank Herb, Nathan, Jack and Ezra, our gardeners, for their hard work and dedication in making the garden the fantastic feature that we are all about to see.

As I am making my speech, Taria is putting into play our secret plan to get a guest to the front without it being obvious. Waving and attracting Madison's attention, Taria offers her a front-row seat to see the new garden, and being the innocent that she is, Madison falls for it, hook, line and sinker.

Once we have our victim in place, we swish open the curtains that have been covering the open doors to the garden and everyone gasps at the sight before them.

Paving leads out into the garden from the ballroom doors and a pedestal holds a plaque announcing the name of our latest feature,

Madison's Walled Garden. Directly behind this is a large pond, and in the center is a statue featured as a fountain. The statue depicts a young lady holding an umbrella, keeping the rain off a pair of frolicking pups. The young lady is an image of Madison that is so lifelike, it is uncanny.

Bringing her to center stage, I inform the pack of the reason for the dedication of the garden and a blushing Madison is clapped and cheered by all. She stands there, tearful but happy as she excepts the pack's heartfelt thanks for taking such care of their pups.

Taking an arm each, Taria and I walk Madison through her garden and although not everything is in bloom yet, Herb and his team have managed to get enough in place that it isn't difficult to imagine it in a few weeks and in all its glory.

By the time we return to the ballroom, Chef Ash has worked her magic with her team and the scene is set for a sumptuous banquet. Once again, Chef Ash holds everyone back and offers the first plate to myself, then her Luna followed by the council members. As we have come to expect, the food is beyond excellent and I see Flint chatting with Chef Ash, no doubt trying to poach her services for the council.

From the corner of my eye, I see a council warrior stalking through the guests and when I pay closer attention, I see it is Miles. Looking further ahead, I see he is moving towards Xander, Eve and Coal, and they haven't seen his approach. Calling to Flint, I ask why was Miles allowed to attend this event with the possible implications of his presence. Flint blusters that he should not have been part of the council's detail and that following Taria's comments on our last phone call, Flint had issued orders that Miles was removed as a council warrior until all the correct procedures had been followed.

Taria is one step ahead and has Gamma Wesley and Ember moving to step in should they be required. Miles reaches the group of his son, ex mate, and her new mate, but doesn't cause the scene I was expecting. Merely standing before them, he talks to them, but due to the noise in the room, neither myself nor Flint can hear his words.

Seeing Gamma Wesley and Ember tense, his words cannot be of a pleasant nature and I expect one or both of them to take action at any moment. Suddenly feeling a mind link from Xander, I hear the words, 'my apologies, Alpha Bronze' and then I see him take Miles by the throat. Miles' hands grasp onto Xanders wrists but it is to no avail, it only takes a few seconds and Miles is dead.

Gamma Wesley and Ember step forward, take Miles's body between them, and drag him out quickly. As they do so, I hear them loudly proclaiming that the poor shifter has fainted at seeing his son after such a long time, obviously the shock was too much for him. No one seems to be aware of the real drama that has taken place, and I will thank Gamma Wesley and Ember later for their quick actions.

Walking quickly over to Xander and his family, I almost drag Flint with me.

"What happened, Xander?" I am confident that he would not have acted in such a manner without good cause.

"My deepest apologies, Alpha Bronze..." Before he gets any further, Eve speaks up.

"Alpha Bronze, Miles was threatening myself and Coal, that is why his life was ended. I would have done it myself, but I was so shocked that he would threaten his own flesh and blood. Before that, however, he stated that he had been a spy for the rogues in the Eclipse pack and that he was protected now from any repercussions of his actions." Looking directly into Flint's eyes, she continues, "How can that be, Councilor? Who has the power to protect a rogue spy from his actions? He blatantly spoke of it, and he thoroughly believed his words."

Flint is totally lost for words, and I speak on his behalf. "We don't have the answer, Eve, at this time, but we will have an answer and in a very short time." Turning away, I walk Flint back to the other council members, including my parents, and ask them to join me in the alpha office immediately.

Once there, I waste no time informing them of the incident, of his words, and that this was allowed to happen at my pack. Without directly ordering them back to Grand Rose Mountain, I strongly suggest that they depart at their earliest opportunity and discover who it is that believes themselves above reproach. Taria stands by my side throughout this brief speech and although I sense her own anger, she does well not to let it out.

Once we are alone, I pace the office floor to release some of the tension. "You handled that perfectly, both as an alpha and as a male. You made me proud to stand beside you, my Alpha, my love."

"It was probably the most difficult thing I have done thus far as an alpha. Having you with me helped, and I could sense that you wanted to add to their discomfort. Thank you for your restraint, my Luna, my darling."

Taking a few more moments to regain our composure, we leave the office to return to the festivities. Gamma Wesley and Ember are outside the door waiting for us and confirm everything that Eve told us. Returning to the ballroom, Xander, Eve and Coal are nowhere to be seen. Thankfully, everything else appears to be continuing as normal with no one any the wiser.

Mingling with everyone, it seems that the ballroom, walled garden and Madison's dedication have been a monumental success. The pack is extremely happy and once the food is consumed and we have the ballroom cleared, I make another announcement.

"As we are all gathered together, except for our border warriors, of course, who I shall make it up to at some later date, I declare a pack run for all those able to take part. Let us rejoice not only as our human selves but share our joy and happiness as our wolf selves, too."

Shifting to Titan takes but a moment, and Maya is only a fraction behind and then stands at our side. Looking into each other's eyes, Maya nods and I begin to howl, joined moments later by my Luna.

Ahwoooooooooooo

Books by J.E. Daelman

SATAN'S GUARDIANS MC

Book One - Brand

Book Two - Shades

Book Three - Odds

Book Four - Torch

Book Five - Ace

Book Six - Nash

Book Seven - Ink

Book Eight - Shadow

Book Nine - Christmas at the Clubhouse - Novella

Book Ten - Whisky

Book Eleven – Halloween at the Clubhouse - Novella

RAGING BARONS MC

Prequel - Truth and Lies

President - Axel - Book Two

Silver - Book Three

Fox – Book Four

Grease – Book Five

Hammer – Book Six

BS – Book Seven

Target – Book Eight

Knuckles – Book Nine

Stitch – Book Ten

Forest – Book Eleven

Meat – Book Twelve

TwoCents – Book Thirteen

Rock – Book Fourteen

Jig – Book Fifteen

TRIPLE KINGS MC

Book One – Hawk

Book Two - Eagle

Book Three - Falcon

PARANORMAL ROMANCE SERIES

KINGDOM OF WOLVES

Wolfsfoot – Book 1

Blackshadow Pack – Book 2

Blood Pearl Pack – Book 3

STANDALONE NOVELLAS

When Life Sucks!

WoMen and Revenge [WAR] Club

Acknowledgments

Firstly, thanks to Richard, who Edits & Alpha reads. You work so hard, and I'm so grateful for all you do. You have so much to put up with, my questions, throwing ideas, and having you read chapters back to me so I can hopefully see the story from the reader's point of view. Love you sweetie xx

My business manager and brother, Vic, thank you, taking a load off my shoulders has been incredible and gives me more time for my imagination to flourish.

Alpha Readers: Gabi, you take the pressure from me finding all the little plot holes I may miss and of course my misspellings when my spellchecker tries to be American.

Proofreader: Linda who double checked all was good to go.

Proofreader: Marie, you didn't like shifter stories until you read Tatiana's story.

For my BETA Readers, Jenni and Stacey. Thank you for finding all those errors that could easily slip through the net.

Those in my ARC Team who took this journey along the shifter path with me. Thank you.

Thank you to Elaine for running the street team, and ARC team manager. Plus, the ladies of the street team for jumping in to help and keep me seen on social media.

Lastly, thank you to my readers for taking the chance on reading my shifter stories. Thank you 🖤

Made in the USA
Monee, IL
05 March 2025

You can find me here

Facebook Author page:
https://www.facebook.com/Jan.SGMC

Facebook Reader page:
https://www.facebook.com/groups/335434258378835

Twitter:
https://twitter.com/daelman_author

Instagram:
https://www.instagram.com/jandaelman_author/

MeWe:
https://mewe.com/i/jandaelman

Blog:
https://jdaelman-author.blogspot.com/

Goodreads:
https://www.goodreads.com/author/show/21391970.Jan_Daelman

BookBub:
https://www.bookbub.com/authors/j-e-daelman

Website:
http://jedaelman.com/

SIGN UP FOR THE NEWSLETTER
https://www.subscribepage.com/u9r7b4

COPYRIGHT © 2025 J.E DAELMAN. ALL RIGHTS RESERVED.

COPYRIGHT PROTECTED WITH WWW.PROTECTMYWORK.COM,

REFERENCE NUMBER: 16538110225S033